TWO FOR JOY

Isabel Fielding is back.

SARAH A. DENZIL

TWO FOR JOY

Sarah A. Denzil

Copyright © 2018 Sarah A. Denzil

All rights reserved, including the right to reproduce this work, in whole or in part, in any form. This is a work of fiction. All characters, events, organizations and products depicted herein are either a product of the author's imagination, or are used fictitiously.

Print cover and book design by Mae I Design & Photography

E-book cover design by Sarah Dalton

ALSO BY SARAH A. DENZIL

Saving April
The Broken Ones
Silent Child
One For Sorrow

TWO FOR JOY

PROLOGUE

This bathroom is unfamiliar, but I stumble my way to the sink to wash my hands. There they are: two pale lumps in the dark. Two trembling, alien-like things that don't seem to belong to me, and yet they do. Perhaps the reason they appear odd to me is because these two pale things are all covered in red. More red than I've ever seen before. It smears when I run the tap, but I need the water to wash it all away.

There it goes, down the plug hole. Water chasing the blood away. Getting rid of the guilt.

You don't know this, but I dream of the blood. I dream of causing pain, of taking lives. It makes me feel powerful. But I could never tell you. Never admit it.

I'm ashamed of who I am.

And yet I don't want to stop.

So here I am, washing away the blood. Washing away the evidence.

CHAPTER
I

ISABEL

Do you think about me? Dream about me? I dream about you almost every night. But in my dreams, you are a beautiful bird. Why won't you let me make you beautiful, Leah? You come to me as a ghost, pale and shimmering, stalking me as a shadow would. But the absence of you hurts me. Why would you want to hurt me?

After a decade of being forced into the company of others, I found myself alone for the first time, and it frightened me. That night on the moors, when you let me go, I was cold and injured, and you left me there like an unwanted dog. My cruel owner, taunting me all those months with promises of friendship, only to leave me like that.

But as usual, you underestimated me, Leah. You thought I would fade away into the darkness, slipping out of your life like any good inconvenience would. If I were a bug, would you step on me and grind me into the dirt? Would you think twice about extinguishing me from your life?

Don't you see that I wanted to make you beautiful? You're mediocre. You're dull and dirty, like the stream I washed myself in on the moors that night. I want to take you from that mediocrity and transform you into the magnificent bird you have the potential be. You're my canvas, Leah, empty and waiting for genius. When I find you, I'll turn you into a work of art.

Don't you understand that I will find you? It doesn't matter what it takes. Do you think I care about my freedom? About my life? I can't live in this world anyway, because the world has already rejected who I am. I don't have anything to live for except you.

Leah.

CHAPTER 2

E for Elizabeth. L for Lizzie. B for Beth. I have three choices, and I hate them all. My name is Elizabeth James, which is boring enough for me to escape notice, and different enough from Leah Smith that Isabel won't think to search for it. The officers who arranged my move into the witness protection programme decided to give me a name with enough variations that I could choose one I like. Lizzie isn't a million miles away from Leah, but all my formal paperwork is under Elizabeth.

So here I am, in a grey little town on the Scottish border, with a new name and a new life.

But it isn't going to last.

The first suggestion for Tom's new name was Anthony, which could be shortened to Tony if he wanted. Anthony James is a pleasant name, and Tony isn't too far from Tom, but he hated it. We went through Owen, Samuel, Harry, and finally settled on Scott. Scott and

Elizabeth James.

Our new house is mid-terrace, with old-fashioned furniture and unattractive wallpaper. Everything was arranged before we arrived, with beds made up, and milk and bread in the kitchen, but we were told not to get too comfortable. There's a chance we won't stay here. This is the first house we've been moved to, but the third new place since we left Hutton. First, we stopped in a hotel in Lancashire. Then we were taken to another hotel in Gateshead. And now we are in a rented house on a drab street with dusty curtains and radiators that clang at night.

Neither of us has a purpose while we live here. We're in limbo. My trips out of the house are to fetch our shopping, but we're given little to live on each week. Food is almost all I buy, except for two new shirts from a charity shop for Tom. We squeeze in a cheap self-defence class once a week, but lately these have been making me so anxious that I think we'll have to stop.

What you need to know about the witness protection programme is that it is not allowed to be an incentive for anyone. Not many people make it into the programme after being a victim of a crime; most are an informer, grassing up their mates in organised crime. Which means that the biggest rule of the programme is that no one gets more than what they had before.

The problem is, we had nothing before.

My scars itch.

There's rain in the air, and my hair is frizzy from the extra moisture. The handles of the plastic shopping bags cut into my palms as I walk along the street. I should have taken up Tom's offer of help, but for the first time since we moved here, he's reading a textbook instead of browsing the internet on the new laptop his foster family bought for him.

That's the other rule—we leave everything behind. We don't

create a Facebook account with any photos on it, or our names, we don't have Instagram accounts or Twitter, or anything else that would leave even the smallest of digital footprints. We are ghosts, living on the outskirts of society, while life happens all around us. We can't join in; at least, not yet. It isn't safe. They haven't found her yet.

Tom used to think that she died on the moors somewhere, fallen deep into a ravine that the police are unable to search, but I know better than that, and lately even he jumps when there's a knock on the door or someone leans over to say hello on the street. Isabel is the cockroach you can't kill, that scuttles into the gaps in the bricks and camps up, watching you carefully and getting ready to jump out when you least expect it. I connected with her in Crowmont Hospital. I made her feel something, and I don't think Isabel will ever forgive me for that. She will never give up. She'd rather die than give up. She will come for me.

My palms begin to sweat as my thoughts drift back to Isabel, as they always seem to do, and I become more aware of the birds above me on the telephone wires, flapping their wings and occasionally squawking. What are they? Ravens? I try to remember what Isabel would say about the omen of a raven, but I can't remember.

And then I abruptly come to my house. Not mine, but at least the place where I lay my head at night. The door opens directly into the living room where I see Tom standing in the centre, staring at the window. There's a small smear of blood and a smudged outline that I didn't notice as I was searching for my keys.

"What happened?" I ask, letting the bags drop to the carpet.

"It was a magpie," Tom says. "Can you believe it?"

I turn to face the smudge on the glass and realise that I can make out the basic shape of a bird in flight. The realisation hits me as hard as a fist to the abdomen, followed by a cold sense of dread spreading from my ears down my neck.

"Are you sure?" I step over to the glass and peer out. Why didn't I see the magpie on the ground outside the house?

"It's not there anymore," Tom says. "It flew away."

The smear of blood is bigger than a pound coin, but not by much. I would certainly expect a bird to be too injured to fly away after such an injury. But I didn't see anything on the pavement outside.

"Are you sure?" I ask.

Tom's jaw tenses as he snaps, "Why would I lie?"

He has a point. What would Tom gain from lying to me? What would he even do with a dead magpie?

"Do you think it's her?" he asks.

I shake my head. "It's a coincidence. As clever as Isabel is, I don't think she could train a bird to fly into our window. It's just a horrible coincidence, Tom." I place a hand on his shoulder, which is much broader than it used to be, and tell myself that I'm right. Surely, it was beyond the realm of possibility. Even in Crowmont Hospital, when Isabel tamed Pepsi, her friendly magpie, she couldn't train a bird to fly into our window. I take a deep breath and try not to think about my nightmares, then I reach down and pick up the shopping. "Are you hungry?"

"I should clean the window," Tom replies, speaking more to himself than to me.

"While you do that, I'll make us sandwiches."

"Fine."

Tom stalks from the room with his head bent low. My secret son. He's filled out since the night on the moors, and he appears older, despite only a few months having passed. He's taller now, with some of the weight shifted and redistributed into muscle. There was a point a few weeks ago when we were a team, closer than ever, protective of each other, but since then we've drifted away again. And now here he is, sullen and spotty as he ever was before. I'm not sure whether it's a good or a bad thing that he considers me his annoying older sister again.

I just wish I'll be able to tell him the truth one day.

It doesn't take long to fill our kitchen with the food. A few tins of soup, beans, a loaf of bread, biscuits, and pasta, and the cupboards are brimming. Though Tom and I keep to ourselves, I know that a family with three children live a few doors up, and I can't imagine living in such a tiny space with all those other bodies. There was a time I lived in a squat with my ex-boyfriend, and even now, when I think of the dirty mugs and the smell that emanated from lazy bodies lying around the floor, I want to gag.

Sounds carry easily in the house, and the squeaking of the cloth against the window tells me that Tom is washing away the blood as he promised. I cringe at the thought of the bird pressing against the glass, peering in with its beady eyes, pecking at the window. But none of that happened; it flew in, fell, and flew away. I cleaned the windows yesterday out of boredom. I obviously cleaned them too well.

Tom walks into the kitchen as I'm buttering bread and throws the dirty cloth into the peddle bin. I can't help but notice that his forehead is damp with sweat. Fear? Or simply exertion from his task?

When he turns back to go into the living room, I notice a feather poking out of the back pocket of his jeans. The sight of it makes me pause in the middle of my task, my hand hovering above the opened packet of sliced ham. Why would he keep such a memento? Tom is as afraid of birds as I am, after everything Isabel put us through. At least I thought he was.

A sharp ring jolts me from my thoughts, sending an electric shock of adrenaline through my veins. I rattle the plate as I reach for the kitchen counter to steady myself, my pulse racing. When will I get over the way surprises make me feel? When will I be normal again? I imagine Seb's silent presence at my side, hand inches from mine, never touching, just there as solid as a brick wall but as soft and comforting as a blanket. After my heart recovers, I take another deep breath in through my nose and out through my mouth and retrieve my mobile phone from my pocket.

"Hello?"

"Elizabeth. It's Adam."

One of the officers who helped us move away from Hutton following Isabel's attack.

"Do we need to pack our things?"

A long sigh. Does he seem tense? His voice is clipped, and he's sighing heavily. Something is wrong. "I'm sorry, but yes."

"Is it Isabel?"

"Honestly, we're not sure, but we need to get you out to be safe. The police in Newcastleton have found a body. A young woman, dark hair like yours, and the corpse has been mutilated."

My fingers grip the rounded edge of the kitchen counter until my knuckles are white as milk. "Are you collecting us?"

"Yes," he said. "Tomorrow morning at 6am."

"We'll be ready."

"Okay. See you then."

I disconnect the call and slump against the kitchen counter. He gave me no word about where we're going, but then he wouldn't do that over the phone. As terrifying as Isabel is, I can't imagine her bugging my mobile phone, but there was a time when I couldn't imagine Isabel cutting the flesh of a dead six-year-old or stuffing a bird into the mouth of a decapitated head. My meagre breakfast attempts to rise, but I ignore it. There's no time for that. I have to get Tom ready.

As soon as he sees my face, he knows I'm afraid.

"We're leaving again tomorrow morning. The officer is collecting us at 6am."

"Why?"

"They found a dead body here in Newcastleton. Mutilated."

Tom snatches the TV remote from the arm of the sofa and programmes the channel to BBC news. They're interviewing a politician about an expenses scandal, but underneath I see the headlines scrolling across the screen.

Woman found dead in Newcastleton. Strangled and mutilated.

"Strangled," Tom repeats. "I wonder when she died."

I wonder when she died as well. Was it last night? The night before? I try to pry my eyes away from the screen, but I can't stop staring at it. *Woman.* That's all she is right now. *Woman strangled.* The strangled woman, mutilated.

That can't happen to me.

CHAPTER 3

We hit the motorway and keep going, with trucks swooshing through the rain around us. Tom is restless in the back seat, fiddling with his phone, occasionally exhaling through his nose and shaking his head. He's reading the news reports, I can tell.

Adam glances nervously at me from the driver's seat. "I'm hoping this will be your last place," he says. "There's no indication that Isabel actually found you. The murdered woman could be an unhappy coincidence. She wasn't found on your back doorstep, after all. But, still, too close for comfort."

I nod, not feeling reassured by his sterile words.

"They've released the name," Tom says from the back seat. "Alison Finlay."

Hearing her name does little except make me feel numb. There it is—the name, Alison Finlay. Was she murdered because of me? Did

Isabel kill her because she couldn't kill me? Did Isabel kill her because I couldn't kill Isabel when I had the chance? All those months ago on the moors when I had her. I *had* her, and I let her go. I could have killed her in the abandoned farmhouse. I could have tied her up, even. I could have done *something*. But I was too scared to touch her. I just wanted to get Tom out of there to safety. Sometimes I hate myself for those actions.

"It's called Clifton-on-Sea. On the southeast coast near Margate. I think you'll like it there. It's very different from the places you've already been. It's quiet, and there's a small beach. We've got a detached house for you to live in. A little bungalow with a sea view. There's a nearby care home, Elizabe—"

"Lizzie," I cut in.

"Right, Lizzie. There's a care home with a position for a receptionist. Say the word and it's yours."

"The word," I reply, trying to smile at my feeble joke. I glance at Tom in the backseat through the rear-view mirror, but he's engrossed by his smartphone. They provided us each with a new mobile phone when we joined the programme, and luckily for us, they actually gave us an upgrade for a change. But now Tom barely lifts his head from it.

"That's good," Adam says with an approving smile. "I'm glad you've decided to get out there and work. I know it means interacting with more people than you've been used to for a while, but I think you're ready for it. Do you feel comfortable with your new identities?"

"Well, it's obviously very strange," I reply. "But I'm getting used to it."

"And do you and Scott use your new identities at home?" Adam asks. He likes to test us with this question every now and then.

"Yes." Lie.

I glance at Tom again to share a conspiratorial smile, but he's still glued to the phone. The smile fades from my lips. But as he's distracted, I allow my gaze to roam over him. He's different now, with shorter hair, no longer dyed black, his piercings removed, and his body shape more defined. But I'm not contemplating those changes right now, I'm searching him for the feathers he took. Did he bring them with him? Is he obsessing over what happened in Hutton? I need to know.

For most of the very long journey, I rest my head against the passenger window and drift into an unsettled sleep, never quite relaxing to the point where I can truly sleep, only ever remaining on the edges. I feel every bump in the road, hear Adam as he clears his throat, hear Tom's tuts in the backseat as he reads more articles on the dead woman.

Alison.

Strangled.

Does that seem like the way Isabel would kill? Though she is terrifying, she's also small. Could Isabel wrap her hands around a woman's throat and strangle her to death? Unless she used rope, or plastic, anything she could fashion into a garrotte. It's like Isabel to be prepared. But wouldn't the cause of death then be asphyxiation? Perhaps I'm overthinking this. How do I know that the media have all the facts? They might have reported strangulation when what they meant was asphyxiation. I can't trust what's written in the tabloids, not that I read much of them anymore.

Adam pays for a Little Chef lunch, stretches his legs walking around the service station, and then drives us the rest of the way to our new home: Clifton-on-Sea. The road winds through the small town, following the beach, before snaking up a hill to the cliffs that overlook the North Sea. The rain has finally stopped, but I can see from the bend in the grass along the verge, and the lonely crisp packet making its way up the hill, that it's very gusty outside.

Five minutes' drive away from the sea, Adam parks the car

outside a small bungalow with a sloped drive, pulls up the handbrake and nods towards the house.

"You should have a bit more room here. It's a lovely little spot. A much better place to start a new life. Or at least a temporary new life until we catch Isabel, anyway."

There's a snort from the backseat. Both Adam and I ignore it.

"Thanks for this. We appreciate everything the programme has given us. I don't think I'll ever feel safe while she's out there, but this helps."

When I climb out of the vehicle, the wind slaps me in the face, taking my breath away. I have to battle through it to walk up the small hill to get to the house, and once I'm there, I carry on until I'm around the side of the building, moving towards the back garden. It's there that I can see the unsettled sea churning below the cliffs. France isn't far away from where we are now, though I can't see it.

Adam was right about this being a change from what we're used to. I've never lived by the sea, and I didn't grow up with seaside holidays, sticky ice-cream fingers and pockets full of seashells. We were never *that* family. But the change in scenery is a welcome one. At last, this place seems a million miles away from Isabel.

But is it enough?

Adam leaves us with a small amount of spending money for extra furniture, money and clothes. A hundred is set aside for me to buy a smart outfit for an interview at the care home he told me about. He also leaves me the name and contact details of my new therapist. Everyone in the witness protection programme gets their own therapist.

That leaves us with the afternoon to unpack the small number of boxes we brought with us. Tom connects his phone to the wireless speaker, and we listen to Funeral for a Friend as we put away cutlery and shelve books. Seb's copy of *Do Androids Dream of Electric Sheep* is mixed in with mine, and I think about finally sitting down and reading it. I can't send it back to him, anyway. I don't want to send it back to him. I want to keep a small part of him here with me.

The bungalow is old-fashioned, and I suspect from the faux stone around the fireplace and the wood panel cladding on the living room walls that it hasn't been updated for a few decades. But it isn't dirty, and even the kitchen has been cared for. I'm already thinking of ways to transform the place. My interview outfit won't cost a hundred pounds; I can use half to buy paint and coat the kitchen cupboards in sunshine yellow to brighten the place up. We can buy a coffee table, perhaps a comfy reading chair, and new cushions for the faded floral sofa.

Tom chooses the bedroom at the front of the house because it has more room for his guitar, and we can fit a small desk in there too. My room faces the sea, with the land dropping sharply away to reveal the choppy waters below. That sudden drop reminds me of a time when my heel caught the edge of a cliff, almost throwing me down to the rocks below. It reminds me of the cold hand I released from my grip and the pale face falling through the dark.

You always wanted to fly.

I'll paint this room sky blue, I think. Bright sky blue.

Both of us restless with worry despite the tiring journey, Tom and I make our way out of the house and into Clifton. It's not a quaint English town, more of a city suburb placed by the sea, with takeaway restaurants, Spar shops, and pubs with grubby signs. We could be somewhere in London, where people overflow out of the apartments above those small shops, and ten different languages are spoken on the streets. But once we've left the long strip of takeaways, we decline down a steep hill to the point where a cold sandy beach meets the sea. Here, the wind assaults me with its damp, salty scent, and the dirty shops are replaced with empty arcades. It's out of season, early-

February, chilly, grey with gusty winds that penetrate my jeans and chill my thighs.

"What do you fancy for tea?" I ask.

Tom shrugs his shoulders.

"Well, we're at the seaside. Fish and chips?"

"All right."

I spot a place farther along the promenade, crossing the road to come closer to the beach. A lone man is walking his dog along the sand, his large, waterproof coat flapping in the wind.

"Do you think we'll move again?" Tom's voice is thin against the wind, but for once it's as though I'm in tune with him, like I could hear him even if he whispered through a hurricane.

"I don't know," I admit. "We're a long way away from her, though. I can feel it."

"Are you psychically connected to her now?"

I roll my eyes at him. "That's not what I mean. Maybe it's this place. I dunno. For the first time in a while, I'm more relaxed. Are you?"

"No," he says.

He didn't have to think about it. And, really, do I need to think about it to know? My words aren't a lie to Tom; I *am* more relaxed, but that doesn't mean that I've stopped thinking about Isabel for even a single second, wondering where she is, wondering what she's doing, wondering if she's still coming for me.

"When she had us trapped in that house," Tom continues. "She said she didn't care about being arrested. She just wanted to hurt you. After all those years in the hospital, she was free, and the one thing she wanted to do was hurt you. She never wanted to escape and live her life. She wanted to escape and find a way to kill you slowly."

His words make me uncomfortable. Never at any point have I wanted to hear Tom talk about such dark events. The worst part is that I know he's right. Isabel could have taken her freedom and got away from me, from Hutton, the hospital and the police. Instead, she risked it all to try to murder me.

"She can't find us," I say, my own voice thin against the wind. I sound tinny, weak, unconvincing. "We've been careful. The programme is careful. They're professionals; they know what they're doing. They hide people from criminals all the time." But I'm not convincing myself. They haven't worked against a person like Isabel before, someone so conniving that she lost weight and made herself resemble me in order to escape from a high-security hospital. "We're going to continue to be careful. That part is our responsibility. We've been given a chance to make a new start, and I think we should embrace it." I stop walking and place my hand on Tom's elbow. Before we met Isabel, I would have pulled him into a hug, but since that night, neither of us has enjoyed much human contact. "We're going to be okay, you know. Do you believe me?"

I see from the sadness in his eyes that he doesn't. He doesn't even believe that *I* believe it, and I think he's probably right.

But he knows he needs to appease me. "What are you having? Cod and chips?"

I loop my arm through his. "Battered sausage."

"Classic choice."

"They're hiring," I note. "They need extra hands for when the season starts."

Tom leans towards the window, reading the sign. "Maybe I should apply."

I'm surprised. Pleased, but surprised. "Yeah, why not? See, things are getting better already."

CHAPTER 4

A feather brushes against my cheek, and my eyes snap open. Within my tightened chest, my heart pounds, causing my pulse to thud in my ears. Every one of my muscles is cold and stiff, and my toes are numb. I place a palm down to ground myself and push myself into a lounging position. I'm on the lawn behind the house, lying on my side, facing the sea.

A scream builds in my throat, dying to be released into the wind coming off the sea. *Not again, not again, not again.* My mind refuses to cease racing. I lean over and push my hands against my knees, bracing myself against the cold gust of wind.

I'm in my pyjamas, which I pat down to discover that my phone is still in my pocket. 5:02am. At least I woke early enough to hide this from Tom, because he'd worry. In a heartbeat, I'm on my feet and running back to the house. What did I do yesterday evening after I went to bed? Did I steal out of the house, walk ten minutes to the

24-hour Spar shop and walk back with bottles of wine? Did I drink them and pass out? Did I break my promise to Tom? I need to know.

The back door is unlocked, but at least I didn't leave it wide open. I step into the kitchen and begin opening the cupboards, searching for empty bottles. I try the fridge and the bin, but there's nothing there. I take each mug left on the side and smell them, inhaling deeply. There's only the lingering scent of coffee and a trace of mint from my herbal tea. I check the living room. I even check my bedroom. Nothing.

I'm not sure whether to be relieved or more afraid. I'm not drinking again, but I am sleepwalking, just like I did during my psychotic episode in Hutton. But I haven't missed a single dosage of my medication. Why is it happening again?

Finally calmer since waking on the grass, I think through what I need to do. First, I need to check that all the doors are locked. Then I need to make an appointment with my therapist. My *new* therapist: a Dr Jennifer Qamber. Then I need a shower and breakfast, and finally I need to go out and buy new clothes for my interview. Today is going to be tough, but at least I know I'm not hungover. I'm not hungover, but I'm also not right. How do I know I'm even in control?

If Tom knows about my sleepwalking, he doesn't mention it for the rest of the day. But he does agree to get the bus to Canterbury for a clothes-shopping trip. The programme hasn't left us with enough money to buy a car on top of our furniture, but I'm glad not to have one. It would just be one more thing to worry about, and the bus service seems fine.

It's clear that we're not in London anymore, but I like the quiet now, and Canterbury is smaller, less hectic, but still has Whitefriars—a decent shopping centre near the High Street. I find a cheap but smart pencil skirt from Primark. Tom chooses a new shirt from Next. Later that day, we decide to buy paint online rather than try to find a DIY shop within walking distance of our bungalow, and then I do some research into the nursing home I'll be interviewing for.

Geriatric nursing is not my speciality, and I'm not even sure I want to go back to nursing, which means the receptionist job is a bit of a relief. Though the environment will be similar to the hospitals I've worked at in the past, the job is completely different, and there's a small nagging doubt that I won't be able to do it. I made mistakes at Crowmont Hospital. Big mistakes. The kind that put people in danger and maybe even got poor Alison Finlay murdered. At least as a receptionist I won't have the opportunity to make those mistakes again. I'll never meet anyone as dangerous as Isabel in a nursing home. I find it hard to believe that I'll ever meet anyone as dangerous ever again. I'm not sure there *is* anyone as dangerous as her.

According to Google, Ivy Lodge is a fifteen-minute bus ride from the small bus station in Clifton. I decide that on Monday I'll leave an hour before the time of my interview just to be sure. From the photographs on the website, the place appears pleasant enough, but you can rarely tell from the pictures. Most focus on the well-tended gardens outside. What is inside like? As a nurse, you hear horror stories about nursing homes, where patients are treated badly by overworked, stressed, or just plain cruel members of staff. I don't want to be in that environment. I want to join a well-organised establishment with a good manager.

Perhaps I'll get lucky.

After spending a little time researching Ivy Lodge and brushing up on the basics of geriatric nursing, I find myself searching the internet for more information on Alison Finlay, the woman found strangled and mutilated. When was she killed? Where was she found? Since leaving Scotland, I've become foggy on the details, focussing more on the here and now. But after waking up on the lawn, I need to know. I need as much information as possible, because since the night I was attacked by Isabel, my thoughts have been... troubling. Violent. And my dreams...

I don't even want to think about my dreams.

"Less than a thirty-minute walk from our house in Newcastleton."

The sound of Tom's voice causes me to yelp in surprise. "Christ on a cracker, you're as quiet as ever. Do you walk around on your tiptoes, kid?"

The old Tom would have flicked my earlobe, or rolled his eyes, or smothered a grin, but this new Tom merely leans over my shoulder to continue reading the news article.

"Why doesn't it say what kind of mutilations were found on the body?" he asks. "There's no detail whatsoever."

"It helps with the investigation to hold things back from the media."

"You should ring that detective and find out," Tom suggests. "What was his name? Murphy. We need to know if it was Isabel. Don't we deserve to know? I mean, for fuck's sake."

"Tom! Language!"

"Don't you mean Scott?" He grips the back of the chair and pushes me. The motion is too forceful to be playful. "That's who I am now. I'm Scott James. What a stupid fucking name."

"Do you think I like Lizzie James? I sound like a Victorian prostitute."

Still no flicker of a laugh.

"Come on, Tom. We need to make the best of this."

He backs away from me. "No, we need to be preparing ourselves for Isabel to find us. We need to be ready. I think I'm going to go for a walk. Get some fresh air."

"Do you want company?"

He shakes his head.

Ivy Lodge is as small and neat as the photographs suggested. I'm relieved that the place is small, which means fewer patients. The carpark is almost full, despite my arriving before nine, which makes me feel relieved that I'll be travelling by bus if I get the job. And then it's a short walk up a drive towards the actual house. It's the kind of manor house I'd imagine a wealthy family living in a hundred years ago, with large windows, a wide front door, and ivy creeping its way up the bricks. There's a stillness that I rarely acquaint with nursing, as though things move at a slower pace here. But it's wise to reserve judgment until after you've entered a care home. There might be more bustle once I'm inside.

I press the buzzer and am beeped in. When I close the door behind me, the entire frame rattles, and my cheeks flush warm from making such a loud noise in a quiet place. I'm early for my interview, so I sit and wait, smoothing my Primark skirt and hoping that no one will notice how cheap the material is. Mum used to say that a good iron transformed an outfit. We wore second-hand clothes most of the time, but Mum washed and ironed them as though they were expensive designer outfits. We were always clean and tidy, even if our clothes were never trendy.

The reception area shields the rest of the care home from view, but as I wait, I can't help but crane my neck to try to catch a glimpse through the doors at the end of the corridor. Is it clean? Tidy? Static white? Are the patients happy? I take a deep breath to try to calm myself. The last time I saw doors like these, I met Isabel.

That can't happen this time.

There are no murderers here, just older people who need help. This isn't a place for the criminally insane. This isn't Crowmont Hospital. But why does it feel like that? I tap my fingers on my knees and try not to stare at the woman sat at the reception desk. Would I be replacing her? Is she temporary? Perhaps they'll tell me in the interview. When I glance back at the entrance, I can't help but think about how I could get up, turn around, walk out and never come back. But then how would I provide for Tom? What would I do with my life?

"Ms James?"

When I turn my head, I'm convinced that I'm sweating profusely.

"Yes." As I stand, I knock over my handbag, and a pen rolls out. "Sorry." I bend quickly and retrieve the pen, feeling dizzy as my pulse quickens from the embarrassment.

"Not to worry." A woman in her forties with a kind smile waits patiently for me to regain my composure. "Hi. I'm Eileen Hargrave, the manager of Ivy Lodge. Would you like to follow me? I'll give you a little tour of Ivy Lodge, then we'll get on with the interview. Your background is psychiatric nursing, is that right?"

"It is."

"Did you fancy a change?"

"Yes, well, also, I just moved to the area with my little brother Scott. Ivy Lodge is close to where we live, and it seems like a lovely place." While the woman is busy opening one of the doors with a pass, I quickly wipe away sweat from my forehead with the back of my hand.

"How are you finding Clifton?"

"The sea views are beautiful. It's just what we needed."

As we walk down a short corridor, I could blink and be back among the Crowmont corridors, walking the hallways to Isabel's room. The image of her bent over her desk drawing her birds will forever be etched on my mind. *Today I drew a crow, Leah. Do you like it? They're lucky.*

No, I won't indulge those thoughts.

"Have you got family in the area?" Eileen asks.

We arrive in a communal space decorated with lots of reclining armchairs and sofas. A few of the patients are dotted around, playing cards or watching television.

"No," I reply. I'm cautious, but decide to say it. "Actually, I've been placed here with help from a domestic violence charity." Adam suggested that I use this as an excuse to make it easier when explaining why we've moved. People don't tend to ask any further questions.

"I'm so sorry," she replies. "Of course, we'll be very discreet." Eileen pauses. "I noticed you don't have an awful lot of administration experience, but your application was excellent. We'll be throwing you in the deep end with a fundraiser to organise if you do get the job."

"I'm a quick learner," I say. "Being trained as a nurse has prepared me for pretty much everything."

Eileen raises her eyebrows. "I can imagine."

But no one could imagine what I've been through.

CHAPTER 5

ISABEL

All that time, you were holding out on me, Leah. You never told me about the hunky farmer, did you? I watched the two of you together, hidden away on the moors, always a safe distance away. And there you were, like two newlyweds, longing gazes aplenty. In love.

I was hurt to see that you'd kept quiet about your private life. All that time, pretending to be my friend, while hiding a huge part of your life from me. Were you ashamed of him? Or didn't you want to get too close to me? Were you faking it all those months?

My mediocre Leah with a man.

Since then, I've had to leave Hutton because you made sure it wasn't safe for me. I was the fox and the hounds were snapping at my tail, but once I managed to clean myself up, I found a way to get out.

Do you know what it cost me? Do you know that you've reduced me to a petty criminal, stealing from people's bags, hunting through rubbish bins? There comes a point where survival takes over, and it eradicates the person you were before. That happened to me. I almost forgot about you as I was sleeping on the streets, searching for leftovers in a café bin, staying away from any main roads where CCTV might be in operation, climbing over garden walls to take clean clothes from washing lines, walking off the beaten path, hoping I was heading in the right direction to get away from Hutton and the manhunt that surrounds it. I couldn't go to a train station because of you. Stealing a car was too risky. I had to walk for miles in filthy clothes until I found the next town. It became all I lived for. I walked and I walked until I was close to collapsing, then I found a town. I snuck around that town at night, stealing in the moonlight, and then I walked through fields and forests until I found the next town.

Do you know what else I did? I saved my stolen money. I bought hair dye. I watched people, and I changed the way I walk, talk, stand. And then I bought a box, the kind you use at the post office. I wanted to buy the box rather than use an abandoned box because I didn't want it to stand out. I wanted my parcel to appear very boring indeed, because I didn't want anyone to check it.

I went to the post office with my box, and I posted it. Then I went to the bus station, and I bought a ticket and got on the bus. Halfway through the journey, I got off the bus in the middle of nowhere, and then I started walking again.

I walked for a very long time. My heels are hardened now, but back then I had many blisters, and there were points when I walked through fields and forests without shoes on because the pain was excruciating. But I walked and I walked until I found a new town, big enough to disappear into, but small enough to go unnoticed by the police, and then I thought about what his face would look like when he opened the box and saw my present.

Leah, when I next see you, will you tell me what Seb thought of the dead magpie I sent to him? I desperately want to know.

CHAPTER 6

Today, we start new jobs. Tom is going to the fish and chip shop on the promenade, and I am going to Ivy Lodge. We walk to the bus stop together, and I want to hold his hand and pull him in to me. But he's sullen and stiff. This new buff version of my son even has a new gait. We don't fit together like we used to.

"I have an idea," I say, breaking the silence. We walk down the hill leading into Clifton with the wind coming off the sea. We're quickly learning that Clifton is almost always windy, but I don't mind, because I like the fresh air after our cramped conditions in Newcastleton. It brings with it the scent of seaweed and crabs, sand and stone. For the first time since I left the moors, nature is close to me, and I miss Seb so much that my stomach aches for him.

"Well?" Tom avoids my gaze, which does little to assuage the anxiety building up through my body.

"You were right the other day. I think we can do more to protect ourselves in case Isabel does find us. We can't hide away and assume it will never happen. But, at the same time, we need to be happy. Why don't we give one of those fitness things a go? You know, like a boot-camp? I don't know about you, but if Isabel does find us, I want to be able to defend myself. Maybe we could join a self-defence class too? I know I got a little uptight about it last time we tried, but I think I can give it another try."

We come to a halt by the bus stop, and Tom leans against the post with his hands pushed deeply into his pockets. "I guess we could do that."

"And we could get a home surveillance system hooked up. I know we have the burglar alarm, but we could get CCTV cameras set up at the front and back doors. That way, we'll see anyone who comes to the house."

Tom nods approvingly. "Good idea." His body relaxes, and his shoulders drop. For the first time in a long time, I reach forward and squeeze his elbow.

"I'm right here. Everything you feel, I feel it too."

Tom drops his head and half-nods. "I know. I'm just… angry, I guess."

"We have a new therapist now. I've booked us appointments to see her." The therapist is mandatory for all participants in the witness protection programme. "Scott and Lizzie are going to get better. And they are going to lead normal lives, I bloody swear it."

He lets out a small laugh, which is music to my ears. Then the bus comes.

There's hope for us yet, I think, as the bus winds its way through the narrow street into the town. Tom leaves me after a few minutes to get to the chip shop, and I stay on until I come to the stop nearest Ivy Lodge.

Do I still believe in hope? Do I still believe in life? Do I think I'll have a normal life?

Yes. And no.

I will never stop seeing Isabel's face in a crowd, seeing her pale skinny hand slip away from mine in my nightmares, and I will never stop worrying that when I part from Tom, I'll never see him again, because I came so close to losing him. The sound of flapping wings will forever send a shiver down my spine, or worse, initiate a panic attack. I'll forever hate the dark, and I hate to live in a house with an attic or a cellar, and I will walk through hospital corridors and think of Isabel in her room, with her back to me.

But I still believe in hope.

My new job at Ivy Lodge is a learning curve. Rather than administering medication or cleaning bed pans, I have to schedule appointments, show visitors into the home, listen to complaints from family members of the patients. A thin-faced woman called Caroline shows me the ropes and introduces me to the patients in the hospital. All the time, I can't stop thinking about when my grandma was in hospital following her first heart attack. She looked me squarely in the eye and told me to never grow old, that growing old brought with it more and more pain and little joy. Her words had frightened me, as I was fifteen and afraid of her protruding veins and liver spots. I wondered how I could avoid growing old without dying, and hoped that scientists would invent some sort of youth serum I could take before I reached middle-age.

But age is inevitable, and avoiding it only isolates the most vulnerable. I never shied away from the criminals in my care at the high-security hospitals, so why should I recoil from old age? As I make my way around the home, I meet a woman who asks me why her husband isn't back with the milk yet, and am mistaken for a younger sister. Another thinks I'm stealing from him. A woman recovering from a hip replacement chats to me as I fetch her a cup of tea, telling me all the places she's had intercourse around Clifton. Apparently, the beach in midsummer is a prime spot for doggers.

By the end of the day, I've met many family members, all of the patients, written a dozen emails and answered the phone without messing up the standard greeting. It's a small success for an ex-nurse suffering with PTSD. I've even discovered my favourite patient. George still has all of his faculties. He's at Ivy Lodge because of his bad hip and the fact that his daughter is disabled herself and can't take care of him properly. As I'm tidying up the communal area, he asks me how long I've been working at Ivy Lodge.

"Today is my first day."

"Are you going to stick around? We get a lot of new faces here. I try to remember everyone, but my mind isn't what it once was."

I tidy up an abandoned game of Scrabble and remove dirty mugs from the coffee table. "You seem sharp enough to me, George."

"You should've known me fifty years ago!" He chuckles brightly.

"Are you flirting with me, George?"

His chuckle turns into a throaty laugh. "I'll have you know, I was married for forty years, and I wouldn't flirt with anyone except my Judy. Not even a pretty young thing like you."

"Sorry," I say. "I know you weren't flirting, really."

"You're all right, sweetheart. It's good to see a smile."

It's good to smile, I think to myself.

"Are you comfortable there? Need anything? A nurse?"

"A pint would be nice," he replies. "A nice trip to the Queen's Head." He laughs and then sighs. "No, no. I'm all set for my physio whatsit later."

"Ahh," I say. "Are they taking care of that hip of yours?"

He nods. "Yes, I suppose. It's not like I can shuffle my way out of here. I don't see how I have much of a choice about the matter, anyway."

"Oh, it won't be so bad," I reassure him. "I'll tell them to go easy on you."

"On your first day? The hell you will. Not that they'll listen to you, anyway."

I raise my eyebrows. "Sticklers, eh?"

He nods. "You a local lass?"

I shake my head. "Just moved here, actually."

"I didn't think so. You've not got the accent. I've lived here my whole life. What do you think of our little town by the sea?"

"I think it's just what I needed," I say.

He nods again as though understanding something I don't understand myself. Then he points towards the hallway leading back to the individual rooms. "Are you busy, Lizzie? Do you have a moment to help me back to my room?"

"I have a few minutes," I say. "Come on. Let's go."

George loops his arm through mine, and we make our way stiffly to his room. He's quiet as we move, concentrating on moving his legs. Once we're there, I help him onto the bed, using my nursing experience to get him comfortable.

"You're a sweet girl," he says, patting my hand. Then he points across to a display cabinet. "I wanted to show you something. Pass me that photograph, there."

I step across the room and retrieve the framed photograph on top of the cabinet. The black and white picture shows two children, one girl and one boy.

"Is this you?" I ask, pointing to the adorable boy with a broad grin. I see around the eyes that it's the man lying in the bed.

"That's me. And next to me is Abigail, my sister."

"I can see the resemblance," I note, observing the same straight nose, wide smile, and close-set eyes.

"We did look alike," he replies. "I miss her."

I pass George the photograph, suddenly understanding why it's a picture of the two of them as children. Did Abigail not get a chance to grow up?

"They say that time heals. But why is it, seventy years later, I still feel the same pain?"

"I'm sorry. What happened to her?"

"It was a fire," he replies. "Someone set our house on fire, and I never saw Abigail again."

I leave George's room a little shaken, needing some air, but the charge nurse, Sandra—a bullish woman with a thick neck and ankles—calls me to one side.

"Is everything all right with Mr Hawker?" she asks.

"He's fine. He was just telling me about his sister. It sounds like a tragic event."

"You were in there more than ten minutes." She places her hands on her hips and narrows her eyes, reminding me of an uptight villainess in a Disney movie.

"I'm so sorry. I think time got away from me."

"It's fine, Lizzie. But you're not a nurse. You shouldn't be spending that much time with the patients. You should be covering reception. We're short-staffed right now, what with that second temp quitting, and I need you to be where you should be. Okay?"

"Sure. I get it."

She lets out a long breath, and her shoulders drop. "How's the first day going? Settling in all right?"

As I tell Sandra about my day, the white walls of Ivy Lodge seem to fade away. Even though my mouth forms words, my mind wanders away as though meandering from a path.

Am I making the same mistakes again? Am I getting too close to a stranger? If I am, is there a reason why I keep repeating this behaviour?

CHAPTER 7

"And the birds?"

"They're an extension of her. They're searching for me, just like she is. And in my dreams, their claws always find me. Their wings beat next to my ears, blocking out the sound of my heartbeat, and they peck and peck until there's nothing of me left. My body is a feast for them to satiate their hunger. Nothing more."

"Take a deep breath."

I follow Dr Qamber's directions, breathing in until my lungs are full.

"Now, breathe out slowly." She motions with her pen for me to follow. "Good. I felt you were getting a little worked up, there. How are you feeling?"

"Better," I admit. "Talking about the nightmares is hard. I suppose it's normal to have nightmares after… Well, you know."

"It is normal to experience nightmares after trauma, yes. And what about when you're awake? Is there any anxiety then?"

"Nearly all the time," I admit.

"Have you experienced any panic attacks?"

"Yes."

"Shortness of breath? A sudden increase in heart rate? Constricted chest?"

"Yes. All of those."

She scribbles in her notebook and nods. "What about the hallucinations you experienced before the attack?"

"It's hard, sometimes, to figure out what's real and what isn't. Especially when I see birds everywhere. But my previous therapist told me to concentrate on the way things interact with the world to try to figure out what's real and what isn't. I don't think I've seen anything that isn't real."

"Good." More scribbles. "Is there anything else we need to discuss? You've left family and friends behind to come here. You're caring for your younger brother. You've just started a new job. That's a lot of stressful changes to deal with at the same time."

"I…" I swallow, pausing to collect my jumbled thoughts and assemble them into something coherent. Behind Dr Qamber's head is a shelf filled with psychology textbooks. Her office is neat, painted a dark blue, and carpeted with a deep pile that my feet sink into. Dr Qamber herself is put together well, with her black hair pulled into a chignon at the base of her neck. "Before Isabel attacked me and Tom, I had issues sleeping. I would sleepwalk, wake up in strange places, and find that I'd been on my computer. Sometimes, I'd been drinking alcohol. I still don't quite remember those moments when I was half-conscious. They stopped happening when I began the anti-psychotics. But since I entered the witness protection programme, it's been happening again." When I stop talking and stare down at my hands, I find that I've gathered the sleeves of my cardigan into my fists.

"Deep breaths."

I close my eyes and inhale, breathing in the faintest scent of the sea. Perhaps Dr Qamber has a scented candle somewhere.

"We'll talk through some breathing techniques to help with the anxiety. And"—she hesitates—"perhaps it's also time to go to your doctor and discuss your medication. I can send over some notes if it might help."

She's glancing at her watch as I nod my head. The hour is almost up, and the therapy session is over for another week. Now I can leave, wobbly-legged and with a head full of nightmares.

My paranoia always intensifies after a therapy session. All the way home, I check behind me, determined that all eyes are on me, and somewhere in the middle of all those eyes is Isabel, waiting and watching. From the line of people at the bus stop, to the teenagers cycling along the promenade, to the whistle of the wind as it sweeps in through the windows on the bus, every small noise has my nerves jangling. These sessions bring back all the fears I had before, during, and after the attack, not that those fears are ever very far away.

It's early evening when I get back to the house, and the sun is fading. After I open the front door, I have to put on the light to properly see what I'm doing, holding my breath in that briefest of moments before the lightbulb comes to life. The coat rack is going, I tell myself. It looks far too much like a tall person looming over the corridor, shapeless and wrong, like a spirit in a horror movie, though I'm far more terrified of earthly dangers than I am the unearthly.

The silence tells me that Tom is still at the chippy, and when I glance at my phone, I remember that his shift ends in half an hour. At least I won't be alone in the house for too long. That's a good thing, considering that I'm still a little shaky from the therapy session.

I hang up my coat on the rack and hurry into the kitchen to make a cup of tea. It was Mum who always put the kettle on in times of crisis, which usually meant when my father was drunk. I hush my thoughts as the water rushes into the plastic kettle, drowning them out with the sound. That chapter of my life has ended, and it does no good to bring it up in my thoughts again. Dr Qamber is right: I do need to make changes, and after this cup of tea, I'll be well on my way to figuring out what to do next. That's all life is, isn't it? Getting through one moment and then figuring out what to do next? It doesn't matter how long that moment is. For some people, a moment can be years. They're organised enough to know exactly what they're doing for the next decade. Others take it second by second. I think I fall into the latter category, especially after everything that happened with Isabel.

I take my mug in one hand and tuck the laptop under my arm so I can move to the lounge and sprawl out on the sofa. As the adult in what's left of my family, it's up to me to figure out how Tom and I are going to get through this. I've been in a fog since we left Hutton. I haven't allowed myself to feel comfortable or think about staying in one place permanently, but now I have a job, as does Tom. We live in a nice house. This town is pleasant, and we're far away from the moors where I ran naked and bloody away from the girl who terrorised me and changed my life forever.

First, I search for camera systems for the house. CCTV, nanny cams and video doorbells could help make us feel safer here. There are alarm systems, too. None of this is cheap, but if I remain frugal with my wages, we should be able to manage for a while. There's such an abundance of options that my tea is long gone before I've compiled a shortlist to show to Tom later. Then I move on to strength training and martial arts. Isabel's strength hardly lies in her physicality, but she's clever enough to ensure that that's not a problem for her by using weapons and the element of surprise. I still wake up in the middle of the night drenched in sweat, with the memory of that sharp knife pressed against my throat.

If I were stronger, perhaps I could disarm her. If I had the confidence, or the knowledge, to wrench a knife or gun out of her hand, unlike last time, when I just froze up.

I'm on my second cup of tea and down half a packet of chocolate digestives by the time Tom comes in. I can't deny that I've been anxiously munching on the biscuits, knowing he was late coming home after the end of his shift. But when he comes into the room, I hide that anxiety and smile.

"How was your first day?"

"All right." He slumps into a chair and flicks on the television.

"My day was fine too," I say, rolling my eyes. "Thanks for asking."

He glances in my direction and sighs. "Sorry. Just tired. Think I might get a shower. The chip fat stuff stinks."

"Did you go out after?"

He gets to his feet and nods. Is it possible that he's taller than yesterday? "Yeah. There's a couple others working there, so we went for a drink at the pub after."

"Oh, that's cool. What are they like?"

"Seem sound," he replies.

"Good."

"I'm going to go for that shower now."

"All right."

Tom leaves the room as I shovel another biscuit into my mouth, telling myself that it's good he finally has some friends. It's good that he's getting out of the house and has a job and is moving on. This is a good thing.

CHAPTER 8

Over the next couple of weeks, I'm too busy organising a fundraising event at Ivy Lodge to focus too much on Tom, but I do manage to persuade him to try out the "plank challenge" with me in order to help with strength training. We're up to 50 seconds of agonising pain and I can feel a slight change in my arms, but I really need to get some weights and work out properly to feel the full effect. At least we're doing it, even if the plank inevitably ends with carpet burns on my elbows and a sweaty collapse onto the floor.

Outside work time, I've managed to install a video doorbell and a camera at the front and the back of the house. Late at night when I can't sleep, I sometimes sneak into the living room and turn the TV channel to our camera just to watch and make sure there's no one there. But I haven't been sleepwalking anymore. Also, therapist, psychiatrist and GP have all teamed up to change my medication, meaning that I should be on track to being normal again. Whatever "normal" is.

Tom works part-time at the chip shop, and the rest of the time, he seems to be in the pub with the other teenagers who work there. The manager reckons he'll be able to go full-time soon, which will be good for an injection of cash (if Tom doesn't start spending it all on beer) but not great for my son's prospects in the long term. Every time he talks about going full-time, I can't help thinking about his A-Levels and what he's going to do with the rest of his life. But Tom is young, and long-term plans are a dull affair to him. I don't even feel like I can argue, after what we endured last year. Let him blow off steam until he's ready to come back to reality. As long as he comes back…

The Ivy Lodge fundraiser is an afternoon tea event with a bake sale and a little ballroom dancing by a couple of local dancers. Eileen gave me a few contacts, a budget, and let me get on with it, which meant I could decorate the social room however I wanted. After getting a few opinions from the nursing staff and the residents themselves, I decided on a vintage theme and bought colourful bunting and patterned tablecloths. This morning, I arranged for the tables to be moved to the outside of the room to create a small dance floor, and placed vintage teapots on every table with trays of scones, jam, cream, and cakes. There are stalls with more cakes in front of the nursing home on the garden.

For once, there is a lively buzz about Ivy Lodge as the residents come to life. Brittle fingers tap the arms of wheelchairs as Vera Lyn plays on the stereo. There are claps and cheers as the ballroom dancers waltz around the room. Some of the younger residents and their friends and families take to the dance floor themselves, attempting the Charleston with the professionals. We even have a few children nicking brownies from the tables and licking chocolate from their fingers.

For the first time in a long time, I'm at ease. Too busy to be looking over my shoulder every minute.

"Hello, there."

I lift my eyes from the laminated schedule in my hands to see George, the most charming of the residents, standing in front of me. "Hi, George. Are you having a good time?"

"I am. A little bird told me that you organised this shindig."

I nod. "With help, of course."

"Well, you've done a good job."

"Thank you."

He smiles and shifts his weight from one leg to the other. "I'm not as quick on my feet as I used to be, but I can still waltz. Fancy a dance with an old codger?"

"George, you're not an old codger. But, yes, I'd love to."

His eyes flash with mischief as I leave the schedule on the nearest table and allow him to take me by the hand onto the small makeshift dance floor. Though his movements are stiff, I can tell he was once a good dancer, and imagine that he was quite a hit with the young women of Clifton. I, on the other hand, have never waltzed before, and almost trip over poor George as we navigate our way around the room.

"There you are," he says. "You're picking it up."

"This isn't what I usually dance to, but I like it," I admit, thinking about the London rave clubs I stumbled out of when I was eighteen and stupid. The "dancing" was more like jostling other sweaty bodies on a sticky floor before snorting lines of powder in the bogs, and waking up the next day with no memory of what had happened. But that was another Leah, another time. Lizzie likes to waltz with gentlemanly OAPs. She didn't grow up with an alcoholic father or live in squats with lazy artistic drug addicts. She's together, normal, not haunted or stalked by a psychotic murderer.

"My grandson is here today," George says brightly. "I'll introduce you to him. He's a good boy."

I always feel like I can't tell whether some of the residents at Ivy Lodge are describing their grandchildren or their pets. "Lovely!"

The song ends, and George walks me back to the table. "And handsome," he adds.

"Are you trying to set me up, George?" I let out a nervous laugh. The last thing I want is an awkward situation with a man.

"Oh, no, dear. He's courting."

As the band starts up a new song about bugles, a young man with ashy blond hair and bright eyes, who I imagine George would have been the spit of if he were twenty-five, comes over and taps George on the arm.

"Nice moves, Grandad."

George surprises me with a few tap-dancing moves before clutching the nearest chair. "I think that's my limit. Mark, I'd like you to meet Lizzie. She's the one who organised this event."

Mark directs his easy smile to me. "Everyone's having a fantastic time here. You've done a great job."

To my horror, a flush of heat creeps up my neck and into my face. "Thanks. Everyone pitched in."

"Mark comes to visit me in between working and taking care of my daughter. She's paralysed after an accident a few years ago," George says.

"I remember you telling me. I'm sorry. That must be difficult for you all."

"It's not as bad as it sounds," Mark says. "She's very independent, but the wheelchair does complicate things. I know she doesn't get out of the house as much as she'd like to. The world isn't catching up to accessibility just yet. It can be a bit frustrating at times."

"I'm sorry," I say, immediately feeling like an idiot, as we all do when confronted with an unusual topic of conversation. "Again." And then I shake my head at myself.

"It's okay," he says, showing a little amusement.

"So, what do you do?" When in doubt, change the topic.

He shrugs. "Office monkey. Not very exciting. I work in administration for a local school."

"Same. I joined the administration team here a few weeks ago."

"Well, you've certainly had a good start by setting this up," he remarks.

"I've been telling Lizzie all about Abigail," George chimes in. "I thought maybe you could talk to Lizzie about it. It doesn't hurt to spread the word however we can. Maybe someday we'll figure out what happened."

Mark leads me away as George goes on the hunt for more sandwiches. "I'm sorry if he's been bending your ear about this."

"Oh, no," I say. "I love talking to George. Don't tell the other patients, but he's my favourite."

"I can believe it. Grandad could charm the birds from the trees. My grandma used to say that. But lately, as he's been getting older, he's been fixated about this fire that happened when he was a boy, and I'm afraid he tells everyone the story, I guess in the hopes that someone will help. I would hire a private investigator, but we don't have the money, and I've not had enough time to delve into the past, what with taking care of Mum and working full-time. I know he's desperate to find out what happened to Abigail, and since he's been at Ivy Lodge, well, he worries that he hasn't got much time left."

I nod. "I've only just moved to the area, so I don't know people, and I don't know local history, but I do have some free time." I think of Tom working long hours in the chip shop and my craving for wine in the evenings after the sun has gone down, when my mind drifts to thoughts of Isabel and I watch the footage from our CCTV cameras. A distraction from that might be nice. "Maybe I can help."

"That's… I mean, that's such a kind offer. I don't know if we can—"

"Honestly, I don't mind. I actually need some sort of hobby right now. I'm pretty bored, to be honest. You'd be doing me a favour."

"Thank you," Mark says brightly. "And now you know me at least!"

I return the smile, thinking that George was right about his grandson.

"Anyway," Mark says, bringing the conversation back. "The story is a tragic one. My grandad was ten when there was a terrible fire in the house. My grandad and his sister Abigail slept in a room down the hall from his parents' room. After my great-grandparents woke during the fire, they burst into Grandad and Abigail's room to get them out. Grandad says he was scooped up into his father's arms and taken downstairs, but they couldn't find Abigail. My great-grandfather took Grandad outside to save him, but as he was getting Grandad to safety, my great-grandmother ran back upstairs to try to find Abigail. The flames engulfed the house. Grandad's father couldn't get back in, and his mother died. It all happened during the war, when things were already fraught. I think maybe the police didn't investigate as heavily as they should have. Abigail's remains were never found, and it was clear that the fire had been started deliberately. They could all have died that night."

"I can't believe he lost his mum like that. It's so sad." There were pinpricks down my arms as I imagined the panic and terror of being trapped in a burning building.

Mark frowned for the first time, and a small line appeared between his eyebrows. "I know that night has been hard for my grandad to cope with all these years. Especially with the way Abigail disappeared."

"And the police didn't investigate?"

"The fire burned everything to ash. Because it was during the war, the fire department was smaller than usual. They tried their best, but the fire tore through the house and annihilated everything. They found the remains of my great-grandmother, but there was nothing left of Abigail. She was only twelve years old and small for her age, and it was 1944, so forensic science was not as good as it is now, but it still seems odd that no bones were found. Nothing. No scrap of the nightdress she was wearing that night. Though I must admit I don't know how well the police searched for her. I don't know the circumstances because I wasn't there, and Grandad was only ten. He barely remembers the fire at all. I've searched out some newspaper articles about the fire, though, and I have my own speculations."

"What are they?" I ask.

"Well," he says, leaning forward. "What if the fire was to cover up an abduction? What if someone kidnapped Abigail and then set the house on fire to get rid of the evidence?"

"Wouldn't they be drawing more attention to themselves?" I ask. "Not finding the remains for the little girl is still a huge story."

"But at the time, the authorities assumed she had perished in the fire anyway. They figured that they'd missed something, or that she burned until there was nothing left." Mark grimaces as he says the words. "If someone did kidnap Abigail, they got away with it. As far as I know, the case was closed after a few years. My great-grandfather was depressed his whole life about losing his wife and daughter. When Grandad was thirty, he came home to find his father hanging from the beams. He'd left a note to my Grandad saying that he was a man now and could take care of himself, and that he wanted to be with his wife again."

"Oh, God." I shake my head. There are no words for such a thing.

"I know. It was hard on Grandad, not that he ever let it drag him down. He's the most positive man I've ever known."

I tactfully turn away as Mark quickly blinks away a tear.

"I'd love to go over your research into this one day. I realise you hardly know me and I'm new here, but if you're desperate for help, I'd be happy to lend a hand."

"You know, my grandad has told his story to anyone and everyone who will listen over the years, and you are the first person to offer to help." Mark takes my hand and clasps it in both of his. "Thank you."

CHAPTER 9

ISABEL

Are you happy, Leah? Making friends? Are you using that unassuming charm to create meaningful relationships? Such a good girl. Such a sweet girl.

Guess who made a friend today?

It was purely by accident. There I was, down a dark alleyway, searching through a bin behind a supermarket, as every well-respecting delinquent on the run needs to do, when an overly large man with too many muscles dragged a scrap of a girl into the alley and shoved her up against the wall. This man had no manners. His hands were all over her, greedy and gobbling, wanting to devour her whole. I couldn't let that happen, and luckily, the man with the hands hadn't seen me crouched like a rat behind the bin.

So I crept up on them.

I approached silently, slowly, until I was close to his back and could see the whites of the girl's eyes. I saw the terror on her face and the tension running through her small body. When she saw me, I placed a finger on my lips. Do you know what, Leah? For a moment, she reminded me of you, and I didn't like the way that man was touching her, because I'd heard all about men like him from the women in Crowmont. Nearly all of them had a story about men like him, with their huge fists and hungry mouths. They don't care about creating art or beauty, like I do. All they care about is taking what they feel entitled to.

As I walked up close behind him, I weighed up my chances. You know very well, Leah, that I'm not a large or physically strong person. Truth be told, my father helped an awful lot with James Gorden *and* with you, Leah dear. But that merely meant that I needed to be sneakier, and we both know that I'm the sneakiest bitch around.

His hands were pulling up her top as I crouched low to the ground. I'd spotted a useful object nestled amongst the litter, one that I felt would help both of us get out of this dire predicament. Once my fingers had grasped the object I sought, I stood, took one step closer to the man, and cleared my throat. The girl's eyes widened, pleading for help. She was whimpering but not screaming, which was good. Any sniff of the police, and I would be forced to "leg it" as Tracy from Crowmont would say.

Frustratingly, the muscly pervert did not even notice my signal. Instead, he lowered his face to the girl's neck and licked her skin possessively. My stomach turned at the sight. I folded my arms, rolled my eyes, and kicked the back of his leg. At least the man was suitably startled by the interruption of his assault. I kicked him even harder, and he turned around, now holding the girl with one hand wrapped around her throat.

When he saw me, though, he grinned. "Want to join in? There's plenty of me to go around." In an attempt to menace me, he squeezed the girl's throat, and she made a strangled gurgling sound.

Leah, I have to confess that I enjoyed that sound. I enjoyed it in a place that I do not much care to describe. A dark, dangerous place. A part of my body that no one has touched. At this point, I hesitated. Did I want to save this girl? Wouldn't I have more fun watching her be harmed? Watching her *die*? It was only a fleeting thought, and a second later, I remembered what I was planning to do.

This man had no manners, and he deserved to be taught a lesson.

"No, thank you. Please let her go. She doesn't want to be pawed by an ugly, dirty pervert like you."

At this, his head tilted down until his eyes were shadows. I did the same, not one to be outdone when it came to menace. And then I unfolded my arms, where the paint can was hidden, and sprayed paint into those shadowed eyes. I had contemplated the idea that the paint can was empty, but I knew from the weight of it when I lifted it that there was paint left. At this point, the man was yelping like a little dog, and he let go of the girl, letting her crumple to the ground. He threw his hands up to his face, giving me the perfect opportunity to kick him hard between the legs.

"Time to run now," I said to the girl.

The man was doubled over and blind, but he was still bigger than both of us put together, and there was a chance he would recover fairly quickly. Luckily, despite the girl being in a state of panic, she was lucid enough to take my hand and climb to her feet in such trouper-like capacity that once again, she reminded me of you.

Then we ran. Two rats fleeing from a mongrel. We ran, and we survived—as rats tend to do—and, honestly, saving a life was almost as exhilarating as taking one.

Almost.

CHAPTER 10

The news about the murdered girl has died down, and I must admit, I almost forgot her after moving to Clifton, but Alison doesn't let me go; instead, she creeps into my dreams. Bloody from head to toe, she follows me, dragging her muddied feet across the coarse grass. We're back on the North Yorkshire moors and she's opening her mouth to speak, but the wind cuts her off, blowing her hair into her eyes.

"What do you want?" I ask desperately.

But she doesn't answer, only continues on, dragging her toes against the ground, her naked body alabaster beneath the blood and drowned in moonlight. Then she turns around, and I see the wounds. The wings are stretched down her back, like unfolded angel's wings. These are red—scorch marks against her white skin—the edges smeared with blood as it drips from the gashes, giving it a smudged appearance, like fresh watercolour ink. The red tattoo draws in your eye and keeps your gaze firmly on it, every inch longing to be seen, to be admired.

It's beautiful.

The wings drape down to her hips. The marks move with her body as she rolls her shoulders. I could close my eyes and imagine the wings unfolding up to the sky, a beautiful bird in flight, or an angel called back to heaven, still bloody, still crimson, and still covered in moonlight.

I'm jealous.

My eyes snap open. My chest is tight, and my breathing is laboured. Pushing out a raspy breath, I'm relieved to see that I'm still in my own bed and haven't wandered somewhere else. Then I notice that the angle of the window is wrong, and that's when I realise that my head isn't on my pillow. I'm the wrong way around at the bottom of the bed.

At least I didn't walk up to an abandoned farmhouse or spend hours on the internet poisoning my mind with serial killer stories. At least I haven't overslept or woken up at the crack of dawn. It's just the right time to get up and go to work, which I do, after untangling myself from the bed sheets.

But on my way out of the house, I worry about the girl in my dreams, the disturbing sight of her wounds, and about our future. Tom has already left for work, and I didn't see him when he came home last night because it was after midnight. When it comes to caring for Tom, I'm impotent. I don't have the authority over him that either of my parents had. I'm constantly lying to him by not telling him that I'm his mother, and I'm the cause of everything bad that has happened to us. Isabel is obsessed with me, and that's how Tom ended up getting hurt that night on the moors. He probably blames me for all of this, and I blame myself too.

As I take a drizzly bus ride to work, I can't stop thinking about how I am to blame for the death of Alison Finlay. Didn't I allow it to happen by not killing Isabel that night?

If I'd killed her, we'd be free.

But I didn't, and I need to figure out why I didn't do that.

I need to figure out what my dreams mean, and why they're full of blood and violence. Am I the same person I used to be? Or is there a new darkness growing inside me that I can't control?

Ivy Lodge seems deathly quiet after the bustle of the charity event, and I spend most of my morning on the internet searching for clues about George's sister, Abigail. It seems that Abigail's disappearance is something of a legend in Clifton, and a few locals have speculated on what happened to her. There's even a forum dedicated to it.

Some believe that Abigail died in the fire and now haunts the promenade looking for her family. There have been sightings of "Little Abby" over the years. I wonder if poor George is aware of it. Others think that the fire was a misdirection to cover up the abduction of Abigail. This is more interesting, but some of the theories are too wacky to be legitimate. For instance, Clifton_Neal is convinced that Abigail was abducted by aliens, and their spaceship set the house on fire when it zoomed back up to space. Conspiracy_Steve believes he's found a connection between Clifton-on-Sea and the Italian mafia during the 1940s.

But amid the conspiracy theories and ghost stories, there is a thread of something that at least could be a plausible explanation. What if the fire *was* started to disguise Abigail's abduction? Forensic science back then was nowhere near as advanced as it is now, and the idea of faking a death with a fire was far more plausible. Whoever took Abigail thought they were faking her death, and although there was suspicion about not finding her remains, eventually the case was closed because there were no other leads, and it seemed that the most likely solution was that she died in the fire along with her mother.

These people went to a lot of trouble to steal a child. Why?

I decide that I need to find out more information about George's parents and what they were involved in. Perhaps that connection to the mafia isn't as far-fetched as it seems.eAs Asss

My mind begins to wander, and my internet searches veer from George's sister to Isabel Fielding, and that's when I find the posts. There are hundreds of them: #justiceforalison on Twitter, Instagram, and Facebook. Most of the tweets call out the police and their inability to find Isabel, but not all of them. Some call for my name to be released to the press because I was the one who let Isabel go in the first place. The same thing happened immediately after Isabel escaped from Crowmont, but I thought those people had put away their pitchforks and got on with their lives. Not anymore. The death of Alison Finlay has brought them all out of the woodwork.

Who is this woman? Why wasn't she arrested? Why should my hard-earned money go towards funding her in the witness protection programme? I don't pay taxes to fund morons who let murderers out of prison. How do we know she isn't working with Crazy Izzy? How do we know she isn't also a killer?

It goes on and on, and as I read the tweets, I want to shrink down in my seat and disappear. The room suddenly seems too hot, and when the nurses walk past the reception, I feel convinced that they know who I am, that they know my shame. But they have no idea who I am. They don't know that I'm marked. They don't see the scars that make me unclean.

Some of them are not visible. I keep them hidden away.

The phone rings.

"It's me."

"Hey, Tom." I'm surprised to hear his voice in the middle of the day. "What's up?"

"Nothing."

There's a pause, and I immediately know there's something wrong.

"Tell me." I try to keep any trace of panic out of my voice.

"It's nothing… I just… I had to come home."

"Aren't you feeling well?" I still feel lightheaded from reading the toxic tweets, and the edge in Tom's voice isn't helping my anxiety lessen. He's upset, and I can tell that he doesn't want to tell me what he's upset about. But he picked up the phone and called me…

"It's not that."

I stay quiet, waiting for him to open up.

"They sent me home." His voice is defensive now. Angry.

"Why? What happened?"

"It's just stupid. It's nothing."

"Yeah, you mentioned that." I roll my eyes, losing patience.

"I just wasn't in the mood for it." He sighs heavily, and I hear the sound of him moving around. I can visualise him pacing back and forth on the carpet. Feet shuffling. "He was being a twat, not me." His voice rises as anger creeps in.

"Tell me what happened, Tom." I sound like a nurse again, calming down a patient. I don't think it's the best course of action, because Tom knows me, and he knows what my "nurse" voice sounds like, and to him it's just patronising and insulting.

He sighs again, not a sad, exhausted sigh, but a short, angry exhale, which is followed by a long rant. "This twat came in the shop complaining I'd sold him a fish with bones in it. Stupid bastard almost choked, he reckoned. Kept saying I could've killed him. But who doesn't know you can get bones in fish? It's fucking cod, for fuck's sake.

What am I supposed to do about that? It's not my fault he can't fucking eat like a fucking normal human being. Stupid old wanker. It was his fault. *His* fault, not mine. And he comes in ranting and raving at me." At this point he runs out of steam, and his voice cracks and falters.

"Why did they send you home?" I ask.

"Because I told him, didn't I? I told him he was an idiot, because he *was* a fucking idiot!"

"Do you want me to come home?" I ask. There must be a reason why he called me immediately. He must need comfort, or reassurance, or something from me.

"No."

"Tom," I say, speaking calmly, choosing my words carefully. "I'm sorry that someone was rude to you. There's no need for that. But you took a job that requires you to interact with customers, and those kinds of jobs come along with rude people who may shout at you from time to time. It's hard not to react to idiots like that, but you can't get aggressive with them. It doesn't work that way."

"What do you know about it?" he snaps.

"I've worked in healthcare for years. I've been spat at, kicked, punched, screamed at and scratched. But I've never lost my temper."

"Sorry for not being perfect like you."

"That's not what—"

But it's too late. Tom has already hung up.

I place my office phone back onto the handset and lean back in my chair. No part of that conversation sounded like the same Tom I grew up with. The trauma we experienced has changed us both, but I think it's changed Tom even more. Suddenly, a heavy sense of exhaustion sweeps over me. I want it all to stop.

One foot in front of the other. One breath followed by the next. I wait until my breathing is back under control, and then I pick up the phone.

CHAPTER 11

Tom is going to see my therapist even if I must drag him to her office myself. Love is a funny thing—sometimes maintaining love requires cruelty. He hates me for it. He doesn't want help, and he certainly doesn't want to see my therapist, but he needs help, and I'm going to get it for him. He's my ward. My flesh and blood. The only person I have left. I will save him from whatever is misfiring right now.

I make an appointment for him then and there at my desk. Then, later, we argue about it. But aside from the therapist drama, the next few days pass by in relative calm. Tom agrees to continue with our plank challenge. We try another self-defence class together, but I'm terrible and Tom is over-enthusiastic. It's a free first session, and I'm not sure I want to carry on with it.

Whenever I start a search about Abigail, I end up reading more about Isabel and Alison Finlay than Little Abby. #justiceforalison haunts my every move on the web. They want to out me. They want to find me and burn me to the ground because they can't find Isabel. She is somewhere in the ether, intangible and mysterious, whereas I am all too real and the public knows there are people who know where I am. I'm a solid entity they can bully until they feel better.

But they don't know anything about me. Yet.

Spooked by the online vitriol, I decide to call Adam.

"Should I be worried? Will we have to move again?" I ask.

"No," he replies. "Not yet, anyway. If anyone does release your name and photograph to the papers, they'll be arrested. You're under protection by us, and we'll do everything we can to keep you safe."

"Just find her." I shake my head and bite my lip. "I know it's not you running the investigation. I know you're not on Isabel's case. But find her. Please."

"They're doing everything they can, Lizzie."

"Do you know if they're close?" Is there hope in my voice? I'm not sure I can tell anymore.

"Honestly, I couldn't tell you even if I knew, but I don't, because I'm not on that case. I'm sorry."

I'm nodding along, my eyes burning with tears of frustration. "It's okay. I know it's not your fault. We're grateful for everything you're doing for us."

After I hang up the phone, I turn around in the kitchen to see Tom standing behind me with his fingers gripping the side of the kitchen counter. "We're *grateful*? They've failed to capture a murderer, the woman who tortured us both, and you're *grateful*?" He makes a derisive sound and storms out of the house. Leaving me alone. Again.

Tom's words play on loop as I work at Ivy Lodge. An earworm you cannot eliminate no matter what, even when you put the radio on loud to drown it out. Except I can't do that. I have to greet visitors and chat with nurses and help elderly patients down the hallway. There's no sign of George in the lounge today, so I decide to head down to his room for a chat about Abigail. With every footstep, I hear Tom's words: *Grateful? Grateful?* Maybe he's right and I should share his anger, but the exhaustion of the last few months has drained it from me. Or perhaps it's my medication numbing me against experiencing the same righteous indignation as Tom.

When I knock on the door, George hoarsely tells me to come in. He's propped up on pillows at an angle that doesn't seem at all comfortable.

"You all right, George? Do you need anything?"

"A time machine," he says. "Back to 1960. Summer. Judy's sundress." He smiles to himself and then chuckles. "Or a cold pint of Boddingtons, if you've got one."

I shake my head. "No, sorry." I adjust his bedding to cover him a little better and then sit down on the chair next to his bed. "I have a ten-minute break, so I thought I'd come for a chat. You're not in the lounge today, George. Is everything all right?"

"It's my legs." He nods down to them. It pains me to see them lying still and useless, like two long sausages of meat without definition. I can see the edema around his ankles and the redness that indicates a rash. "They don't want to work today."

"Too much dancing at the tea dance the other week."

He laughs heartily. "But it was worth it to dance with a lovely young woman like you."

"Oh, you charmer. Has a nurse been in to check on your legs?"

George lowers his voice. "It was the one with short hair. Looks like a Beatle."

I have to bite my lip to avoid a laugh. Stacey does have an unfortunate mop-top, but it suits her androgynous features.

"She said I wouldn't be dancing again for a little while. I need some rest." He sighs heavily before seeming to realise there's someone else in the room. "But it's nice to have company. Mark has been a bit busy recently. He got a promotion at work."

"That's wonderful."

"It is," he admits. "I'm very proud of him."

I can tell that George is holding back. The unspoken words hang between us. *But now he can't visit as much.* And *I'm lonely.* Other patients, the nurses, me—we don't replace family. At that moment, I realise that I'm lonely too, because the one member of my family that I have left is shutting me out of his life. I don't think I've thought of myself as lonely until that very moment.

I clear my throat and change the subject. "I've started to research your sister's disappearance on the internet."

"Oh, yes?" he says, his head lifting and some shine coming back to his eyes. When George's eyes twinkle, it's obvious that he was once a very handsome man.

"Mm-hmm, but I haven't found much. Just a few conspiracy theories. I need to go to the library and find the newspapers to research it a little better."

George's lips form a tense smile, and he nods once. His brow is furrowed, and his eyes seem unfocussed. I'm about to check that he's okay when he lifts his finger and points to the top drawer in the cabinet at the foot of his bed.

"Open that drawer, will you, Lizzie? There's something I want to show you."

"This one?" After standing up from the chair, I place my hand on the drawer in question.

"That's the one. Open it up. There's something I haven't told you about yet. I wasn't sure if you were interested at first, so I left it. But it might be important, you know, for the investigation you're attempting. Reach in. There's a bundle of old photographs." George's finger trembles as he continues to hold out his arm.

I reach in and find the photographs he's referring to. The drawer is sticky to close, requiring a good shove with my shoulder.

"I have them." I sink back into the chair next to his bed and hand the bundle over.

George tuts. "I can't see a thing these days. Be a dear and pass me that magnifying glass."

After I hand him the glass, George holds it in one shaking hand and peers down at the stack of black-and-white photographs.

"No, no," he mutters to himself. "That's my father and his mother on the pier. Oh, and that's our old dog Bruce."

I take a look at Bruce—a black lab pup lying on the grass with his tongue lolling out and his head tipped to one side, adorably large ears and paws, and big puppy-dog eyes gazing into the camera. I bet Bruce was a lot of fun. A great family dog. My heart aches for George after the life he's lived. I don't want to know whether Bruce existed before the fire, or after.

"Here we are." George lifts the photograph higher to get a better view. "This is the one."

I lean over his shoulder. The image is of a smiling young woman leaning against a tree with a wide trunk, like an oak tree, though I can't be sure because the leaves aren't in the picture. Her long, wavy hair has plenty of volume at the roots, and is tossed back to show her large loop earrings. Her skirt is dangerously short, and her high-heeled boots reach almost all the way up to her knees. She is wearing a roll-neck jumper that swamps her chin. It's a relaxed pose, like something you'd see on Instagram, but it's obviously from the sixties with that fashion and her exaggerated eyeliner. George turns the photograph over, and I see a note in the corner: *Mary, 1962.*

"She's pretty," I note. "Is she a relative of yours?" I see something of George around the eyes and the shape of the nose, though I only recognise it because I've seen photographs of George when he was younger, and because those same features were visible when I met his grandson.

"She might be," George says. "Truth is, I don't know who she is. I received this photograph in the post on a Tuesday morning, April, 1984. There was no note. Only this."

I gaze down at the photograph, my jaw looser with surprise. "Do you think this is Abigail?"

"Yes," he says. "I do."

CHAPTER 12

"It was a relief to see her like this," he says. "Though the photograph was twenty years old by the time it reached me."

"Did you take it to the police?" I ask.

He nods. "They tried to trace the postmark on the envelope, but I think they thought I was some sort of local nutcase. They had other things to deal with at the time, what with the miners' strikes going on and whatnot. There was a pit closed five miles out of town. There was plenty of trouble in those days." He puts the magnifying glass down and strokes the photograph. "I tried again a few years later. But I was married, had a daughter about to go to university and a life. I wanted to find my sister, I did, but there was nothing to go on. The post stamp was Leeds, and there were too many young women called Mary for a police detective to go through. I tried a private detective at one point, but Judy told me to cut it out. We needed that money for our mortgage."

I gently take the photograph from George's hand and examine the young woman in the picture. She appears happy and healthy. Did she know she'd been kidnapped as a child? Could she remember her life before? Did she remember George?

"There's not much detail in the picture. It's zoomed in too close. I can't see any buildings behind her. They could be in a park, or a field, or a wood. It's hard to tell. But the postmark says Leeds, which could be worth investigating. Maybe I could check out parks in Leeds and the surrounding areas? Maybe Mary lived somewhere close to the park in the photograph."

"All these years and I never found her. If I'd had the money, I would've kept on with that detective, but I couldn't. And then the years went by in a flash. I never stopped thinking about her, though. I wondered what she was doing almost every day. At least she seems happy here. Doesn't she?"

"She does," I admit.

"And that's what matters."

I take the photograph back to my desk and scan it. Then I drop the picture back at George's room. By this time, George is tired, drifting in and out of sleep. I leave him be and return to my desk. Later on in the afternoon, I take visitors through the home, noticing that Mrs. Cartwright, who suffers badly with dementia, is wandering the corridors in her slip. I'm not sure how she got past the nurses, but I know that patients can be sneaky when they want to be, not that Mrs. Cartwright will have intended any malice by escaping her room.

"Let me take you to your room. Come on." I put a gentle arm over her bony shoulder.

"Get away from me." She shrinks away, shaking her head.

"Murderer."

Though I'm used to difficult patients, the venom in her voice shocks me, as does her accusation. I stand there aghast for a moment before pulling myself together. She's a lady with dementia. Nothing more. "You must be confusing me with someone else. I'm Lizzie. I work on the reception desk. Come with me. We need to get you back in your room."

"You're not Lizzie," she says. "Murderer."

When I take a step closer, her arm swings out, and she hits me squarely with her palm on my cheek. The blow is hard enough for me to stagger back in shock. We stand there for a moment, face to face, me stroking the soreness of my face, tears springing to my eyes in shock—no matter how many times you get hit, a slap to the face is always such a shocking event that tears spring up immediately—and her, defiant, with her fists clenched. She looks strong, like a woman facing down a demon.

"Mrs. Cartwright"—my voice is small—"I'm not a murderer."

She takes a step to the right and walks around me, all the time her eyes focused on me, challenging me. And then she continues along the corridor, leaving me alone, clutching my cheek.

I realise that Mrs. Cartwright is not herself, that she has been taken over by an illness that can change a person, change the things they say or even believe. It can change a person's personality. And yet… Can truth come from madness? Out of the mouths of babes, they say, and right now Mrs. Cartwright is more like a baby than she has been for decades. She is the twisted form of a child moulded from an adult's brain, with an adult's experience, but without the ability to *be* an adult. She's lost, but that doesn't mean she can't occasionally speak the truth.

Sometimes I think I am a murderer, and not because I let Isabel live. Not just because of that. No. There's more. More that I don't even want to admit to myself.

Can I trust any of this? Mrs. Cartwright's ramblings… my own thoughts, feelings, and dreams. What's real and what isn't? Alfie leaning against the wall of Crowmont Hospital smoking, telling me about the serial killers who lived in the hospital. He wasn't real. He was a figment of my imagination. I know this because I checked. There was no one called Alfie working at Crowmont.

My cheek stings from where Mrs Cartwright hit me, but can I trust that feeling? Can I trust my memory of what happened? Did she call me a murderer? Or did I call myself a murderer?

Dr Qamber scribbles her notes as the oppressive silences presses on my chest like a bowling ball resting on my ribcage.

"I thought I was better," I say, desperate to break the silence.

"Better than what?" Dr Qamber replies with a smile. "I know it's difficult. This whole process is difficult, and you've been through extensive emotional and physical trauma. It could be that the patient you mentioned *did* say those things, but because of your past, you assumed that it was a hallucination."

"If it was real, why did she say that? Do you think she knows who I am?"

"You're not a murderer, Lizzie, are you? Isabel Fielding is the murderer, and you can't control the things she does. This is all about the guilt you've felt since Alison Finlay was murdered. But that guilt is not your guilt, it's Isabel's. She's the person who has chosen to kill other people. She's the one who takes lives. Not you."

"She's ill," I reply. "And my actions led to her escape from Crowmont. And then I allowed her to escape by not thinking quickly enough. I just wanted to get Tom out of there, out of that house. But if I'd tied her up even—"

"And what if Isabel had regained consciousness as you were restraining her? What if she'd then found the strength to hurt you? What if she'd murdered you both? You didn't know what would happen if you did try to restrain her. It was too risky. You made a decision and chose the safest option available, which was to run away to safety and call the police. You're a citizen, not a police officer. You have no obligation to restrain or kill a murderer. None of this is your fault."

I glance down at my hands to see that my fingers are trembling. When Dr Qamber says this to me, I know that she's right. But I also know that once I'm home and I'm upstairs in bed, my thoughts will flood in and I'll begin to doubt myself again. There are things she doesn't know. That I'm afraid to tell her.

For the rest of the session, we discuss medication, and she writes me a new prescription. There's no red mark or bruise on my face, which means it's inconclusive whether the slap actually happened or not, though Dr Qamber does mention that it might be unlikely for me to *feel* a slap if it didn't happen. Most people with psychotic disorders experience auditory hallucinations, which is where we get the "hearing voices" stereotype from. Not everyone sees things. But the brain is complex and individual. There are no two brains that are exactly the same. We all experience mental illness in a slightly different way, which is why these illnesses are hard to diagnose. We're all unique beings. In that sense, we're all alone in the world, if you stop and think about it.

CHAPTER 13

ISABEL

I need to admit something to you, Leah. You're not the only one on my mind. I've been thinking about someone else this whole time, and I suppose I should tell you who that is. I've been thinking about my mother alone in that house, all her children gone, her husband dead. How did her husband die? Oh, yes, you killed him, Leah. You.

You made my mother a widow. Dirty little murderer. Filthy little life-taker. Do you still see his blood on your hands when you're cooking for your *son*?

Why is it that none of the newspapers tell me what happened to Daddy? They won't tell me the details. All I know is that I woke up and found his heart stabbed through, and I know you did it. Admit it.

But I still love you. That's strange, isn't it?

Anyway, the point is, I still think about my poor mother all alone in the house with no one to talk to, and that is why I send her my sketches. I liked to think that when I was rotting away in that drab and lifeless hospital, my mother was still proud of me because I was talented. I think she was, you know. She never said anything. She never visited. But I think she was proud of me, because what mother wouldn't have been proud of a daughter who could create beauty out of nothing?

So I send her beautiful things. Magpies, of course, but also wrens, finches, crows, blackbirds, tits, swallows, sparrows, all your various garden birds. I want her to know that I'm thinking of her, and I'm thinking of the birds that visited our garden when I was a little girl. Because we all think about that time, don't we? Some of us are still stuck there.

Chloe and I stole a car. Now, I won't say that it was as fun as decapitating a blogger, but it was quite a rush. Don't get all high and mighty on me, Leah—we stole that car from a car thief, so really it wasn't stealing at all.

After I rescued Chloe from the sex-pest who cornered her in the alley, I learned that she was in fact a drug dealer as well as a prostitute. A common drug dealer, how about that? I'm no expert on the underbelly of the criminal world, but what I gleaned through overheard conversations at Crowmont, the word "dealer" may be a slight exaggeration in this case. It seems to me that Chloe delivers drugs to punters. A go-between from dealer to customer. A middle man. She doesn't carry an awful lot of the stuff in one go, because if she's arrested, she'll serve less time that way.

We had a little conversation, Chloe and I, after I saved her life and her dignity (though I think that may have been stolen from her long ago), and I proposed that this little drug transportation deal might not be in her favour, and why didn't she set up on her own? The conclusion to that conversation was that perhaps she should. That's how we ended up driving around in an old Ford Escort with a collection of bags of various pills and powder. She did explain to me what each one was, but I have no interest in narcotics. I'm more interested in other thrills. There is some cocaine, speed, meth. The others have silly names. Molly. Ket. I'm not sure what else. They were stolen, too. And now we're in danger.

But it's all rather *Thelma and Louise*. (I watched that in the lounge at Crowmont. Everyone stood and cheered when they drove off the cliff. Death is better than prison.) We drive around in our car peddling our wares, moving swiftly on to another area, buying petrol with drug money. Selling drugs in little folds of paper to bug-eyed boys chewing their lips. We sleep in the car at night, parked in laybys, caravan park carparks, quiet country roads. We're travelling all around the country together. One day I'm in Liverpool, the next I'm in Wales.

It's liberating, Leah. But don't for one moment think that I've forgotten about you.

CHAPTER 14

#JUSTICEFORALISON

When Twitter goes for blood, the knife slices the jugular. They believe that I'm responsible for her death, that I'm the one who needs to be punished.

But what do I think? When I'm alone in my room at night, isolated from my son, isolated from the people who were once my friends, does my mind drift to places of love and light? Or does it fall into darkness? My dreams are not what they once were. They're bloody and bruised. I see a knife slicing through flesh. But whose hand holds the knife?

My mind goes to places I don't care to admit to. And then I wake and I'm somewhere else.

Today, I'm in a field staring out to sea across the cliffs. Skin chilled by the early morning air, hair tangled in weeds as though I'm growing out of the earth. My scars ache like they've been raked with fingernails. For the first time in a long time, Isabel feels close to me again. With breath still caught in my chest, I stand and turn to face away from the cliff. There's no one there, but for a moment I believed there was.

The fragments of my dreams come back to me as I wake up properly. I was being chased by faceless people holding placards with the phrase #justiceforalison. Alison's corpse was being paraded around like a blow-up doll, passed from one person to the next as though she were a prop on a stag do.

And then the hands on the knife…

And then Isabel.

And then darkness.

And then the sea.

I'm trembling from cold and shock as I start walking towards the house, hoping that Tom isn't awake yet. This is something he doesn't need to know. But unfortunately, as I enter the house through the back door, Tom is sat at the dining table trying to feed water to a magpie. The shock of it makes me pause, and my stomach flips with disgust.

"Where did you wake up this time?" Tom asks.

"Near the cliff. I guess the medication isn't working."

Tom merely nods. He isn't the same boy who begged me to stop drinking, who cared about keeping us together as a family. If I were Tom, I'd worry about my big sister going back to her old habits, but he doesn't seem to care anymore.

The bird? Tom knows about my fear of magpies after what happened in the psychiatric ward. He knows that I have nightmares. How could he bring one into our home?

"What are you doing?" I ask.

He shrugs. "I found it outside. I think its wing is broken or something. I thought I'd try to save it. Doesn't seem like it's working, though. Have we got an empty shoe box?" He's all innocence and light, as though last year never happened.

I force myself to lean in for a closer examination. "Tom, that bird is dead."

He prods it with an index finger, and I cringe back. In my mind, I see Isabel's pet magpie land on her shoulder. I see the way she used to flick her hair and smile a broad, genuine smile, hiding her true nature. The way Isabel was incredibly gentle with animals and yet so sadistic deep down makes it difficult for me to see Tom engaging in the same sort of act of kindness. Then I have to remind myself that he isn't Isabel and he probably just wanted to help a wounded animal.

"I think you're right." He sighs. "Well, at least I tried."

"I'll find something to wrap it in, and we'll bury it."

Tom shakes his head. "I thought I could save it."

As I move closer to wrap an arm around him, I'm aware of the t-shirt and knickers I'm still wearing after sleepwalking. Yet again, it takes me back to that night on the moors when Isabel and her father stripped me down and tortured me in front of Tom. Perhaps it's that hesitation that Tom picks up on when he jumps to his feet and pushes his chair away.

"Don't bother," he says. "I'll sort it out. You hate birds, anyway."

"I don't hate them," I protest. "I'm afraid of them after what happened. You know what I went through."

"Yeah. I was there."

"I know," I reply. "I know, Tom. Why don't we talk about it? We haven't sat down and talked through what happened. Not properly, anyway. Don't you think that'll help?"

"Why? Won't everything just go back to normal? You sleepwalking, hallucinating, drinking and fucking up? Me on my own with no parents. Isabel out there waiting for us. Hunting us. Killing women who resemble you."

"Tom." My eyes burn with the sensation of unshed tears, and I realise that this might be the perfect moment to tell him what happened with our father. To tell him that I'm really his mother. That he does have a parent. I'm right here.

But then I'd have to admit to him that he was a child of rape. And I couldn't do it.

"What?"

"Tom, I know you've been avoiding it, but you *have* to go and see my therapist. I've arranged an appointment with her."

"Fine. Whatever."

He snatches the bird from the table and walks out of the dining room into the garden. As he walks away, I notice a few feathers sticking out of the pocket at the back of his jeans, just like at the house in Scotland. Is Tom going out searching for magpies? Is he seeking them out to taunt me, to torture me?

I suppose there are a couple of options. Either Tom stuffed the bird in his pocket, or he pulled the feathers from its body and kept them. Whichever he did, it feels as though the bird situation has been orchestrated by Tom in some way. Did he kill the bird himself? Or did he find it dead and bring it into the house, then wait for the right moment to perform his theatrics? What was Tom trying to achieve by bringing a dead magpie into our home? Except frightening me, of course.

Perhaps that was his intention all along, as some sort of provocative act of teenage rebellion. I had thought, as Tom approaches his eighteenth birthday, that the teenage hormones would calm down, but they're only getting worse. Maybe it's the trauma. Or maybe it's something much worse.

After showering and changing, I make a cup of tea to calm my nerves before doing some more research on the disappearance of Abigail. I have the scanned copy of "Mary" from Leeds, who certainly seems to be a dead ringer for George himself. But how am I going to track down Mary fifty years later? She could be anywhere.

I try Facebook first, putting "Mary, Leeds" into the search bar and filtering the results by age. But I think Mary is probably too old to have partaken in the Facebook migration, and most profiles are private now, anyway. There's a chance that Mary might have died between 1984 and now. A good chance.

Then I try those family history websites, but most require you to sign up and pay a subscription fee to get any decent results. I can't really afford to pay for them and wonder whether to ask George or his son if they'd lend me the money. At the same time, I felt bad about asking for handouts. What if they suspect that I'd spend the money on myself instead? No, they don't know me well enough to know I'm trustworthy. I don't want to cause problems, and borrowing money always causes problems in relationships. That's just one of the things you learn when you grow up poor.

In the end, I give up and browse the Justice for Alison hashtag instead. It's trending on Twitter right now, with more tweets coming in every second as I browse.

Release the bitch's name. She's in on it. #findthenurse #findisabel #justiceforalison

Are the police blind? The nurse is obviously hiding Isabel. #justiceforalison #isabelfieldingisoutthere

Why should my taxes go towards keeping scum like the nurse safe? #justiceforalison #nursebitch

#justiceforalison The people have spoken. We want to know who she is.

I feel sick to my stomach. I'm living in a pressure cooker, and the Twitteratti are about to lift the lid. Who knows about me? Seb, his brothers, the other nurses at Crowmont... They know my name, and they might have a photograph of me somewhere. I wasn't social when I lived at Hutton, but there was a security photo of me at the hospital. What if they release it? What if my photo gets to the public?

And if they do come for me? Would I deserve it?

I shake my head and decide to check the footage from the

cameras in the house. If Tom did orchestrate the bird scenario, maybe the footage will show something. I check the back camera, clicking on the back arrow, cringing as I enter the house dishevelled and bemused, going further back until the door opens and Tom is standing outside holding a cup of tea. He stands there for a moment before walking farther into the garden, nearer to the sea. Then he disappears out of sight. A few minutes pass before he comes back, the bird in one hand, the tea in the other. Nothing on the footage shows him doing anything to the bird, but I still feel a creeping sense of dread worm its way up my spine.

CHAPTER 15

I spot George in the lounge as I'm showing visitors into the care home. He's out of bed causing mischief with Agnes, a keen poker player. As I'm on my way back to reception, I plan on leaving him to his game, but instead he calls me over.

"Lizzie has been helping me look for Abigail," George says to Agnes, eyes gleaming with what I think might be pride.

Agnes lifts the corners of her freshly dealt cards and eyes them carefully. "Terrible what happened to your Abigail. No one ever forgot it, you know, George. We thought about her all those years, and still do."

A flicker of pain crosses George's face. "So do I. Every day since then. I know she's out there somewhere. Well," he says, glancing down at his cards, "I fold. Are you busy, Lizzie?" Agnes chuckles at that. "Fancy going for a walk with an old man?"

"Come on then, old man." I offer him my arm and he takes it, heaving himself up to standing position.

He pats my hand. "Thank you, dear."

"Don't thank me too soon, because I don't have great news. I'm just not sure where to search for Mary. I've tried the internet, but I'm not coming up with anything. Perhaps I could meet your grandson in the library, and we can do a bit of research together. I don't know my way around Clifton well enough, to be honest." I steer us out into the garden behind the home. It's a lovely sunny day, and it seems a shame to waste it indoors, where everything smells faintly of disinfectant.

"I'll ask him, but I'm sure he will. How are you settling in?"

"Oh, okay."

"Now, don't be offended, but I'm an old man and I don't have much to do. I noticed that you seem a little tired. Is everything all right?"

I turn away from George and focus on the flower beds around the garden before answering. "I live with my younger brother because our parents died recently." I feel guilty about lying to George, but I also don't feel like explaining that my murdering father killed my mother. "He's a teenager, and he's become… difficult."

"Oh, well! Teenagers aren't much fun. You should've known me when I was a lad. I don't look like much now, but I thought I was James Dean." He chuckles. "My father played hell when I bought a motorcycle. It was more of a scooter, if I'm honest. Not a Harley Davidson or anything like that."

"George, I bet the young women of Clifton thought you were a real catch. Were you the bad boy of this seaside town?"

"I thought I was at the time. But, no." He laughs. "Just a rebel without a clue."

Listening to this man lifts my spirits. I laugh for the first time in a long time.

"Now, that is a nice sight. I don't see a smile on your face too often. Be honest with me, Lizzie. Is this task too much for you? I look at you and I see grief etched on your face, and I wonder if searching for my Abigail is taking a toll that one human being should not place on another without a good and true justification. If it is, then please say. Because I would hate to contribute to your troubles."

I take a deep breath, steadying myself. It takes a while to reach a point where I can speak again. "No. You're not. You're taking away from my troubles. Investigating Abigail's disappearance, or Mary if that's her in the photograph, is helping me. It's what I need right now."

"Good," he says. "You're a true friend, Lizzie. We would have been fast friends growing up. Though I only had eyes for my Judy and always will."

What a life I would have, being loved by a man like George. I see myself on the moors next to Seb—terse, tranquil, strong Seb—and my body aches to be back there. Even with the pain that comes along with my memories of Seb, I can't help but miss him.

"The library might have more information on Abigail's disappearance," I say. "I need to check out the newspaper articles from that time and see if there's anything I've missed. But I'm not sure how I'm going to track her down after the fire. At least you have that photograph. Perhaps there's a marriage certificate for a Mary of that age in Leeds. If it is Abigail, it could be that she had a birth certificate forged. Otherwise, she would have had problems getting married, getting jobs and bank accounts and so on. I'm not sure. It was a different time then, with different rules. I have to show three forms of identification for a gym membership."

"All you can do is your best, Lizzie."

Perhaps he's right.

I don't want to be the big sister/mum who checks up on her brother/son, but I have to know if he turned up to his therapy session with Dr Qamber. When I speak to her, I'm relieved to hear that he did, but she won't tell me how the session went. Still, that's progress. But perhaps I should have pushed him sooner. I shouldn't have listened to what he was telling me and paid more attention to his mood and behaviours. But it's hard to do that when living has become making it through one day and then the next. When you're hanging by a thread, it's almost impossible to think of anyone but yourself. I'm trying.

All you can do is your best, Lizzie.

#justiceforalison

Am I a good and true friend? Or am I the terrible person that the internet has deemed me to be? I'm not sure I know.

It's early evening, and Tom is at work. I've wolfed down macaroni and cheese and am about to curl up on the sofa with reality television when the phone rings.

"I hear you're Elizabeth now."

The connection breaks up for a moment, and in the space of a heartbeat I hear the voice as female. After freezing like a cat caught in the headlights, I realise that the voice isn't female at all. It's male.

"Detective Murphy."

"You sound surprised," he notes.

"I am. I didn't think you were given details of where we moved."

"I wasn't," he admits. "But the team decided to let me in." He pauses, and the silence hangs when I realise that there must be a valid reason for the programme to give DCI Murphy my information. *Have they caught her?* "There's been a development, and I felt that I had to tell you myself."

My palms begin to sweat, but I can't pinpoint my exact emotion. Am I afraid or excited? Is this the moment when I will finally hear that Isabel has been caught and will be brought to justice for the murders of James Gorden and Maisie Earnshaw? Or is it bad news? Does Isabel know where I am? Is she out there on the cliffs, drawing me a new bird to post through my letterbox? Or is she in the attic, like last time? Sharpening her knives. Waiting for me to sleep before she slips one under my chin...

"Because Isabel has indicated that she's obsessed with you, we've had surveillance in a few different areas. At the Braithwaites' farm." I hold my breath as he speaks. *Don't let her have hurt Seb.* "Tom's— sorry, Scott's old school, his foster parents, your family home in Hackney, and your mother's grave."

"Have you found her?" I ask.

Murphy hesitates again before answering. "No."

There is weight behind that word. I hear the exhaustion in his voice. "No, we haven't."

"Okay. Tell me what's happened."

"A few weeks ago, several bird illustrations were sent to Anna Fielding's house. She was understandably upset. We moved her to a hotel and increased surveillance on her house for a few weeks to see if Isabel would try anything. But in order to do that within our budget, we had to let a few officers go from another surveillance spot."

Oh, God, please. Not Seb.

"Okay." My blood pumps so hard that I'm convinced he can hear it.

"We decided that your mother's grave would be the least likely place she'd try anything. The other areas of surveillance were all protecting people, and we had to make sure those people were protected. But unfortunately, my officers have noticed a disturbance at the grave."

"A disturbance? What kind of disturbance?" My first thoughts are of Seb. He's okay. Isabel hasn't gone after him. Then the horror of what Murphy is telling me sinks in. Isabel has done something to Mum's grave. She's *disturbed* it in some way.

"She... She dug it up."

"She did what?"

"We assume it was her," he says. "I can't imagine why anyone else would... do that. But the soil around her grave has been... transferred. And we believe her coffin has been opened."

Despite everything that Isabel has done—delivering the head of my ally, hiding in my attic, killing a *child*—this still shocks me. She dug up my poor mother.

My stomach flips, and my mouth fills with bile. I take the phone away from my head and gag, almost throwing up on the carpet. My head is light and my legs are weak and I'm all too aware of the ground beneath my feet and my body wanting to sink into it.

"Leah?"

As I fight the nausea, I barely register his slip-up, calling me by my real name.

"Are you all right?"

I place the phone back to my ear. "Not really."

I'm relieved that no one *living* has been hurt by her, but... my mother. How could she?

"I know how difficult this is. And I'm sorry. If it's any consolation, as terrible as that might sound, your mother's body has not been... stolen. Our forensic team is checking over the remains now, but there was no sign that she has been... tampered with. Was your mother buried with any jewellery or heirlooms?"

"Her wedding ring," I admit. I'd agonised over it. What do you do when your father murders your mother? Do you pretend her alcoholic arsehole of a husband never existed? Or do you bury her with the one piece of jewellery she wore every single day, no matter how many bruises he gave her? I decided on the latter. She was faithful to him to the end, and I believed she would want that ring.

"It's gone."

So there it is. That's what she wanted. A piece of my mother. A piece of *me*. She's still as obsessed with me as always. After moving away from Hutton, I hoped that her attention might have been directed elsewhere. Survival, perhaps. Preservation. Because it couldn't be easy out there on her own.

Fuck.

Am I sympathising with her now? Am I feeling sorry for this girl who could at best be described as deranged and at worst a monster? Is there anything human left of Isabel Fielding?

"I've got a team down there now. If she comes back to the grave, we'll find her."

"She won't," I reply, my voice flat and dead. "She took what she wanted and left. You were too late."

I hear Murphy sigh down the phone and again feel the exhaustion in that sigh. I imagine him crumpled up. Stooped.

"I'm sorry, Leah." Leah again. It's nice to hear my real name spoken out loud. "We're doing the best we can."

"I know."

But is their best good enough?

"There's no reason to believe you aren't safe where you are."

"Okay. But what if the Justice for Alison people get hold of my name? Then someone might recognise me here and put my location up on the internet."

"I heard about that shitshow," he says. "I'm sorry about that. There's not much we can do about the actual posts—free speech and all that. But if anyone does share your name or photograph, they'll be arrested, and the image and or name will be deleted."

Nothing is ever deleted from the internet, I think. Just ask Beyonce.

It's not much reassurance, but it might be the best I'll get under the circumstances.

"How are you?" he asks.

The question takes me by surprise. I've never thought of myself having much of a relationship with DCI Murphy. But I suppose there's been something of a bond, especially when he visited me in York Hospital. I still remember him sat by my hospital bed, guilt and worry on his face as he admitted that Isabel had disappeared.

"It's nice here," I admit. "I have a job I enjoy. Tom is… struggling. But I'm okay. Actually, I'm helping an elderly man search for his sister, who disappeared during a house fire. I know how busy you are, but if you could look into it…"

No hesitation this time. "Sure. What's the name?"

"Abigail Hawker," I reply.

"When did she go missing?"

I tell Murphy some of the details about Abigail and the fire. Even about the photograph of "Mary" that turned up years later.

"Cold cases like this don't always turn anything up," he says. "But I'll have an officer take a look." For the first time, there's a little hope in his voice, and I realise how obligated he feels about Isabel's case, and how determined he is to help me in any way possible. This is a man who has been crucified by the press for being incompetent. But I know the truth. Isabel is *just that good*. It's not DCI Murphy who's the problem, it's her.

CHAPTER 16

ISABEL

Hello, Leah. I have a story to tell you today, and I think you'll enjoy it.

Chloe and I have been continuing on our road trip for a few days now. It's proving to be quite an experience, with lots of highs and lows. The highs, for instance, involve a white substance we snort up our noses every now and then. Chloe likes to do it much more frequently than I do, because I like to remain in control. However, I did decide to have a go. One never knows when one might return to one's secure hospital facility, after all. The lows include waking up in the morning with Chloe's dirty feet shoved in my face. Her hygiene leaves something to be desired. But I can handle it. After all, I did use the showers at Crowmont Hospital. I'm no clean freak.

But I digress.

We were heading south, dear Leah, and I said to Chloe that I had a friend who used to live in the south. Being from the north,

I wasn't too sure how to get to this place via car, seeing as the last time I went was on public transport; a train journey in a baseball cap, like something out of a spy thriller. So Chloe bought an A-Z road map because we didn't have a smartphone for sat nav. We briefly considered stealing one, but I decided that was too risky.

It should be noted here that Chloe has no idea who I am and why I'm homeless. I've avoided answering her questions, and I think she assumes that I'm the victim of some terrible crime. Bless her damaged little soul.

We continued on our little road trip to the south, reaching our destination after a few petrol station stops, after selling small bags of white powder, after snorting a few lines and eating McDonald's out of paper bags. We reached our destination relatively quickly.

Do you know where we went?

We went to a place close to your heart. Your home town! We went to Hackney, Leah, because there was someone I wanted to visit.

But the visitation was tricky. Firstly, I couldn't tell Chloe what I was going to do. I also needed to check that it was safe to visit. That involved us staying at the town for a few days before I made the visit, and Chloe complained about this *the whole time*. While the whinging and whining was getting to me, I decided to allow her some grace, owing to her difficult past. You have to make allowances for some people, don't you? And Chloe has been good to me. She follows me like a little puppy dog, my willing slave. Hanging on my every word.

It was nice. You used to be like that, Leah.

Anyway, there we were in Hackney, waiting for some sort of sign that the coast was clear, as they say in *Scooby-Doo*. My appearance is quite different now compared to when all the trouble began, meaning I was hopeful that I could slip away without being noticed.

And I was right.

There was no one there, Leah. I expected at least one dark car parked in the vicinity. At least one dodgy-looking vehicle clearly monitoring the place. But there was no one.

I slipped in through a side entrance. You know the ones. Every cemetery has a side entrance and a path that leads through the graves to another road. They are locked at night, and I had to make sure there wasn't a CCTV camera attached to a streetlight or something first. I got Chloe to drop me off close to the entrance because I was carrying various pieces of equipment needed for my task. She was certainly spooked to see what I was taking to the cemetery, but I assured her that it wasn't nefarious. It was business.

Though it was a little nefarious.

The last time we saw each other, Leah, I told you about how I visited your mother's grave. Well, I created a mental map of that cemetery. I know, I know, I'm a genius with an extraordinary memory. We both know that.

Again, I was wary of cameras. I knew you would have mentioned my visit to your mother to the police when you escaped from me. I knew they would observe this spot in case I decided to come back. That's why I was surprised. I was prepared to call it off, just like I called off my visit to your farm-boy and to my mother. But this was free and easy. There was nothing. No camera on the gravestone. Nothing. Perhaps it's illegal to whack a CCTV camera on a gravestone; I don't know. It was dark enough that if there were any others in the area, they wouldn't pick up my face. I just had to hope that they weren't manned 24/7.

I had one chance to visit. This was it.

It shames me to admit it, but I'm not a physically strong person. As you know, I had help from my father when we taught James Gorden to stay out of our business. Digging, for instance, is not a pastime I've done particularly often. Not since I dug a hole on Blackpool Beach. But I'm a determined little sod when I want to be. No pun intended.

And trust me, Leah, I wanted to be.

I wanted to see the worms, feel the earth, see the bones and the decaying flesh, smell the mould, the rot, see the structure of her, the structure of you. I wanted to see where you came from.

As the soil came away from that most sacred of places, I lay down in it. Rubbed it on my skin. Spread it up my arms. The farther down I got, the damper it became. And then, after blistering my hands, sweating through my shirt, and almost crying tears of frustration, I reached wood.

Leah, I met your mother. And she's beautiful.

though I have seen the source!
CHAPTER 17

I meet Mark on the steps of the library with my laptop bag slung over my shoulder, already sweating through my long-sleeved shirt. Spring feels as though it is around the corner now, and I haven't dressed appropriately. On the other hand, he appears thoroughly ready for summer in a t-shirt and light trousers.

"Hey," he says, crinkling his bright blue eyes, just like his grandad's.

"Thanks for meeting me." I extend a hand, not sure if this is a handshake moment, but feeling like I need to do something to acknowledge it. He takes it, and we quickly shake.

"No, I should be thanking you. You've cheered my grandad a great deal by helping him like this. He told me that he showed you the picture of 'Mary.'"

"Yeah."

We make our way into the library, Mark leading the way.

"When he first showed me that photograph, I felt like my mind had been blown. I mean, I never believed Grandad's crazy theories about Abigail until that point. But she *looks* like him. And it can't be another female relative, because she's dressed in sixties clothes, you know? She's the right age to be Abigail, and she has some of my grandad's features." He shakes his head. "It's weird. But I didn't know where to start tracking down people who might be her. I wish we could afford a private detective, but we can't. I know this isn't even close to your job, but I think Grandad is getting desperate. He's asked everyone who's walked into his room. You were the first to say yes!"

I laugh. "Really? But he's such a charmer."

"He is." Mark leads us over to a library computer and places his bag down on a chair. "And a good man. He deserves to find out what happened to her. I think it would give him some peace after all these years. He doesn't want to die before finding out."

We boot up the computer and begin to check the archived newspaper clippings that have been scanned and saved. *Fire in Clifton. Two dead in house fire. House fire deemed to be arson.*

"We've always known it was arson," Mark says. "Grandad told us what the police found out. There were scraps of bedding covered in gasoline that had been fed through the letterbox. The arsonist dropped several matches on the bedding, and the entire house caught fire. It's a miracle any of them survived."

"Why would someone do that?"

Mark shakes his head. "We don't know. As far as I'm aware, Grandad and the rest of his family were friendly with everyone. His mother volunteered at the local school as a dinner lady. My father was popular in the local pub. Grandad and Abigail had friends at school. They struggled a bit with money, but not to the point of poverty. No one would be jealous of them. They were regular people."

Quietly, we read through more articles about the fire.

It began in the early hours of Thursday morning. Claire and Anthony Hawker woke to find their house on fire. Anthony recalled hearing his ten-year-old son, George, crying and rushed to his children's bedroom. But at this point, his twelve-year-old daughter, Abigail, was missing from the children's room. Anthony told police that he thought little Abigail might have wakened in the night to get a glass of water or go to the toilet. Anthony took George in his arms, and they hurried downstairs. It was then that they realised Abigail wasn't downstairs either, and Claire rushed back up the stairs to find her daughter. Anthony recounted to the police how he had attempted to stop his wife from going back, but Claire wanted to rescue her only daughter. Anthony then managed to fight his way through the blaze to rescue his son through the back of the house. With his son safe in the garden with a neighbour, Anthony attempted to re-enter the house but was unable to due to the flames.

Unfortunately, Claire perished in the fire before firefighters could reach her. Her remains were found in the upstairs hallway, where she must have been rushing in total chaos to find her daughter.

The remains of Abigail Hawker were not recovered.

There were also more recent articles about the case where amateur sleuths had attempted to piece together the mystery.

Did the police fail to find twelve-year-old Abigail Hawker's remains, or was she kidnapped from her own home? On the 14th of April 1944, the Hawker residence went up in flames, killing thirty-two-year-old Claire Hawker and possibly her daughter, Abigail.

I scanned over the information I'd already read in previous articles. Abigail's remains were not found. The perpetrators of the arson were not found. Then...

Shortly after the house fire, a family moved away from Clifton-on-Sea after living there almost all of their lives. Clive and Marie Pierce moved suddenly away from the town, abandoning a job, renting out their property before selling it, and telling only a few people that they were moving. I spoke to Clifton resident Maud Stevens about the Pierces, and she felt that the situation was odd.

I glance across at Mark. "Have you read this? It's an opinion piece, but it's very interesting."

Mark leans over my shoulder to read the article. "No, I've never seen this one before. I mostly read the clippings from the time of the fire. I never thought to keep going. And I've never heard of the Pierce family, either. I wonder if Grandad remembers them."

Maud Stevens, described as ninety-two at the time of the article in 2005, claimed that Clive Pierce was an "oddity" and his wife "quiet". The person interviewing Maud prodded for more information, aiming at juicy gossip, but there aren't any clear details about who the Pierce family were or where they moved. Still, it's certainly an avenue to investigate further. The timing was definitely suspicious.

I think about the strange Pierce family disappearance on my way home. The farther away from the library I travel, the more I wonder if both the article writer and dear old Maud were reaching for something that wasn't there. Perhaps it's nothing more than a coincidence. But then, after listening to James Gorden talk about Isabel, I'm not as quick to dismiss conspiracy theories anymore. I wanted to stay and continue the search, but Mark had to leave shortly after we found the article, and we didn't have time to go to Ivy Lodge and ask George about the Pierces.

Back home, I do a little more research, seeing if I can find out anything else about Clive and Marie Pierce in Clifton, but Facebook doesn't bring up any results, and I'm unsure where else to search. Without knowing where they moved, it's impossible to guess.

The house is quiet, warm, scented by the sea breeze. Everything smells faintly of salt here, from the wind coming off the sea to the fish-and-chip shops along the pier. There's something comforting about it, reminding me of one nice memory with my family, a holiday to Scarborough before my father's drinking grew out of control.

But Isabel ruined the comfort of this place. The silence is tinged with a foreboding sense of unease. The breeze lifts the hair on the back of my neck and makes me feel as though I'm being watched. Where is she right now? What is she doing? When I am alone like this, I wonder if we are connected in some way, that if I closed my eyes, I'd see through hers. Perhaps if I were hypnotised, I'd reveal her dastardly plans, like Mina Harker and Dracula.

I long for a glass of wine to calm my jangling nerves, but I daren't do it. Instead, I check the house, verifying that nothing has been moved. Since moving to Clifton, I haven't done this as often, but now I feel the need to examine the doors for evidence of tampering, to inspect every room. I even check the cutlery drawers and the plates in the cupboard. I'm not sure why she'd move my plates, but I have to know. Isabel is good at mind games. If she wanted to frighten me, she'd know exactly how to do it. Then I check the cameras and zoom through the footage to check that no one suspicious has come to the house.

The longer I check, the more tense I become, and when the phone rings, my heart leaps into action, banging against my ribs. My legs are like jelly as I reach for my phone. Before lifting the landline to my ear, I take a deep breath, because this could be yet another phone call to tell me something is wrong.

"Hi, Lizzie. It's DCI Murphy."

"Hi." It sounds strange to utter a greeting as mundane as "hi" when I'm expecting terrible news. I can already tell from his voice that this isn't a telephone conversation to inform me of Isabel's capture.

"I wanted to keep you informed," he says. "We've been watching the cemetery where your mother is buried, and we haven't seen any kind of disturbance. But forensics have confirmed that it was Isabel who opened the grave and that she did take your mother's wedding ring."

I knew all this already, and yet my stomach still flips. I have to hold back the urge to vomit on the floor. If I didn't expect Tom home at any moment, I think I might be sick, but I don't want to alarm him. I certainly don't want him to find out about this.

"She dug up my mother," I say, breathless. "I still can't believe it."

"I'm sorry," Murphy continues. "I'm so sorry this happened to you."

"Can my mother be laid to rest now?" I ask.

"Yes," he says. "But we think it's best to bury her somewhere else."

I nod. I was thinking the same thing. And I've already thought of a place where we went together once, alone, without my dad. I was pregnant with Tom at the time, though I didn't know it. Dad had just left for two months to work on a building site in the south of France. It was bliss. "The Cotswolds. We stayed at a B&B in Stow-on-the-Wold."

Murphy listens quietly as I give him instructions.

"Do you want us to wait and see if we can… retrieve the ring?" he asks.

"No." Perhaps she was never meant to have it. Perhaps this is rectifying a wrong I made when we buried her. And perhaps the police will never find it anyway.

There's another pause where Murphy realises that I have little faith in his team finding Isabel in the foreseeable future.

"I did a little digging about that disappearance for you," he says. The way he says it makes me think that he did it personally, rather than asking another cop of lower ranking to do it for him. For some reason, that makes me feel sad. I'm using this as an escape from the stress of real life, and so is he. "There's a possibility the police didn't do a thorough search of the area and missed her body. It's slim. Unlikely, even. The other options could include her being taken before or during the fire, or someone moved or hid her body. If the body was moved or hidden, the arson might have been designed to cover up her murder. And, I'm afraid, in that case, I would be considering family members suspicious. Now, it could have been an accidental murder. Or it could have been premeditated. Too much time may have passed to ever find out if that is the case. The thing is, if someone did move or hide the body, what would be the point? A fire would destroy evidence, especially back then. Which makes me think that she was abducted."

"I found out some more information," I say. "There was a family who disappeared just after the fire. Clive and Marie Pierce. They didn't have children."

"That's interesting," he replies. "I'll do some more research. See if anything comes up."

I give him as much information as I can from the news article, though it isn't much to go on. "I might know more after I've spoken to George."

"I have a number you can call me on." He recites what appears to be a mobile phone number, and then we say our goodbyes.

He also tells me that I can contact him if I'm ever worried or afraid.

That leaves me little comfort. Isabel is clearly out there, and she wants to find me. She hasn't given up, and even DCI Murphy is worried for me.

CHAPTER 18

Tom leans against the bus window, feigning tiredness and a hangover. I know he just doesn't want to talk to me. However, we have fifteen minutes to kill, and I'll be damned if we're going to do it in silence.

"Are you going out later?" I ask.

"Just to the pub."

"Oh, yeah? Who's going?"

"People from the chippy."

"Do they have names?"

"Yes." He turns his head towards me and rolls his eyes in a dramatic and completely teenager-ish way.

"Good for them."

We sit in awkward silence for a moment.

"Did I tell you that I'm helping an elderly gentleman at the care home? His sister went missing seventy-odd years ago in suspicious circumstances. Maybe I could tell you everything I know so far, and you can tell me what you think."

He straightens up a little. Finally, I've caught his attention. "Go on, then. I bet I can figure it out."

"Well," I say, and then I launch into the whole story, from the fire at George's house, to the police not being able to find Abigail's body, to the Pierce family disappearing, to the picture of "Mary" who bears a striking resemblance to Abigail.

"Obvious, innit," Tom says after I've finished recounting the tale. "The Pierce family couldn't have kids, or they were paedos. They stole the little girl and moved away with her to start a new life. Then this girl grew up and became Mary. They felt guilty, or they were bastards and wanted to taunt George with a picture of the sister he never got to grow up with."

I can't help but smile. "Got it all figured out, haven't you? How could they get away from the area without anyone knowing they had Abigail?"

He shrugs. "Hide her in the boot of their car."

"I guess we'll have to see if they owned a car."

"I guess you will."

"Any more theories?"

"Have you considered alien abduction?"

I can't help but laugh. "Funny you should mention that. One of the conspiracies on the internet goes into great detail about how Abigail was abducted by a race of purple aliens with tentacles who burned the house down with their blasters before the spaceship went back to X9. That was the name of their planet, apparently. In another universe. Which they got to through a black hole in space."

"I take it Stephen Hawking confirmed this was possible."

"Of course."

Tom laughs.

Maybe I can still reach him, after all.

As I'm dealing with patient files, sending emails and answering the phone, I'm actually thinking about the Pierce family. It beats obsessing over Isabel, anyway. The morning drags on until I have a break, but unfortunately, on the way there I bump into Mrs Cartwright, who is delirious again.

"Murderer," she says. "Blood on your hands. Dirt on your skin. Where were you? Where were you when it happened?"

She tuts at me as I edge away from her and down the corridor.

By the time I get to George's room, I'm shaken, and the good mood from the brief bit of banter with Tom on the bus has almost completely disappeared. But none of that matters when I see that George is laid up in bed again, this time with a drip. I quickly examine the contents, but it's just saline and an anti-nausea drug, which is a relief.

"Everything all right, George?" I ask.

"Could do with a holiday. I'm not going to lie," he says.

"Just sit back and relax. Are you feeling a bit under the weather?"

"Can't seem to keep my brekky down," he admits. "Got a dicky tummy. You'd best stay back, Lizzie love. If it's a bug, I don't want you to catch it."

"Don't worry about me. I'll wash my hands on the way out." I frown. George appears very pale and pasty today. "Shall I leave you to get some rest?"

"How did it go with Mark?" he asks.

A few minutes can't hurt. I pull up a chair and tell him the theory about the Pierces.

"Oh, no," he says. "It can't be them. They were a lovely couple. The fella, he volunteered at the school. He used to set up the school play every year. He volunteered at the school all the time. He seemed old at the time, but maybe that was because I was young. Probably in his forties."

"They didn't have children of their own, though, did they? Isn't that a bit of a weird thing to do without having your own kids?"

"I don't think so," he says. "Not in those days. We had a community then. Everyone chipped in." But then his expression changes, shifting into contemplation. "Now, there *is* something I remember about Mrs Pierce. She did have a daughter, but the daughter died very young. There was some terrible gossip at the time that the child wasn't his. She had an affair, they said. I remember my mother chatting about it around the kitchen table with the woman from down the street. Malicious, it was, but you know how people gossip."

They do. And since the internet was created, they do it even more and on a larger scale. The world is one big gossip machine, burning through news fast and destructively. I should know. I'm still at the centre of it.

"Do you know where they moved?" I ask.

George shakes his head, and I can see that he's growing tired. "It was after the fire. We were in a state of shock, what with losing Mum. I don't think we even noticed. I only heard they'd gone when I went back to school. One kid said they went north. Another said London."

His chin begins to drift down to his chest. I lean over and give his hand a squeeze and let him nod off in peace.

Every day, he weakens a little more, and I can see that old age is taking its toll. It's time for me to find out what happened to Abigail, because if I'm too late to tell him, I'll never forgive myself.

Perhaps it was Tom who planted the seed in my mind, but the one detail that jumps out at me is how Mr Pierce directed the school play every year. I decide to research the local school to find out how long it's been open. Over a hundred years. Good. Then I create a fake Facebook profile under a completely different name, and post in a few local history groups asking if anyone remembers the school plays at Clifton Junior School and whether they remember Mr. Pierce. It's a long shot. Anyone who does will be in their eighties. But I also know that people love to reminisce and I hope that even a son/daughter, or grandson/granddaughter might see my post and ask a relative if they remember.

And then I email Mark to arrange a meeting with George's daughter. I hate to admit it, but George is growing weaker and weaker, and his memories might not be as reliable as they once were. Perhaps if she can recall her dad talking about this stuff when she was growing up, she might be able to help.

Mark emails back immediately.

Before meeting with George's daughter, Susie, I have a therapy session with Dr Qamber and afterwards need to pick up a new prescription. She isn't happy with my progress. I'm showing signs of anxiety. There are scratch marks on my hands and psoriasis on my wrist. I've lost weight, and my face is gaunt. There are dark circles under my eyes from lack of sleep.

And the big one: I wake up in places I shouldn't.

This needs to stop. There's a chance that my sleepwalking will lead to hallucinations and psychotic delusions. She's very serious about this. Tom needs a stable environment, and if I don't get this under control, he might leave. The thought makes me feel sick: being alone in that house without anyone to talk to, waiting for Isabel to find me.

I pick up the prescription and take the pills, barely even bothering to learn about what they are. Perhaps it's because I'm not nursing anymore, but I've lost my desire to keep up with the medical profession.

It's a short walk to Susie's house from the bus stop, but it's up quite a steep hill. Despite my half-hearted attempt at the plank challenge and a few self-defence classes (which Tom has now given up on, and I probably will soon), I struggle to get up there without a long break halfway up. But the street itself is quaint and pleasant, lined by blossom trees, dotted with drives that lead up to painted semi-detached houses with big bay windows. I could live here if I had a family to enjoy these large houses.

I wonder how Susie manages living on this hill while being in a wheelchair, but when I reach the appropriate house, I notice that the drive and the ramp leading up to the front door have been arranged with her in mind. The door is wider. The house is actually on the flat top of the hill, and there's a car parked outside in a bay lined with yellow paint.

Susie's front door is almost as yellow as the paint marking the disabled bay. A large brass knocker sits in the middle, and above the door is a colourful stained-glass depiction of daffodils. There is a saying about yellow doors symbolising happiness, or hope, or something like that, but I can't remember it now. I only think that it's bright and colourful, and I hope Susie is the same way.

I hope this because I'm nervous about meeting her, though I'm not sure why. Perhaps it's because I've come to know and love her father. We're connected intimately by a thread, and it's a strange sort of intimacy to have with a person, to know a family member well enough to share thoughts and feelings with them. I didn't grow up in a house that shared that kind of thing. Maybe I'm craving it now, looking for validation from a new family to replace the one I lost.

Not a great time for epiphanies, Leah. I have a job to do for a man I care about.

Mark opens the door after I knock, smiling as always. He shows me in through the hallway and into a small but quaint kitchen with emerald-green walls and potted herbs on the windowsill.

Susie and her wheelchair are positioned next to the dining table, with a teapot set out ready next to a plate of assorted biscuits. The little touch of hospitality reminds me of the yellow door with the colourful flowers. I immediately see George in her, around the eyes, in her smile. In the house, even, full of natural light. Ah, if only I'd been born into *this* family.

"You must be Lizzie," Susie says, extending a hand. I ignore the twinge of guilt about not being able to give them my real name, and take a few steps forward to shake her hand. "Nice to meet you. Dad's very happy that you're helping us. I am too. I know this isn't your job, but I can't tell you how nice it is to have some help. It makes you think better about people, doesn't it? When they help you out for no reason. Sorry, I'm rambling. I do that. Sit down, won't you? Mark, pour the tea. Do you want tea?" She regards me questioningly.

"I'd love one. Milk, no sugar, thanks."

"Grab a biscuit," Mark says. "No, seriously. They're my weakness, and you have to move fast."

Mark is like a tall weed, with barely an ounce of fat. Either he's exaggerating to make me feel more comfortable about taking one, or he has an enviable metabolism. But I take a chocolate digestive anyway.

"Mine's crisps," I admit. It's also wine, but that isn't quite as fun to admit. Not when you've given up.

"Dad says you're making good progress. I talk to him on the

phone most nights," Susie tells me. "I would go to the home more often, but after the accident, I... Well, I'm in a lot of chronic pain, and the painkillers can send me a bit..." She mimes a loop next to her temple with a finger. "That's why Mark helps me out, you see."

"I understand." I sip on my tea before adding, "I'm just sorry that I haven't managed to find much out so far. There's one small detail that cropped up when I went to the library. Did Mark tell you about it?"

"Yes," she says. "The Pierces. Now, I think I do remember people talking about that. Obviously, it was well before I was born, but this is a small town, and any strange occurrence will be remembered for decades. Grandad talked about it sometimes, too. Not often, because it happened around the same time as the fire, and he never wanted to talk about that."

"What did people say about the Pierces?" I ask.

"Every now and then, I'd be at the dentist's, or on the bus, and a couple of older folks would start talking about it, usually saying something like, 'Do you remember the Pierces?' And then they'd gossip about the disappearance. One of the prevailing titbits of gossip was that the wife had an affair and got pregnant and that the husband forced her to have an abortion. But I don't know how true it is. Don't know where they went, either. No one ever seemed to know."

"Your dad mentioned that they lost a child. Could that piece of gossip have come about because of a miscarriage? Sometimes rumours are twisted versions of the truth."

"Yes, definitely. She could have had a miscarriage, and it could all have been very tragic. But for some reason, people genuinely did believe she had an affair."

"Were the Pierces liked?" I ask.

Susie shakes her head, but not in a "no" gesture, more as though she's trying to dig up old memories to answer the question. "I don't think I remember what they actually said about them as people. To be honest, I don't think they said an awful lot about them. There was something else, though." She frowns now, before sipping her tea. Even the action of tipping the cup appears to bring her pain. She winces before placing the cup back on its saucer. "This is a very malicious rumour that I only heard once. I was a child, perhaps ten years old, waiting at the doctor's surgery with Dad. There were two women behind us, and Dad had nipped to the loo, so he didn't hear. Otherwise, I think he would have told them to shut up about this around a child. I don't know who the women were, because I never saw their faces. The topic of the Pierces' disappearance came up, as did the topic of the affair, and then one of them said, 'Belinda MacDonald said he touched her during the school play.' She went on to say that this Belinda claimed he was a pervert." Susan's gaze flashes guiltily across to Mark. "I shouldn't be talking about this in front of you, should I?"

Mark, mid-bite through a biscuit, rolls his eyes dramatically. "I'm twenty-seven, Mum."

"I know, but still. This is horrible stuff."

"No, it's important," he reminds her. "Keep going. It might help find out what happened to Abigail."

"Well, not much happened after that. The other woman shut her down, saying it was a nasty accusation and she shouldn't say things like that. One thing I do remember, though, was that the first woman seemed offended by being called nasty, as though she wouldn't usually talk about such matters if she didn't have a reliable source."

"Bloody hell," I say. "So they were childless, and there was a chance that the husband was a paedophile? How come no one investigated their disappearance?"

"I've often wondered what happened back then," Susie says. "I'll never be able to find out, because most of the people who were around have passed on. But I'd imagine the police tracked them down

TWO FOR JOY

and questioned them, at least."

Perhaps DCI Murphy would have access to the police file to find out. It might be a big ask, though.

"There's another thing you don't know." Susie splays her fingers against the wood of the table and stares down at them for a moment. "Dad doesn't even know about this. Not long before the accident, I was researching Abigail's disappearance, and I did some digging into our family background. When I was poking around, I found out that my grandmother was divorced before she married my grandfather. It was a short marriage. Barely lasted six months. My great-auntie Sally was still alive at the time, though she'd been living in Australia for several decades. I phoned her up and asked about this first husband. According to Sally, the man was mean. A 'wrong 'un', she called him. She said he was abusive and possessive. Very controlling, and very jealous. She said that Grandma married Grandad to get away from him. I checked the dates, and they're very close together. As is Abigail's birth."

"Oh," I say. "You think this controlling man was Abigail's real father?"

She nods. "I'm sure they kept it very hush-hush if he was. No one ever told Dad."

That makes me wonder whether George should be told sooner rather than later. But it isn't my place to say.

"Surely, this ex-husband would have been the number one suspect."

"According to Great-Aunt Sally, he was. She said, though she was very old at this point—in her nineties, bless her—that the man had an alibi."

"Do you remember his name?" I ask.

"Yes," she says. "Simon Blackthorn."

CHAPTER 19

The time flashes on my phone screen. 3am. I'm awake, but I don't know why, and I'm so tired that my eyelids feel as though they're glued together. Something woke me. What was it?

I quiet my breathing in order to concentrate harder, my mind finally sharpening, and my eyes prising open. Now that I know I was awakened by an unknown sound, my body is on high alert for danger. Moving quickly, I turn on the lamp next to my bed and retrieve the knife I keep between the mattress and the bed frame. If Isabel is here, I want to be prepared.

But my room is empty. The window is shut, as I left it, and there is nothing lurking in the shadows. No slip of a girl waiting with her sharp knives and sharper smile. Finally, I can let go of that breath I've been holding in. Perhaps it was a bad dream that woke me. I've had plenty of those.

And then…

A scream.

It wasn't a bad dream that woke me. It was Tom crying out. Without a moment's thought, I leap out of the bed, cross the room to my door, and snatch it open. The knife blade glints in the moonlight, gripped in my fist of whitened knuckles.

I'm coming for you, Isabel. Keep the fuck away from my son.

Tom's door is closed, and inside I can hear him screaming. The sounds are nothing like the kinds of screams you hear in horror films. They are low and guttural and desperate. I'm convinced that he's in pain.

As I open the door, I hold my knife aloft, ready to pounce on the girl who feeds my nightmares, ready to defend my son. I flick the light switch on, relieved that I have at least one advantage: knowing the house. But when the light fills the room, there's no one else there. Just Tom, writhing in his bed linen, his head moving from left to right, his eyes screwed shut and his legs kicking. I *was* awakened by a nightmare, just not my own.

With adrenaline still pumping through my veins, I leave the knife on Tom's desk and hurry to him, shushing him, cooing soothing words. *It's all right. It's going to be all right.* But Tom is hard to wake. I place a hand on his shoulder, but he wrenches it away in his sleep. When I try again and grip harder, his eyes flash open, and everything happens extraordinarily quickly. In the seconds that follow, I have to allow my brain to piece it altogether. He opens his eyes, turns his body towards me, and his right arm twists around and lands a punch just above my right cheekbone.

It's hard enough to knock me back onto the floor. I sit there like a toy with the stuffing pulled out, crumpled and vulnerable, in a state of shock.

"Leah." Tom's eyes are wide and white. "Are you okay? I'm sorry! I'm *so* sorry. I was having a nightmare, and I thought you were Isabel. Are you okay? Do you want me to call an ambulance?"

He strokes my hair and puts his hands on my shoulders. All I can think about is how close he is to me, and how pale he seems.

"I'm okay," I manage, though my face is sore. A bruise will be forming as we speak, and I'm dreading my day at work. "It's... fine. An accident."

"It was," he says. "I'm sorry." His expression contorts and his brow furrows, his mouth turns down, and there's moisture on his eyelashes. When his hands ball into fists, I can see that he's trying very hard not to cry.

"It's okay, Tom."

But he leans away from me and rocks back on his heels, bringing his tight fists up to his eyes. He shakes his head and mumbles something incoherent against his wrists.

"Tom, really. Stop. It's okay. I'm fine. It's just a bruise." I'm scared now. He's withdrawing away from me, tightening up into someone I don't recognise. He pushes back on his heels and rises. "Hey. I mean it, you know. Everything's going to be okay." I climb to my feet in order to close the gap between us.

Tom paces the room, still muttering to himself, his face red and blotchy, a throbbing vein protruding from his neck. He hits himself hard on the temple with one of his screwed-up fists and roars with such ferocity that my first instinct is to back away in fear. But that's ridiculous, isn't it? This is my Tom. My sweet, gentle little brother. My son. Pushing my fears aside, I rush to him and put my arms around him, cradling him tightly to stop him hurting himself again.

"She's not here," I say. "I won't let her hurt us again. I promise."

"You can't promise that." His body convulses as the tears finally come. "You don't know." More tears, more sobs that wrack through his body. "You don't know anything."

"No," I say. "I can't. But I swear I'll do everything I possibly can to stop it happening again."

As I hold him in my arms, I make a promise to myself. If I ever get the opportunity again, I will kill Isabel Fielding.

Covering up the bruise with foundation and concealer reminds me of my mother. While my father would avoid her face as much as possible when he flew into his rages, there were often still a few marks to cover up. Finger marks around her throat. Cigarette burns on her forearms. This is different, though. Tom wasn't in control. He wasn't himself. Is that what my mother told herself, too?

I'm angry. My mother's wedding ring is in the clutches of that murdering bitch, Isabel Fielding. When I was the one she had hurt the most, I could cope with it all. I carry the scars. I have the nightmares. I'm the one on medication, the one who experiences anxiety, the one who can't deal with birds anymore without hearing her voice in my ear. But I'm not the one she's hurt the most. That's Tom. I knew he was traumatised, and I knew he was angry, but I didn't realise how broken he was until the moment he began pacing that room. Now, everything aches inside me. Now, I see the utter devastation she's caused my family. Even my *mother*. My long-dead mother.

I stare at my reflection in the mirror and wonder: *What can I do? What can I do to make this right?* But the answers aren't there.

George is asleep when I enter his room. I fuss around a little, tidying his magazines, opening the curtains, removing empty cups. When he stirs, he smiles at me.

"Pretty Lizzie," he says.

I could cry. I've reached the point where any kindness shown to me makes me want to break down. It could be the new medication, or maybe I am becoming an emotional wreck.

"Morning," I say brightly, moving towards his bed in order to chat.

But I immediately see that that was a mistake when his smile fades. "What have you done to yourself?"

Self-consciously, I raise a hand to my cheek. "It was an accident." Knowing that nothing I say will sound like a successful lie, I've decided to be vague. There's a part of me that can't stand the idea of making up a lie to tell people, in the same way Mum did. Walking into doors, falling down stairs, tripping on Tom's toy truck, a swing at the park.

"I hope that wasn't a fella," he says again, his voice stern, like he's about to give me a life lecture. "There's no one on God's green earth worth getting bruises over. Mark my words."

"I know. Don't worry, it isn't like that."

"Oh," he says. "It never is."

As I sit next to him listening to his words of wisdom, I feel utterly guilty about knowing what his mother went through when he doesn't know himself. But it isn't my place to tell him. I can't. As much as I want to.

"I met your Susie the other day." A change of subject might help things along. "She's lovely. Reminds me of you."

"Is that right? Oh, no. Susie takes after her mother."

"Got your eyes, though."

He laughs. "Ah, you might be right about that."

"Susie remembers people talking about the Pierces, so I'm going to research that. But it made me think. We've not talked properly about your mother yet. I know it must be hard to think back to that time, but do you remember anyone being around your mum? Anyone suspicious or threatening?"

"Ooh, now. It was a long time ago," he says. He coughs a little and pushes himself up against the pillow slightly. I had a chat with the nurse before coming in, and I know he's still a little delicate, but the worst of his bug is over and he's tired but better than he was. "There's not much I remember at all."

"What do you remember? Maybe talking about it will jog something."

"She was pretty; I remember that. Brown hair, like yours. Blue eyes. Always wore a dress and stockings, as ladies did back then. And she slept in her rollers. The lipstick she wore was red, but it wasn't a strong red. It was subtle. I used to be able to smell her perfume whenever I thought about it, but it's gone now. So is her face, I think. I have to rely on photographs for that, and not many survived the fire.

"Now, what was she doing the day of the fire? She made breakfast in the morning. I fought with Abby about who would get the last piece of toast because I was hungry. She told us to cut it in half and share. We did it, but we weren't happy about it. Oh, yes, and she burnt her hand on the kettle. That wasn't like her; she was a very careful woman. She burnt her hand because she was absent-minded that morning. Not much like herself. Now I think about it, she'd been funny for a few days. She forgot to pick Abby up from her swimming lesson. I had to remind her, and we ran all the way down Rose Street to the baths to collect her. The teacher gave her such a telling-off that she was in tears all the way home. And…" George's eyes glaze over, as though he's somewhere very far away. "The phone calls."

"Phone calls?"

"Yes. Well, I never. I'd forgotten all about them. I was home from school for a few days. This was about a week before the fire. I had tonsillitis. Abby was fine, so she went to school, but I was laid up on the sofa, listening to the radio. We had a telephone in the hallway, on one of those little tables you don't see much anymore. I was trying to listen to the radio, but the blasted telephone kept going. Every time, my mother would rush into the hall and snatch up that phone. Then I'd hear her saying things like, 'stop calling here', 'leave me alone', 'leave us alone'. Honestly, I thought it was the mortgage people or the tax man, or one of the other things my father would complain about at dinner. But now that I think about it, I'm not sure."

"It sounds like someone was harassing your mother," I say.

"You might be right. But I can't think of anyone who would want to hurt Mum." George pauses and frowns. "Whoever it was probably started the fire. They're the murderer."

CHAPTER 20

ISABEL

I suspect that this might be true for you, Leah. I suspected it the first time I met you, and it's something we have in common. We don't have many friends, do we? We're not the social butterfly type. We're more the kind that sit in a room at night and think about darkness. My darkness is different from yours, though. I accept that. You seem to me like a self-flagellator, someone who is in a constant state of guilt. What's shame to you? Tuesday night? Monday morning? A sprinkle of social embarrassment with your cornflakes? Did you cry at school when you got a bad mark? Did you feel guilty about letting Mummy and Daddy down?

I know you did.

We don't have many friends. But my reason is quite simple: once I get to know them, I inevitably want to kill them. Some may call this "a shame". However, I see it as an opportunity.

That opportunity arose last night in a motel that takes cash payments, somewhere outside Watford. We were close to a main road, and the constant hum of traffic was giving me a headache. I stared at Chloe, and I realised we'd reached the point of repetition when things stop being interesting. Visiting your mother was a lot of fun, but since then, it had been little more than drug deals, drug use, sleeping in cars, and cheeseburgers. I'd finished with my room service burger, and I felt sick.

I looked at Chloe, and I felt sick.

We were watching television together for the first time—this was our first motel stay. It was some sort of soap opera I remember the inmates of Crowmont Hospital watching religiously. All the women loved it and gathered round to watch insignificant people with Mancunian accents wail and flail over cheating husbands and wives. I was bored.

The soap finished, and the adverts came on and then the news. Chloe was a little worse for wear at this point, having injected herself with what I can only assume was heroin. There was a temptation to try it myself, I have to admit, but I'd seen the track marks on the arms of the people at Crowmont. I'd seen the destruction marks. I'd also seen Chloe lose control of herself after taking it, and I'm not one to lose control. I'm one to take it.

As Chloe sank into her high, I leaned against the headboard of the bed and watched the news with interest. I've been following the murder of Alison Finlay and am fascinated by what the police think. But up to this point, I'd done this by stealing newspapers and reading them while Chloe was asleep, then throwing them away before she saw a picture of old muggins here within its pages. Chloe is not one to take interest in the headlines. She cares more about drugs and burgers than she does the most wanted woman in Britain.

But what I should have thought about, which I failed to do, was the fact that *I* am the news. The news is all about me, because there's nothing else of interest in this shithole of a country. So, as Chloe lay there with her eyes half-open in drug-addled bliss, a photograph of me popped up on the screen.

Oh, shit.

Well, even geniuses have a bad day.

I switched the channel over as quickly as possible, but Chloe turned to me and her face attempted to frown, though it was still relaxed from all the heroin.

It was at that moment, Leah, that I realised what I would do about my boredom.

CHAPTER
21

There's a moment just before the dawn when I could swear that my dreams are real. Here is my father, sitting in a chair, laughing at the woman I've become. There is Isabel, sharpening her knife, her eyes quick and intelligent, waiting. And there is Tom, naked, bathed in blood, his hands outstretched towards me. And then there is the body of the woman, #justiceforalison etched on her body. She's changing, and her hands aren't hands, they're claws. Bird claws. I wake, and I think—did I do this?

Am I responsible?

The magpie beats its wings.

No. It's my heart. My heart is racing.

Since I changed medication, I've found that I sleep through the night in my own bed, but my dreams are more vivid than ever. Some of the anxiety has lifted, but I'm groggier, clumsier, like I'm only 80% of myself. Perhaps I leave the other 20% in my dreams.

It's Saturday, and I have a day when neither I nor Tom needs to work. When I stumble downstairs, he has a pot of coffee waiting.

"Want one?"

I eye this creature with suspicion. What kind of teenage boy offers someone coffee? Perhaps the teenage boy I used to live with until an angry and bitter monster took up camp.

"Sure."

"Sleep okay?" he asks.

"Apart from the nightmares, yes," I reply.

Tom places the coffee on the table. "Honesty for once. Maybe those new pills are working."

I take a sip of coffee. "You know I never lie to you."

"Lying is still lying if it's by omission." He shrugs.

Ah, the angry, bitter monster is definitely still in there.

"Is everything okay?" I ask.

Tom takes a sip of his coffee and regards me with hooded eyes. "It's just refreshing for you to admit that you have nightmares. You always seem to think that you have to make everything okay. That you have to protect me all the time."

I think about reaching out and taking his hand. At one time I would have, but now I hesitate. Are we past that? "Of course I want to protect you. That's what... That's what big sisters do."

"I don't need it," he says, and he sounds tired. "I want you to treat me like an adult."

My breath catches in my throat. "I thought I was."

"Did you?"

"Yes."

Tom lets out a hollow laugh. "Huh."

"Yeah, I guess I made a bad job of that." My shoulders drop in disappointment. I sip on the coffee and hold in a sigh. "Are we okay?"

"Sure."

He says it too quickly, like he's holding back. I squint, but I can't figure out if he truly is okay, or whether he's simply placating me.

"Hey, want to help me with something today?" I ask. "You know my friend George at the home? And how I'm doing some research to try to establish what happened to his sister in the forties?"

"Yeah."

"I need to track down more information about his mother's ex-husband. I know we're not supposed to create Facebook accounts, but I could create a false one under a different name and a stock photo and ask for more information. Join some local groups. What do you think? You're better at this stuff than I am. Will you help me? I had a go at it myself a while ago, but I don't think I did a very good job."

"Okay, but only until I have to go meet the others at the pub later. There's a burger and a pint deal."

"Nice. Can I come?"

He regards me, horrified.

"Only kidding!"

He almost laughs. Almost.

We create a profile page for a lady called Evelyn, and choose the most natural-looking stock image for a woman in her eighties that we can find. I even create a new email address to ensure that nothing can be traced back to either Lizzie or Leah. It's like I've been split into three. First, I was Leah. Then I was Lizzie and Leah. Now I'm Lizzie, Leah and Evelyn. Which of us is the better woman? My money is on Evelyn.

After doing some research, Tom adds me to a few groups. We find a group for the local school, and a group for local history. There's another group for making friends and keeping in touch. Then I go through several profiles and add those people as friends, hoping they'll add me back without trying to research poor old Evelyn, who of course doesn't exist. But whatever we can do to find Simon Blackthorn is worth doing, and even better than all that, it means I get to spend some time with Tom.

"Look at this," Tom says. I left the computer to pour another cup of coffee. The wooziness from these new drugs is hard to kick. I move back and lean over the computer. "This person has the same last name. She's friends with several people called Blackthorn, and there are some photos on her page of her relatives. Look: this is a scanned photo of a black-and-white picture taken long ago. Under the photo, she's put Blackthorn as the caption."

"Rita Blackthorn. What if she's his granddaughter or something? Add her as a friend."

Tom clicks on the "add friend" button, and we both stay staring at it as though she'll add us back immediately.

"Good thing she had her settings to public. Who does that these days?"

"Trusting people," I say. "People who haven't been attacked by a psychopath?"

"We're joking about it now?" Tom raises an eyebrow. "I guess that means something is healing."

"Yeah, maybe you're right. Or maybe it's this new medication making me weird."

"I think you were pretty weird already."

"Good point." I smile and sip my coffee. "Do you think we're going to find out what happened to George's sister? How amazing would that be?"

Tom cocks his head to the right and regards me with a strange expression on his face. The mid-morning sun catches his birthmark, turning it even more vermillion than ever. "Why do you do this? *How* do you do this?"

"Do what?"

"You know… find a cause and fight for it. And I'm not just talking about Isabel. Remember Gavin, that druggy artist boyfriend of yours? You almost dropped out of your A-Levels, working two jobs to support his habit. You thought you could fix him, didn't you? Why do you keep trying to fix everyone else except us?"

"That's not true!" Though I try to keep a friendly smile on my face, the words sting like lemon on a cut. "Fixing both of us is… is almost all I think about. This is my distraction so I don't drive myself crazy. Again."

"You're running away. Escaping. Getting lost in business that isn't yours."

"That's not fair. He asked for my help."

"And despite everything that's going on with us, you still gave it to him." Tom stands, and the chair squeaks against the floor. "Don't you have the energy to fight for us?"

"I fight for us all the time. I fought for us at that abandoned farm—"

"I seem to remember I did the fighting." Tom's eyes are like marbles. Dark, emotionless marbles. Cold and small. "Why didn't you kill her, Leah? Why didn't you kill her when she was unconscious in the farmhouse?"

There it is. There's the resentment.

I've thought since that night that the wedge between me and Tom is down to the fact that I've never told him I gave birth to him, but as he asks me that question, I realise the truth. That's what has been pulling us apart.

"You know why." My voice is soft and cool, ignoring the hot storm beneath my skin.

"No. I don't."

"I'm a nurse, Tom. Not a murderer."

"I killed her father," he says. His voice is emotionless. Terrifying.

"To save me," I say. "He was trying to murder me. When Isabel was unconscious on the ground, she was helpless. It would have been *her* murder. I would have been just like her." My stomach twists, and for a terrifying moment, I think I'm going to be sick. But then I pull myself together and run my fingers through my hair to steady myself. "You seem to forget me pushing her off a cliff. You keep forgetting that. I fought her, and I won. I pushed her, and she shouldn't have survived."

"Alison Finlay is dead because of you. Because you couldn't finish it."

My scars itch. The coffee swirls in my stomach. Tom stares at me with the dead eyes of a magpie.

"It wasn't that hard, you know." He takes a step towards me and lifts a knife from the block on the counter. "It went in much easier than I thought it would. All those bullies at school called me fat. A blob. Bad at sports, un-athletic, stupid. But I proved them all wrong when I drove that knife into David Fielding's back. Didn't I?"

I take a step back. "You did it in self-defence. It was brave, Tom, but the act itself isn't something to be *proud* of. You should be proud that you defended us, saved us, but the actual act... Tom, you know better than that. Don't you? You know that?"

Tom places the knife back down. "Of course."

He stands there with his hands by his sides, staring down at his feet. I take a tentative step towards him. "Tom, is there something you need to tell me?"

He shakes his head.

"I'm here to help you. I'm your friend... I..." Everything sounds lame. Cliched. "I won't judge you. I know we don't talk about that night, and I can see now that I made a mistake in not talking to you about what happened. You're traumatised by having to kill David Fielding, and perhaps we should address all of that. Do you want to sit down and talk about it?"

How has today ended up going horribly wrong? We were sat together working on a task, joking a little. Even a few laughs. And yet… all of this was bubbling under the surface, waiting to be released. Why didn't I see it coming?

"I want to talk about Mum," Tom says eventually.

"Okay. What about her?" Alarm bells are ringing in my head. What does he know?

"You didn't know I was in that day, did you? But I was. I heard you talking to Murphy. I heard you discussing how Isabel dug our mother up and stole her ring. How could you *not tell me*?"

He seems tall, broad, almost terrifying in the small kitchen. No one tells you that about teenage boys, do they? They're *terrifying*. "I wanted to spare you that. God, Tom, when I was told, I wanted to be sick. I felt disgusted, violated. What she did to Mum was abhorrent. I… I couldn't tell you because I didn't want you to feel the same way I felt."

"Lies, Leah. All lies. You want to keep it all to yourself. The drama. The horror. The violence. You love it, don't you? Remember how you researched all those serial killers? You can't get enough of it." He places his hands on my shoulders. "You let Isabel go because you love her. Don't you see that?"

CHAPTER 22

ISABEL

I do wish I could send you these letters, Leah. No, I wish I could see you, touch your skin, smell your scent. Was it your shampoo that smelled like lavender? Or do you use some sort of old-fashioned perfume? Since I've been free, I've noticed that only women in their eighties smell as strongly of lavender as you, but it doesn't surprise me that you're old-fashioned.

How I'd love to tell you this story in person and see your expression. I remember the glint of fascination in your eyes as I lured you into my room with promises of depraved tales about my childhood.

You're as dark as I am, Leah, and don't you ever forget it.

Here's a little depraved tale for you.

Once upon a time, a girl was born. Her family were strange and eccentric. They didn't watch movies together on the sofa or have perfect family dinners on a Sunday. They hunted and killed together.

The girl learned that destruction was the greatest of all arts, but society didn't care for her kind of art. She was locked away and told she'd never leave, so the girl learned to play a new game, one that needed the right prey in order to work. The girl chose her prey and played the game to her best ability until one day she decided that she would die happy by creating one perfect piece of art, even if it meant giving up her newfound freedom. The girl's family helped her, and she almost completed it, except for one problem. The prey turned on her.

The girl escaped from the prey's clutches and managed to run away. She hid in the dirt and shadows, hungry and alone but free, and then she made a friend. The friend showed the girl a new world. She showed her where to eat and how to get high. But it turns out that the new world was boring to the girl. She wanted destruction.

She wanted to create.

The friend was slowing her down. She was a burden. The friend didn't have two brain cells to rub together, but eventually she figured out that the girl was infamous and that there was a reward for turning in the girl.

I caught her with her ear to a mobile phone the next day. I think she thought I was still asleep, but I wasn't.

"Who are you calling?" I asked.

When she turned to me, her skin was waxy and yellow, like a candle with condensation on the surface. There were deep purple bruises beneath her eyes, and her hair was greasy and disgusting. When I first met Chloe, I thought she was pretty, in a rough kind of way. But now she was hollow and jaundiced, unhealthy and grubby. I wanted to get away from her.

"Just a friend."

"I didn't know you had any friends." I sat up in bed and reached over to her, then gently pulled the phone away from her ear. "I thought I was your friend."

"You are," she said. Her words came quick. Desperate little utterances. The voice of the cowardly. The begging. The pathetic.

"Let's go and get breakfast, shall we?" I suggested.

"I think I need to go—"

"No, you don't." At this point, she needed a little persuasion, so I took her wrist in my hand and held her tight.

"Okay."

We dined on fried chicken, because it was the nearest restaurant. Chloe barely touched her food. I think it was at this point in the day when Chloe resigned herself to her fate. She stared down at her fried chicken and decided that she didn't have much of a life, anyway. Sometimes a little fighting spirit won out and she raised her head and regarded the people in the restaurant with wide eyes, which was when I jabbed a knife into her thigh under the table, just enough to let her know it was there. Chloe, poor dim-witted, drug-addled Chloe, was the kind of person who just needed to be scared a bit. She didn't take much persuasion at all. She didn't have your streak of self-preservation. Maybe that's why you're much more interesting prey.

We went back to the car after our greasy breakfast, and Chloe begged me to let her go. She was crying. She promised many things: that she wouldn't tell the police, that she wouldn't tell anyone. She asked me what I wanted. Did I want money? Drugs? Sex? I didn't want any of those things, and I believed her when she told me she wouldn't tell anyone. Well, I believed she wouldn't tell anyone for a while. But one day the fear would ebb away and she would believe herself to be safe, and it would be on that day that she would blab all about her experiences with me.

That isn't why I did what I did. I want you to know that. I did it because I was bored.

I drove. It was the first time I'd driven the car, because I don't have a license, of course. I'm not a good driver, Leah. I barely made it out of Crowmont with your car. That was always the part of the plan that I was frightened of. Would I make it out of the carpark, even?

I digress. Anyway, I drove us away from the chicken restaurant and away from the main roads. I drove all day, in fact, with a full tank of petrol dutifully paid for the night before. I drove and I drove as Chloe cried quietly in the seat next to me. I avoided roads with too many traffic lights, but when I did stop, I held on to her to stop her leaping out of the car door. Eventually, I allowed her to take enough drugs to calm herself down.

She was passive then, and she made barely a sound when I stopped on a country road by what appeared to be a forest of thickset trees. It was night by this point. I don't know how long we'd been driving. But finally we stopped at this isolated place, and I pulled her from the car.

Chloe wasn't prey. Prey needs to put up a fight, and the fight had been knocked from this girl many years ago. But she was about to serve a purpose. Her life wouldn't be a waste, after all. I was going to transform her into something greater, something far more beautiful than she'd ever been in her life.

I led her by the hand into the trees, keeping my knife in the other hand. A different knife from the one I held beneath your chin, Leah. This one I bought from a department store, wearing a disguise. A black wig and a beret hat. Nothing too conspicuous. Not a balaclava or anything like that. I bought it with money Chloe had earned from her drug deals, as she was slumped, high, half-conscious in the backseat of the car.

Poor girl. If only she'd noticed more, she might have prevented her own death. Well, never mind. Now she would get to transform, as I said, into beauty.

I was lucky enough to find a stream. Chloe was dirty and greasy from her drugs and from the terrible food we'd been eating. I stripped her like a mother does her baby before a bath. Then I bathed her in the stream. She shivered and made little gasping sounds, but she didn't try to run away. I gave her another hit of her favourite narcotic, bound her hands and feet, and then I got to work.

Do you think about our time together in the farmhouse, Leah? I do. Often. One of my deepest regrets is not completing my work. Chloe provided a new canvas for me to work on, but it wasn't quite the same as you. When I was finished, I felt… underwhelmed. At least when I untied her and pushed her into the stream, her arms and hair spread out in an attractive way. It was then that I realised her hair was almost the same colour as your hair, Leah, and that made me a little happier. Until it made me sad.

I won't be satisfied until you, my most worthy prey, have been transformed into my best creation.

I need you, Leah, and I will find you.

CHAPTER
23

Rita Blackthorn finally accepts my friend request. I've been checking Facebook all day, but it isn't until the evening that I receive the notification. As soon as we're friends, I view every photo, status and comment that I can, greedy for more information. The more I read, the more I believe she is a descendant of Simon Blackthorn. Some of her relatives even live nearby. I cross-reference members of her family with people's names I saw in groups about Clifton, and everything seems to check out.

Now, I sit in front of the laptop with my hands hovering over the keyboard. I need to message her if I'm going to find out anything more about Simon Blackthorn and his relationship to George's mother, but I'm nervous. She could become incredibly offended if I suggest that her grandfather, or great-grandfather, was a man capable of murder and kidnapping. Or even of domestic abuse. And what if I have the wrong person, anyway? Or, what if I reveal my identity in some way? What if I slip up?

This is for George. I decide to compose a quick message pretending to be Evelyn's granddaughter, who is trying to learn more information about Simon Blackthorn. There, it's done. Back to waiting.

Against my better judgement, I can't help checking the hashtag that makes my skin turn cold. I check both Facebook and Twitter, relieved to see it isn't quite as active as before. Maybe the fuss has died down. Or maybe they've moved to some other social media or website arena to discuss ways to kill me slowly. They don't see the scars I wear. They don't know me.

They don't know what's in my nightmares.

Some days, I'm not sure I even know myself. Some days, the secrets I keep inside myself threaten to overflow. Sometimes I worry about myself and what I'm capable of, what I've been capable of in the past.

I log out of Facebook and then remember that I wanted to check out another one of Rita Blackthorn's friends. But this time, when I go to log back into Facebook, I discover that there's another email address linked to a Facebook account. Tom's email address.

My stomach drops. Tom knows he shouldn't have a Facebook account, certainly not with the email address that contains his real name. I consider shutting down the laptop and talking to him later, but I don't. I log in under his email address.

I know I shouldn't be doing this. The way my palms begin to sweat suggests I'm all too aware that I shouldn't be doing it. But Tom is at the pub with his friends, and I'm alone in the house with a mind that cannot stop looping back to the moment he picked up that knife from the kitchen table and held it towards me. Those black magpie eyes had been staring at me… My mind is stuck in that moment, asking me what I actually know about my son. Perhaps this is an opportunity to find out.

I log in without a hitch—the password is saved on this device; that's sloppy by Tom—and his page appears. There's no profile picture. No status. Perhaps this is just an empty account he left active by accident. I'm about to log back out with a sigh of relief, but before I do, I can't help clicking on the inbox icon.

And there I see them. My first assessment was wrong; this account isn't empty at all. It's used for communication. I screw my eyes tightly shut and place my face in my palms, shaking my head. How could he do this? How could he put us in danger like this?

There are six messages in total, and they span over a period of three or four months. Every single message is to and from the same person: Isabel's mother. I lean back in my chair, reeling from this new revelation.

Hi Anna,

This is a hard message to write. I don't know if you know who I am. I'm Tom Smith, Leah's brother. I think you know Leah, because she is the nurse who let your daughter escape. She even went to your house once, didn't she? She came back shaken, afraid of your husband.

We are protected now, because your daughter is still obsessed with my sister. We're protected, but we don't feel safe. I wondered if you feel the same way? I guess I needed someone to talk to. Leah doesn't talk about what happened much.

There's another reason why I messaged you. I am the person who killed your husband, and I'm very sorry about that. I wake up at night and feel like I've done it again. Like I've murdered someone. I feel like a killer.

I'm sorry.
Tom

There are tears in my eyes as I read his first message to Anna Fielding. I hadn't realised how much pain Tom was in after the night on the moors. We're both traumatised. We're both damaged. And we both seem to be moving in different directions rather than healing together. I wipe the tears away and read Anna's reply.

Dear Tom,

I'm sorry for my late reply. I stopped checking my Facebook account after my family were outed as murderers. It has been a very painful time for me, and though I get messages of support, some are not so kind. People expect me to have seen what was going on, but… Well, I was never truly there. I'm an addict. Alcohol and prescription drugs. The last few decades have been a hazy mess, but now I'm receiving help.

You see, I never realised how David encouraged my addiction. He poured me wine, recommended doctors to treat my anxiety. Tucked me into bed after I passed out, and then did what? Murdered innocent people. I was the perfect wife for him.

To everyone outside the family, we had the perfect life.

Until Maisie was killed.

I do not blame you for killing my husband. He did not deserve to live. But I still grieve for him. I grieve for them all.

I am sorry for what my family did to your family. Keep in touch if you would like to.

Best Wishes,
Anna Fielding

The loneliest woman in the world. I thought that the night I spent eating dinner with the Fieldings. She was alone all that time, lost in her haze of booze and drugs. I wonder if she will ever be able to live a normal life ever again. Tom was the one to reach out, and I understand why. She is the only person who can relate to our lives. Why didn't I see it before? We've been through the exact same circumstances. My father took away my family, my mother. Her husband destroyed her family. We both had violence in our lives. We are survivors of abuse and addicts, and we're riddled with the guilt and shame of not being able to stop the violence.

There is no way I can be angry with Tom for reaching out to Anna. It's dangerous to do so, of course it is, but I understand what he needs. I need it too.

I'm about to close the laptop when Tom's most recent message catches my eye.

Hey Anna,

How is AA going? You must be proud of your progress. My sister is also doing well with sobriety. But she is on medication for her psychological problems, and I don't know if it's working. She thinks I haven't noticed, but I see her sleepwalk in the night and wake up elsewhere. Once, I remember her leaving the house and coming back with blood on her hands. That was when we lived in Scotland.

I can't stop thinking about Isabel. Where is she? What is she doing? Why does she have those violent impulses? Do you think it's anger? Sometimes I wonder if we all bottle up darkness and rage until it explodes. Are we all capable of murder, do you think? I think we are. There's a killer inside everyone.

I know there's a killer inside me.

I'm sorry to be so dark and depressing. I guess that's what's on my mind right now.

Leah has made me start going to see a therapist. Looks like I need one! Anyway. Keep writing.

Tom

Parts of that message remind me of young Tom. The breezy sign-off. The kindness and consideration to ask about her AA meetings. But the rest is someone else entirely. The Tom I know doesn't talk about violence and murder as though they are daily occurrences, or about the way everyone could kill another person. The Tom I know is gentle.

And then there's the part that makes my stomach churn. *Once, I remember her leaving the house and coming back with blood on her hands.* I close my eyes, count to ten, and steady my breathing. There was a night. One night. I did have blood on my hands, and I couldn't find a cut anywhere on myself. At around 4am, I woke up on the kitchen floor in a panic, in the midst of a terrible nightmare. I hurried to the bathroom, showered, hid my bloody clothes, and went back to bed. But I thought it was a secret. And I've never found out where the blood came from.

It takes several cups of tea before my fingers stop trembling. While on my third, I receive a message from Rita Blackthorn.

I'm very sorry to hear about your grandmother's illness. Of course, I'd love to help you in any way I can. I did a little family research recently and did learn more about Simon Blackthorn. I don't know a lot, but I can try to help. What is your grandmother's connection with Simon?
Rita

She sounds nice. Normal. Trusting. Of course I feel terrible about lying to her, but I can't exactly tell her the truth. I send a quick reply.

Thanks so much! Do you fancy grabbing a coffee? I live in Clifton but can travel to you.
My grandmother knew Simon as the husband of one of her friends, Claire Hawker. The Hawker family suffered a tragedy in the 40s, and she's

desperately trying to remember more about that time.
I really appreciate you doing this!
Lizzie

Rita responds within five minutes. She must be online.

Great! I live in London. Could meet in King's Cross and grab lunch?

We arrange a time and date. I shut the laptop and take a deep breath.

"Good morning, sunshine."

I pull open the curtains. "It's raining, George."

"Ah, not when you come to see me," he says.

"You old charmer, you." I'm rolling my eyes as I manoeuvre the chair closer to his bed, but his kind words warm me on a cold and wet Monday morning. "I have some news."

"Good, I hope," he says.

I nod. "I think so. I've managed to track down a descendant of your mother's ex-husband. I have a feeling that the animosity he showed towards your mother after the break-up is an important lead. She might not know anything, but it's a place to start."

"You've found out more than anyone else," George says.

"Simon Blackthorn could have been the person phoning your Mum before the fire. Then again, he might not be. If it's nothing, I'm going to check out the Pierces. I still think it's odd that the family all left at the same time. And Mr Pierce sounds dodgy."

"Does he, now? What makes you say that?"

For some reason, I hold back about the overheard conversation in the doctor's office. "If wife did have an affair, he might have psychological issues." I pause, wondering whether to tell him my suspicions of Simon Blackthorn being Abigail's real father, then decide not to. That's a family matter. "I'm going to give Mark a call later and see if he can come with me to meet Rita. That's the name of the woman related to Simon."

"Getting on well, are you? Has he shown you around Clifton yet?" George asks. Of course his eyes are twinkling with mischief, and I can't help but wonder whether part of his plan is to set me and Mark up together, along with uncovering the mystery of his disappearing sister.

"No, not yet. Now, don't get excited. Trust me when I tell you that you wouldn't want a granddaughter like me."

George thumps the bed with his fist. "Don't you be saying that, Lizzie love. You're a good person."

I straighten up his bedding, plump up the pillows and leave him to nap. *A good person*. What is a good person, really? Is a *good* person good all the time? Can I be bad for years and then become a good person? Or will I always be bad? My naiveté, addictions, and psychological issues all led to a convicted criminal escaping from her imprisonment. I'm not sure I'm a good person at all.

I have blood on my hands.

Ivy Lodge is setting up a new database for storing client details, which means that for the rest of the day, I'm consumed by the thrilling task of transferring names from one part of the system to another. To be honest, I don't mind it at all, as it's a welcome distraction from what I found on Tom's Facebook account, though I can't help letting my mind drift back to thoughts about Anna Fielding.

The end of the day comes around quickly for a Monday. At lunchtime, I call Mark, and we agree to meet at the train station on Wednesday morning and travel down to London together. I book the day off work without any trouble. I get a few hundred people moved into the correct database, copying and pasting until my fingers are sore. If I didn't have that constant niggle at the back of my mind, the one that likes to remind me about Isabel and Tom and Anna Fielding, and even Owen and David Fielding, and of course, my mother and father, I'd be happy.

"You in?" I call as I walk through the door of the bungalow. No one answers, but I hear the sound of the television running in the lounge. Typical teenager, not answering when call. I slip off my shoes, dump my coat and bag, and make my way into the living room. "Tom?"

He's sat slouched forward with his thumbnail between his teeth. Before I have chance to ask if anything is wrong, I notice what he's engrossed with what's on the screen. It's the news.

"… another body of a young woman was found in a woods. The body was mutilated and dumped in the stream in a forest area near Kidderminster. That's all we know at the moment. More information is coming in, as we remain live near the scene. This is the second murder that could be connected to Isabel Fielding since her escape from Crowmont Hospital…"

"Fuck."

Tom finally turns around to fix me with those cold magpie eyes. "She's killed another one."

CHAPTER 24

When Tom turns back to the television screen, I excuse myself and rush to the laptop, where I pull up Google Maps. Geography isn't my strong point, and I need to know where they found the body. I connect Kidderminster to our current location and let out a long sigh of relief. Too far. No one living in Clifton-on-Sea could travel there and back in one night.

"Tom, do you want a cuppa?" I call through into the living room.

"Are you fucking kidding?"

"Hey." Angrily, I hurry back into the lounge. "Don't speak to me like that."

"Are you stupid, though?" he says. "A woman has been murdered, and you're putting the kettle on like nothing has happened."

"Oh, for Christ's sake. You know full well that everyone puts the kettle on in times of crisis in this country. What do you think the policewoman did when she found me curled up in a ball, talking to

James Gorden's head? The first thing she did was make me a cup of tea."

The blood drains from Tom's face.

"What did Seb do when I ran to him at the farm, bloodied and cold? How fucking dare you believe I'm moving on like nothing's happened when you damn well know I feel responsible for all of this? Why do you think I'm on medication? Why do you think my mind *fucking broke*? I've indulged this nonsense for too long. I know you're in pain, but so am I. I know you're traumatised, but *so am I*. You accuse me of not talking to you about what happened—well, here I am. What do you have to say to me?"

Tom shakes his head slowly. "I don't know."

"Got any secret Facebook accounts you want to tell me about?" I can't help it. I'm out of control, my anger is a living thing, taking up space within my body, overtaking my brain.

"You've been spying on me," he says.

"No, you idiot. Autofill completed the details on the log-in screen."

I'm not sure Tom could get any paler, but somehow he does.

"I needed someone to talk to."

"So did I," I say. "For some strange reason, I thought I had you, but it appears that I don't."

Tom stands. Taller than me. Broader. Puppy fat almost gone, and a man left behind. Where did my boy go? And those eyes are ice-cold.

"I want to move out," he says. "I want to move on and live my life the way I want to live it. That's not going to happen here. I look at you, and all I see is Isabel."

The words are like a knife to my gut. An image of Tom flashes through my mind: him plunging the knife into David Fielding. I run out of the room, barely making it to the kitchen sink before I vomit.

He follows me in. "Jesus."

My hands are shaking as I pull the tea towel from the oven door and wipe my mouth.

"Are you ill? You're very pale."

"I'm fine," I say. "I just... I think it's the new medication."

Tom frowns, and a line forms between his eyebrows. "Is it the murdered girl? Is it me?"

I look at my son. *My son.* I just don't know what to say to him. I can't find the words. My eyes fill with tears, and I feel like the loneliest, stupidest woman in the world. He wants to get away from me because I've never been able to protect him. Why should he want to stay with me?

He pushes his hands into the pockets of his jeans and waits for me to answer. Finally, I compose myself enough to be able to croak out a response. "I thought we'd be a team. Us against the world. Surviving together. But... what happened with Isabel has pushed us apart from each other."

"I just need some space, that's all."

I nod, thinking about those months when Tom was in foster care and I holed myself up in the cottage, afraid of the world. I don't want to be alone.

"I'm sorry," he says.

I wish I knew whether he means it.

The next day, I get obligatory phone calls from both Adam and DCI Murphy. Both think we're—*I'm*—safe here. The murder was 200 miles away, which seems to indicate that Isabel still doesn't know where we are. I've decided to stay off work, claiming that a migraine has me bedridden. The reality is that I do stay in bed and contemplate life without Tom living with me. I'm afraid of his leaving, both for me and for him. There's much to be done to help him heal, but perhaps he needs to do that alone. Perhaps I'm more of a hindrance than a help: making him angry, causing him to unleash his temper. The last year has seen him grow into a harder, colder version of himself. But perhaps that's normal after the trauma he's experienced.

Some people shut down. Me, I'm rawer and more exposed than ever. But Tom is living in his own hardened shell.

While I hide in my bedroom, I hear him moving around, collecting his things. One of his friends from the chip shop needs a housemate for a small apartment. It's all set up and ready to go. I hear his wardrobe door open and shut, the sound of coat hangers clattering to the floor, bags being zipped. Will he have enough money? He'll need a second job. Can he even keep his job with that temper? Why is this so hard? He's old enough to move out, and yet I know he isn't ready. I know he's still a child. My child, the one I refused to acknowledge as mine as soon as he left my womb. Who am I to make him stay with me?

He leaves without saying goodbye, no doubt hoping to avoid a scene, but I'm all cried out. I'm even slightly relieved that the event is over. It's happened. He's left. And now he has the responsibility of keeping himself safe against Isabel.

But the question is: would he keep me safe?

He sent those messages to Anna Fielding, putting us both in danger. And I have no way of knowing what he'll do when he's out there in the world. Will he tell someone his real name? Will he tell them who I am? #justiceforalison might get a whole lot more dangerous. I never thought I would feel this disconnected and wary of Tom, but we've gone our separate ways now.

Dr Qamber's office is sunny this afternoon. She has the blinds down a touch to stop the light from getting in my eyes. Clifton is bright today.

Even the old shopfronts seemed more cheerful as I passed them on the bus. I must resemble a grey cartoon next to the colourful town.

"He went, and I didn't stop him," I admit. "It made me feel weak, watching him go, but somehow I think it's better for both of us. I make him angry all the time, and I'm not sure I can live with that anymore."

"You call yourself weak for letting Tom move out, but I think it shows great strength. The anger issues you mentioned are important here. Is it possible that you have been in an abusive relationship with Tom since you moved away from your last residence? The way he lashes out at you makes me think that he was becoming your abuser. Stopping that cycle from happening makes both of you extremely brave," she says.

It's like thinking through soup today. My mind refuses to cooperate. Even this simple theory feels like a complicated maths equation. My mouth is dry, and I keep swallowing. Thoughtfully, Dr Qamber pushes a glass of water towards me. I nod my thanks and take a sip.

"Like my father. *His* father."

"We all inherit a few bad habits from our parents," she points out. "But that doesn't mean we have to become them. There's no destiny written that says Tom must be abusive because his father was. It's possible that he learned some behaviour from his father, and he began to cycle into that behaviour. His moving out was a way of stopping it before it got worse."

"So, there's still good in him?"

"That's an odd thing to say." Dr Qamber leans closer. "Why wouldn't there still be good in him? Tom may have anger issues, but hasn't he always been the victim of the things that have happened to you both?"

"Yes," I admit. "But… he's changed so much that I don't recognise him."

"Adolescence is a complicated time. No one truly understands who they are at that age. You might not recognise him because of the steep difference in his personality since he's grown into a man. It doesn't mean you won't come to recognise him," she adds.

"He needs to be away from me in order to grow," I say. "That's what hurts. I'm not good enough."

"I think that's all we have time for today, Leah," she says. "But it might be a good idea for you to do something for me before next week. I want you to make a list of all the things you like about yourself."

That'll be a short list. "Okay, I will."

Dr Qamber purses her lips as though she wants to say more. She probably wants to grab me by the shoulders and shake me until I see sense. I'll play along with her games and write my list about how I'm actually a good person, even though deep down, I know I'm bad. Rotten to the core. How else do you explain the night I found myself covered in blood?

CHAPTER 25

ISABEL

I heard they found poor Chloe. It's all over the newspapers and on the televisions. Of course that means my face is more recognisable than ever. That's why I drove to a secluded spot somewhere between Birmingham and Wales, slept for a day, then carried on until I found a tiny village in Wales to hide away for a little while.

I wonder if you've read the newspapers, Leah. Have you seen my art? I hope so.

Self-preservation is important now. I'm like a new, refreshed version of myself, ready to find you, to complete what started when you first walked through the door at Crowmont Hospital. I could not hunt you looking like I did, the way you probably remember me. Anyone would see me and consider me an undesirable. A vagrant. That's useful for disappearing, but not useful for entering back into society, which I think I might have to do in order to find you. Of course, that's also extremely risky.

I think we both know I'll succeed. I always do.

First, a wash. All I had was a stream and a bar of soap, but it did the trick. My bloody clothing, worn while deconstructing Chloe, had already been burned carefully, away from the murder scene. I thought I'd washed away the blood from my skin, but somehow there was more to find, and it dissolved into the stream and washed away. I used some of Chloe's cleaner clothes to dress in. Her bra was too big, her jeans tight around the thighs. My hair dried as the sun rose. The dye was growing out, and I needed to change my appearance again. This time, I needed help.

Venturing back into society meant getting a proper haircut, clothes, and money. Luckily, Chloe left me the rest of her stash, which I managed to sell to a couple of gormless teenage boys outside a Comprehensive school. It was risky, but I kept a hat low down on my head, did my best junkie impression, and took as much cash as they had on them. Just about enough for petrol and a haircut, though I would need to dye my hair myself again.

The tiny village provided a small hairdresser owned by a plump woman called Carol. The shop is appropriately named "Hair By Carol", confirming exactly who will cut your hair. I sat in the chair and kept my shoulders back, my head held high. This was perhaps the riskiest part of my plan. On the way to the hairdresser, I bumped into an old lady on the street and helped her retrieve her belongings from the pavement. One of those belongings might or might not have ended up going in my pocket, and now I was sporting a rather fetching pair of reading glasses with chrome frames. A pair of glasses drastically change an appearance, or so I was led to believe from Superman cartoons.

By the end of the hour, Carol thought I was a lovely girl. I'm down on my luck, I told her, in search of a job. She told me to ask for Gavin at the newsagent on Bendelow Road, to tell him that she sent me. I was bound to get the part time cashier job if I told him my sob story. We Millennials have a terrible deal, and the older generations are too hard on us, apparently. We can't afford to buy houses, the environment is fucked, and the recession has resulted in a freeze on pay rises in public sector jobs for too long. I swear, Leah, I came out of that hairdresser feeling sorry for *you* in your pedestrian nursing job, with a teenage boy to care for. The world isn't on your side, is it? Do you go to food banks, Leah? No, I don't think you do, because now that you're in the witness protection programme, the taxpayers pay for your cost of living, or so *The Sun* continues to harp on about. They think you should pay for letting me out of Crowmont. They think you should come out in the open and show your face.

I do too, because then I could show my face, and show you my teeth.

With my brand-new haircut—a nice choppy bob that rests alongside my jawline, with a thick fringe that comes down to my brow—I decided to find a more affluent area for my next task. Isabel the vagrant was about to be no more. I'd had enough of drugs and smells and stained clothing. It was fun for a while, but not exactly who I am.

After asking a few older women on the street where was a good place to go shopping, I got on a bus and headed into the suburb of a town that caters to the more high-end clientele. It's here that I realised that Carol's hairdressing shop wasn't my riskiest moment. This was about to be it. And for once, I almost felt nervous about it. There was a lot riding on my abilities. But I was confident I could do it.

No baseball caps or old-lady glasses here. Both would draw far too much attention, and I already stood out like a sore thumb in my cheap jeans and baggy bra. But there wasn't much I could do about that. I also needed to avoid as much CCTV as I could, which is why I chose a small town and not a bigger city. However, I was aware that the shops I wanted to target would definitely have cameras. Perhaps I would get lucky in small independent cafes or bars. I decided on a tiny wine bar at the corner of the main shopping street. I went in and ordered an orange juice before sitting down near to a group of women sat around a chilled bottle of champagne; another already empty bottle was tipped upside down in a bucket by their feet. Also by their feet were several shopping bags in different sizes. These weren't the flimsy plastic shopping bags of the high street, but the tough, reinforced card bags from designer stores. I remembered all the names of the designers from watching my mother struggle through the front door of our house with her bags, already tipsy by lunchtime.

I needed to acquire those bags.

It was 2pm, and they were wrapping up their liquid lunch. Soon, they would be gone, and I would have to stay here, hoping for another group of rich women to come along with their goodies. Two left to go to the bathroom, carrying Mulberry handbags in the crooks of their arms. One of them went to the bar to settle the bill, leaving just one on her own. I needed to act fast. If only Chloe were with me to help. For once, I missed her, and I was almost sad about it. But I had only myself to rely on, which I was used to at any case. The woman was engrossed in playing some sort of game on her phone. The blonde at the bar was tipsy enough to try to chat up the bartender. The bags by their table were strewn so far and wide that one was almost next to my foot. The smallest bag. I dropped my magazine, bent low to pick it up, and scooped up the bag, hiding it underneath Chloe's old coat, which was slung over my arm. The woman didn't even notice.

Then, as I got up from my seat, I bumped her arm with my hip, causing her to drop her phone.

"I'm *very* sorry," I said.

She merely tutted and bent down to retrieve the phone, and as she did, I made my way to the opposite side of the table, closest to the door, hooked the handles of one of the bags around my wrist and walked straight out of the bar without looking back.

For almost the entire length of the street, I expected to hear voices behind me, but none ever came. I carried on walking, carrying my shopping bags as though nothing had happened. And when I realised no one was going to call me back, I went to the bus station and paid for the next bus to the nearest city. Cardiff. Only then did I open the bags and see what I'd "bought". The smallest bag was—as I had suspected—jewellery. A Cartier necklace worth at least a thousand pounds. The larger bag contained a leather bag that would probably cost the entirety of your monthly wage, dear Leah. These were good finds. All I needed to do was find a pawn shop.

And then, Leah, I would have the funds, the will, and the means to find you.

CHAPTER 26

Mark meets me at the Clifton train station wearing black jeans and a smart navy jumper. Every time I see him, I see a little more of the man George must have been when he was young, and for some reason, it makes me feel guilty. Surely, I'm not ready to feel anything for another man? Not after Seb. Not with everything going on. And someone so *young*? There's a pang I can't deny, but Mark is a friend.

"This is going to be a bit weird, isn't it?" For once, Mark is frowning, which is surprising to see. This must be what he's like when he's nervous. "I've never actually got to the stage where I meet someone who might have answers about Abigail. After all these years, we might be able to find out what happened to her."

"I hope so. Did you bring the photograph?"

Mark nods and pats his messenger bag. "I also brought photos of my grandmother, Mum, Grandad and Abigail before the fire. I know

Rita isn't much older than us, but maybe it'll jog something."

We grab coffee, and I try to rid myself of the morning grog. Sleeping without Tom in the house is a challenge, and lately the songbirds have been waking me up in the morning. Every time I'm awakened by a blackbird, I picture the drawing that Isabel made for me. The uncanny likeness of the house I lived in, which she created by simply listening to my description. Another death, Isabel still free, and Tom moved out. I haven't told my therapist, but I've been slipping an extra pill into my daily dosage to help me sleep. Not that it matters. The nightmares still come, and I wake up feeling as though I've been sleeping in a stream of blood.

"Sugar? Leah?"

"What?"

Mark holds out a sachet of brown sugar for me to put in my coffee.

"No, thanks."

"Are you all right?" he asks. "If you're feeling under the weather, we can reschedule."

"No," I say firmly. "Absolutely not. George has been waiting decades to solve this mystery." Besides, I *need* this. I need to get away from my life. Mark's face is so etched with concern that it makes my heart swell. I find myself opening my mouth to speak. "I haven't been sleeping well. I'm the guardian to my younger brother, and he recently decided to move out of the house. It's very quiet without him. Too quiet."

"I felt like that when I moved out of Mum's house," Mark says. "It takes a while to adjust, doesn't it?"

"Yes." There's nothing I can say, of course. Nothing real. That's the barrier between me and the rest of the world now. I can never be real. Never be the real me.

There are only two platforms at Clifton station, which makes it easy enough to board. Then, at St Pancras, the sudden bustle of the city takes my breath away. I'm immediately tense, tight in the chest, and anxious to get out. The faces in the crowd disturb me. A group of twenty-something girls have hair that's too mousy, that same shade of mid-brown that I remember from my time at Crowmont. Then there are the pigeons everywhere. Did Isabel draw me a pigeon once? What did she say? They represent gossip, chatter, betrayal.

Mark leads the way, or at least I'm happy to allow him to. He doesn't know I lived in Hackney for the first twenty-odd years of my life and that I'm more than capable of finding my way around, though I suppose my accent will have already told that tale. But I'm a different person now, and I cannot hear myself think with all this din. The drugs are making me muddled.

The Piccadilly line moves across Central like a snake. We take the underground and find the small coffee shop Rita told us about. Mark orders a latte and a flapjack. I order a tea and a glass of water. And then we wait.

I know Rita as she walks in the door. She's just like her profile picture, except a little shorter than I imagined. Her face is round, with pink cheeks and a small snub nose. Her hair is long, dark, and wavy, but lacks the volume to make it pretty. I can tell she leaves her hair to air-dry rather than blow-drying it. Her skin has not been cared for. There are tiny burst blood vessels around her nose, and as she comes towards the table, I see that it's dry and flaky. Her clothes are smart but inexpensive. Comfortable, right down to the sandals with thick heels.

Mark stands up to greet her, and I do the same. He has the right to the first handshake as the descendant of George Hawker and his parents. But of course Rita thinks I'm also a descendant of a person involved in this mystery. I have no actual right to be here.

"We spoke on Facebook," I say. "I'm Evelyn's granddaughter." Mark has been told about my white lie.

"It's nice to meet you." For a moment, her eyes narrow. "You know, you seem very familiar. Do I know you from somewhere?"

My blood runs cold, and I wonder if we grew up in the same area or went to the same school. If she recognises me, it could turn my life upside down.

"I don't think so," I reply eventually.

She shakes her head. "No, I think I'm getting muddled. I've been so excited about this meeting, about talking more about Simon and the family. I'm probably hoping we knew each other somehow."

"Yes," I say with a laugh. "That's probably it."

Rita settles into the table with a tea and a brownie while Mark takes the photographs out of his messenger bag.

"This is my grandfather," Mark says, passing the black-and-white pictures across the table. "And these are his parents. That's Claire Hawker, who was married to Simon Blackthorn. I don't suppose you recognise her, do you?"

Rita moves the photograph closer to her face for a better view. She sighs. "No. I don't remember seeing any photographs of her. When my father passed away last year, I inherited a lot of his belongings, and there were photo albums included in it all. I brought some with me, actually." She reaches down towards a large tote bag and pulls out a couple of leather-bound photo albums. "Here we are."

Both Mark and I lean closer as she cracks the spine of the album. If there are photographs of Simon Blackthorn, we want to see them. If there are photographs of Abigail… or the mysterious Mary…

"This is Simon," she says. "He was my great-grandfather on my father's side. Dad resembles him a little bit, with the dark eyes and hair." The picture is, of course, in black and white, but Simon's dark eyes are arresting. He's staring directly at the camera with a slight smirk on his lips.

"What was he like?" I ask, a little nervous to know the answer.

"My father said he was a very stern man. A big drinker. He had four wives, apparently. One died in an accident. She fell down the stairs of their house. One left him in the middle of a huge row and was only found again when Simon tracked her down for a divorce. That was my grandfather's mum. He didn't have a relationship with her at all. She left my grandfather when she left Simon. One must have been the Claire that you mentioned. The last one stuck around until Simon died."

"Did Simon move around a lot?" Mark asks. "He must have lived near or around Clifton at some point. Did he live anywhere else?"

"I think he went to a town just outside Canterbury. I can't remember the name, but it was famous for taking in children during the war. There was a home there, I think. Children from London went there, where it was safer." Rita frowns down at the photograph of Simon. "Dad didn't have a very good childhood. My grandfather took after Simon, by the sounds of it. He buried his problems by drinking a lot and took out his rages on Dad. Things move in cycles, don't they? Human beings copy each other." For a moment, she seems haunted, and I want to take her hand and tell her she isn't alone. But it might scare her away. "Is there a reason why you're researching my great-grandfather? Did he hurt someone?"

I let Mark tell the story. It's his story to tell. Rita sits and listens quietly, an impassive expression on her face, all the while fingering the photograph in the album. Afterwards, she only nods.

"I understand now," she says. "I have to say that I think it's unlikely. From what I've heard of Simon, he was a thug with a bad temper, but a kidnapper? I don't know. That requires an awful lot of preparation and planning, and I don't think the men in this family have that kind of acumen. But shall we check through some more of the pictures? See if anyone jumps out at you?"

Rita thumbs through the photo album, giving names to the faces in the pictures. The black-and-white photographs make the people in them seem like actors in a movie. None of it feels real. As she turns the last page, I can sense Mark's disappointment. His voice is thin when he thanks her for her time.

"Abigail isn't in any of those photos," I explain. "But you've been very helpful." I show her the photographs we brought of Abigail and the mysterious Mary, but Rita doesn't recognise either.

"I'm sorry. I wish I could have helped more." Her eyes droop at the edges, tinged with the sadness of not being useful.

"We just appreciate you coming here to meet us," Mark says. "It was very generous of you."

"I wish I could have solved the mystery for you," Rita says. "I can see that it means a lot to you."

"It does," Mark says. "But thank you."

Later, on the train back to Clifton, I sit across from a tired and silent Mark. I make an attempt to rally him. "It isn't completely hopeless. I thought what she said about Canterbury was interesting. If they did take children in during the war, then perhaps Abigail was smuggled into the children's home. I'd imagine it was a complicated time. Identification papers were a lot easier to forge. Maybe Simon kept Abigail there. After all, there's every chance that Simon was Abigail's real father. Why would he let her go like that? Men like Simon see their women as property. He wouldn't like another man raising his own."

Mark purses his lips slightly in interest at my words. I can tell he wants to ask me questions, but he then seems to dismiss the questions with a little shake of his head. He clears his throat and says, "That's a very good idea. Except that she couldn't remember the name of the town. I just don't know. Wouldn't the home need some sort of identification?"

"It must have been a confusing time back then. With children all over the place, some might have parents who had died in the bombing and no living relatives. Did they stay in the homes? What happened to them? Simon could have made it seem like Abigail was one of them."

"But why wouldn't she speak up?" Mark says. "Why wouldn't she tell people she'd been kidnapped?"

"I don't know," I admit. "Fear? Simon was a scary man, by all accounts. He'd already murdered her mother, if he did set fire to the house. Perhaps he told her he'd murder her father and brother too. She was only twelve years old. I could imagine her being very frightened."

"Jesus."

"Sorry. I know this is all very dark."

Mark shakes his head. "I don't know what else I expected. Maybe part of me hoped she wandered away and was found by a nice, childless family who decided to raise her. Some sort of happy ending. But there won't be one, will there? There never is."

There never is. Not for me, I want to say. But I don't, perhaps because I don't really believe that. "At this stage, I'm willing to believe anything is possible. We still need to track down the Pierces."

Mark leans back in his chair, appearing as exhausted as I feel. "How are we going to do that?"

CHAPTER 27

ISABEL

CASH4GOLD is a brilliant place. I took in the fancy jewellery from the drunk lady in the bar, and they gave me money. Next, I found a pawn shop for the designer bag. Next thing I knew, I had a fat wallet full of cash. In a charity shop in another affluent area, I picked up some good-quality clothes for a fraction of the original price, and I kept the rest of the money for coming expenses.

The expense of finding you, dear Leah.

The trickiness to all of this is finding you without attracting attention to myself. I can hardly buy a laptop and set up wifi, can I? Public libraries have become my friends, but it means risking CCTV picking up my image and some eagle-eyed police officer recognising me. Hats and sunglasses are extremely conspicuous. Let's hope the fringe does its job and obscures my features as much as possible. You can do a lot with a change in posture, a little weight loss and a new haircut. I've considered wigs, but they're a bit of a caricature. I have to fit in with society, and yet not look like myself at all.

Searching for you on the internet is interesting. You're a ghost, Leah. No one knows you. You don't exist anymore. No Facebook, no Twitter, no Instagram. Every trace of you has been removed. There's no Tom, either. Well, except for the millions of other Tom and Leah Smiths. None of them are either of you. At this point, I've stop researching your name and have been searching for your face instead. I'm sure you got a new name after you were taken in by the police, but I doubt they gave you a new face. Your name and photograph were never released to the public, were they? You were never hounded by the media. But I've discovered something very interesting as I search for you, Leah. I've discovered that people on the internet, the great British public, blame you for a lot.

#justiceforalison

Very interesting. They want your name. They want to know who you are. After following the Twitter hashtag for a while, I created my own account—a pseudonym, of course—and added my own voice to the mix.

Fkin bitch. She let that syco out. She's in on it. #justiceforalison

And then another account.

Don't give up. #justiceforalison. Find the nurse.

And another account.

Why should we pay for her to be safe? #justiceforalison

And another account.

I heard her name was Leah. Anyone else hear that? #justiceforalison

And then I almost had to leave the library, because I wanted to laugh. Oh, Leah, you poor thing. You do end up in the shit, don't you? I got a little distracted from the Twittering Twats who want your blood and instead Googled Tom's old school, discovered a few kids his age in the catchment area and looked to see if I could find a profile for your little brother—or your son, if what you told me on the moors was true. If anyone is going to fuck up big time, I imagine it's that little dweeb. I tried reading NHS news articles and the websites for hospitals in different areas, going through staff pictures, but I still don't know where you are. I don't even have a radius to begin with.

Then it dawned on me. What if the #justiceforalison mob got your full name? Would it take long for them to find your photograph? And once they had your photograph, someone might recognise you.

I went back to my tweet: *I heard her name was Leah. Anyone else hear that? #justiceforalison*. Then I created another account in order to reply to my own tweet. *Leah Smith. From Hackney, moved to Hutton, where she worked at Crowmont Hospital. Spread the word. #justiceforalison. We'll get her, and the little psycho Isabel Fielding.*

Then I leaned back and smiled. My original tweet already had five retweets and six hearts. Now those retweets and hearts were going up. There were replies back. *Are you sure? This is a game-changer.* And: *Fuck, yes! Finally, someone with balls.* But my favourite tweet is this one: *This is right. I worked at Crowmont Hospital. I knew her. So glad it's out there. Sick of keeping her secret.*

It's only a matter of time, Leah. The people on the internet want you just as much as I do, and now they have your name. Soon, they'll have your new name, and I will find you.

CHAPTER
28

I'm Evelyn again, only this time I'm searching for the Pierces. This distraction is a welcome one. Otherwise, I would be worrying about Tom, who hasn't been in touch for a few days now. The house is quiet and lonely, with nothing but the TV to keep me company. I become obsessed with watching the footage from the camera on the door and then I buy an extra lock, but that just makes me feel guilty about not buying it while Tom was here. I'm not sure why. I've never been great at protecting him, have I? And now I'm here, locked away in the bungalow, while Tom is out there all on his own.

Without Tom here, I've abandoned all attempts at exercise and self-defence, not that I was doing much anyway. As soon as Tom joined the gym, I lost the motivation to do it on my own. At one time I fantasised that if Isabel ever found me again, I'd be ready for her, but now that isn't going to happen. She'll find a mess, just like before.

No, forget Leah and her problems. I'm Evelyn now. I'm searching for clues, because I will find out what happened to Abigail Hawker. The desire to know burns brightly inside me, sometimes competing with my desire to keep Tom safe, to want Isabel out of my life for good, to wish bad things on the people who use the #justiceforalison hashtag.

Maybe not that last one.

Evelyn continues to post in local history groups about the Pierce family. Where did they go? One mentioned Liverpool. Another says London. How am I going to find them in these large cities? The name is not unusual enough. I'll never be able to track them down. Eventually, I give up on Facebook and make a phone call instead.

He answers after just one ring. "Leah—I mean, Lizzie."

"You don't have to call me that over the phone," I say. "I'm guessing your mobile isn't being tapped."

"It would be unlikely," Murphy replies. "But yours?"

"I'm safe," I say. "Well, for the time being, I guess."

"How are you?" he asks. "Keeping all right?"

"I'm okay. Tom moved out, though. He wanted to live with some new friends he's made."

"Oh. Sorry to hear that."

"He wanted space. I guess we all deal with trauma in different ways." I force myself to smile as I talk, and then remember how my mum used to do exactly the same thing when she was in tears. There she was on the phone, smiling, tears running down her cheeks.

"As long as you're safe and happy. How can I help you today?" he asks.

"It's about that cold case I told you about." It feels strange to use the vernacular of a police officer, and for a moment I fancy myself a character in a Hitchcock film. "I'm still helping the elderly man in the nursing home. It's a welcome distraction, to be honest. Otherwise I'd be obsessing over… her."

"You don't have to explain yourself to me," he says. "Go on. Have you found anything out? I'm afraid the lad I had researching this case couldn't find much."

"Actually, yes," I say. "We found out that George Hawker's mother had an abusive ex-husband called Simon Blackthorn. He moved away to somewhere near Canterbury, where I think there was a home for displaced children during the war. I actually need to check that out. But there's also this family that disappeared around the same time. The Pierces." I explain to him what I think, telling him about the unusual husband and the circumstances surrounding their disappearance. I hear Murphy's pen scribbling away as he diligently takes notes. "If I do some research into the children's home, could you do me a favour and check out the Pierces?"

"I will," he says.

"Any news? You know, about her."

"A strange sighting in Wales," he says. "If it's real, it means she's a long way away from you. The... new victim... the girl. It seems that Isabel was with this girl for a while. They stole a car and drove around a bit. The girl was a junkie. She rode around with a bad lot, dealt some drugs, prostituted herself for a while. I don't know how Isabel ended up with her, but when we found the abandoned car, we checked CCTV at a few petrol stations, and Isabel was in the car with her. It appears that they were travelling together. We're piecing things together, Leah. Sit tight for now, okay?"

"I will."

After I hang up, the house feels even quieter than ever.

That night, I dream of blood again. It's on my hands and face, smeared on like lipstick. I wake up thinking of the girl Isabel befriended. Did that girl have any idea about the danger she was in? At what point did she know she was in too deep and that Isabel was going to open her jaws and swallow her whole? At least one thing is certain—Isabel killed that girl. No one else.

Because I was beginning to wonder.

But I won't let my mind go there.

No news from Tom. Perhaps he's lost to me. I remember when I was looking forward to the day he would come out to me and announce that he's gay. I had this fantasy all built up in my mind of a rainbow-coloured cake on the kitchen counter with a heartfelt note alongside the plate. I'd tear up, turn around, see him there with a nervous expression on his face. Then I'd throw my arms around him and tell him that I loved him and was proud of him. Okay, so I was a bit of a lame, uncool older sister to him, but I never doubted his love for me, not until the moment he lifted that knife and held it out to me in a threatening way. That wasn't the Tom I know and love.

Toast for breakfast. Don't think about what Tom is eating. Is he eating? Can he afford food? No, don't think about it, because you'll drive yourself mad. Instead, focus on the Hawkers. The children's home.

The morning flies by in a blur of visitors and paperwork. I've almost completed the database, which means I'll have a little time on my hands if I take the last of the work slowly. In stolen minutes here and there, I search for children's homes operating in the area in 1944. Where is close enough to Canterbury to be the place Rita Blackthorn told me about? Where could this home be? There are four possible children's homes. One has now been converted into flats, a second was turned into a private hospital, the third was knocked down in the eighties and is now a multi-storey carpark, and the last one is now a school. But there have to be records of the children who once lived there. To find those records, I'll have to phone up local libraries or a local registry office and see if they have any information.

Well, I wanted a distraction.

When lunch comes around, I take my tuna sandwich to George's room and sit with him, but he's asleep. I stay there anyway, not wanting him to be alone. George sleeps a lot now, and that worries me. The bedsheets seem looser against his body, and there are dark circles beneath his eyes. Old age creeps up on us all. When I'm old, what will make me feel proud? I see no great acts of bravery in my past, only failures.

"Talk later, George." A small kiss for his forehead.

As I walk back to my desk, I can't stop thinking about Abigail and her disappearance. Canterbury isn't very far away from Clifton. If you were going to kidnap a child, wouldn't you take them farther away? Ideally, out of the country. But not every criminal in history was a master criminal. Some of them got away with it because of the time period or plain old luck. There's no way I can rule out the children's home, but I have to admit, I'm not holding out much hope.

Before I start calling libraries and registry offices, I put everything I've found out in an email to Mark. We've agreed to keep each other updated. He sends me back a gif of a cartoon character dialling an old-fashioned telephone. I send him one of someone falling asleep at their desk.

The afternoon is busier, but I manage to cross one phone call from my list. They take my details and ask what information I need before promising to email me back. Then I find myself swamped by organising doctors' calendars and arranging meetings for the executive staff. I even end up staying half an hour late before heading home. The empty bungalow awaits, and I can't claim to be ecstatic about getting home. At least the bus journey is scenic, with views of the sea and the promenade along Clifton Bay.

"Excuse me."

When I pull myself away from the window of the bus, I see that a woman in her thirties with her hair pulled into a tight bun has leaned across the aisle to come closer to me.

"Don't I know you?" she asks.

"I don't think so," I reply. The way she's staring at me makes me feel ill at ease. Whoever she thinks I am, she doesn't seem happy to see me.

"I'm sure I know you," she insists.

Luckily, a little boy no older than five pulls on her jacket, and she tears her gaze away from me. But once more she turns and glances at me out of the corner of her eye, and I'm sure she's scowling now. My stomach flips over with worry, and my chest begins to feel tight. Rather than stay on the bus with this strange woman, I decide to ring the bell and get off at the next stop, hoping she's not doing the same. The bus brakes suddenly as I'm getting out of my seat, causing me to bump into the woman with my hip.

"Sorry," I mutter as I hurry off the bus, my fingers trembling. I thought the new medication was supposed to help me with anxiety? God knows it makes me feel groggy and out of it enough.

Three stops away from home. I have quite an uphill walk, but the fresh air feels good. Who was that woman, and why did she frighten me like that? Am I reading into things too much? Am I overreacting?

Of course I'm overreacting. I have one of those bland faces that people mistake for their local shop owner, or the person they see at the bus stop, or someone they went to school with ten years ago. It means *nothing*.

The fresh air is nice for a time, but soon the effort of the uphill walk causes me to sweat, and before long, the back of my shirt is sticking to my skin. Cars pass me on the narrow road, and the rumble of their engines makes me tense and edgy. Exhaust fumes mix with the sea salt in the air. I long for the quiet. The empty bungalow now feels like a haven against the stress of the journey back.

But as I approach the bungalow, there's an alien object on the front step that causes me to stop in my tracks and makes my stomach heave. I don't like things on my front doorstep, especially not things like this.

A dead magpie lies there lifeless. I turn around and walk away.

CHAPTER 29

I have nowhere to go, but I know I'm not walking into that house. As I turn on my heel and begin hurrying down the hill, I almost drop my handbag onto the driveway. But I'll need that. I need to keep my wits about me, too; otherwise, I'll be in deep trouble.

Who can I call? Tom? DCI Murphy? Adam?

No. The first person I call is Mark.

I'm not sure why I'm calling Mark instead of Tom. Mark has a car, which of course is useful, but I'm not sure where he lives or works, if he could even see me, and of course how to explain my predicament. How can I? I can't even tell him who I am. And yet I call him.

"Hey, Lizzie, what's up?"

"I'm really sorry to bother you. Are you at work?"

"No, it's okay. I just got home."

"Oh, okay, good. I..." A bus whizzes past, and my breath catches. *Pull it together, Leah.* I think about taking a couple of extra pills, but

I'm not sure I have the dexterity in my trembling fingers to retrieve them from my bag. "I don't know how to explain all of this, but I wondered if we could meet now. For a coffee or something?"

"Of course. Have you found something?"

"No. It's nothing to do with Abigail or George. I... umm, I just could do with someone to talk to."

There's a slight pause before he answers brightly, "Then you called the right person, Lizzie. Shall I pick you up? We could go to mine. It's nice and quiet."

"Thanks." I give him directions to the next bus stop and sit down inside the shelter. Staying still seems wrong, but I can't keep walking forever.

It's just a magpie, I tell myself. But what if it isn't? As I wait for Mark, I contemplate calling Adam and telling him what's happened, but what if he overreacts and relocates us immediately? Would Tom come with me? If he didn't come with me, would he be safe? After another deliberation with myself, I decide to call Tom to make sure he's okay.

He answers the phone after letting it ring nine times. I count them.

"I thought I said not to call for a few days," Tom says by way of greeting.

"I just wanted to check you're all right."

"I'm fine."

"Good."

"Is something going on?"

I take a deep breath, deciding that there are enough secrets between the two of us. "I found a dead magpie on the doorstep, and... well, you know what that means."

"Did it die there, or was it put there?" he asks. "If it died there, there would be marks on the door. It probably flew into the door or something. I found that bird around the back, didn't I? The birds are mental here. Maybe it's the sea or something."

"I didn't look."

"I don't think it's her," he says. "It's not her style."

"How do you know what her *style* is?"

He laughs. "What, you think you were the only one there that night in the farmhouse? When you find my head on the doorstep, that's when you'll know—"

"How can you say that?"

"Grow up, Leah. You probably imagined it."

"Jesus, Tom—"

He hangs up, cutting me off, leaving me staring at my phone. I could throw it into the road and stamp on it until my feet hurt, but the honk of a horn makes me start, and the phone slips through my fingers onto the pavement instead.

"Sorry." Mark leans out of the window and smiles apologetically. "Thought the horn thing would be funny, but it really wasn't."

"It's okay. I'm a bit jumpy, that's all."

"Get in."

I retrieve my phone from the tarmac and climb into the passenger's seat. Mark still seems sheepish after his little joke.

"Sorry about startling you. Is everything all right? You don't seem yourself."

"I'm okay. Just had a bit of a fright, that's all."

"What happened?"

"Oh, it's a long story." I should probably be utilising this time to come up with a good story to explain what's happened to me over the last few days, but my mind is completely blank. Then I consider telling him everything, but that would be stupid. I glance in his direction and wonder, how well do I know this person? Can I trust him? There's no reason not to. Surely, Mark couldn't have anything to do with Isabel. He's just a normal guy living in a normal town who is trying to help his family.

"You can tell me over a cup of coffee. I would suggest a coffee shop, but when you said you wanted to talk, I figured you'd prefer somewhere more private. But if you'd prefer a coffee shop, just let me know."

"No," I say. "Your place is just fine."

Mark's small terrace reminds me of Susie's house. It has that light, airy feel, with bright colours and large windows. He doesn't live like a typical guy, where the décor often contains harsh contrasts between white and dark, glass and metal. His place is softer and even has a few throws and cushions. He has good taste.

"This isn't what I expected," I admit.

"I can't take credit," he says. "Most of it was bought by my ex. But she left suddenly and didn't bother taking anything with her."

"Oh." That revelation surprises me. I had thought he was still seeing someone. "I'm sorry."

He casts his eyes downwards as though the memory is still painful. "That's also a long story, but you're not here to hear mine, you're here to tell me yours." He moves around the kitchen, opening cupboard doors and finding the paraphernalia for his fancy coffee maker, the kind that use little bullet-shaped pods to create different flavours. "Regular coffee? Chocolate? Vanilla? This thing has it all."

"Regular for me. You like your coffee, then?"

"You're looking at a certified coffee addict, I'm afraid."

"We all have flaws."

I take a seat at Mark's breakfast bar and begin to feel a little less on edge. In fact, the magpie was beginning to feel a bit ridiculous, and I wasn't sure what, or how, to explain what had frightened me. I decide on the story I told to my boss back when I first moved to Clifton.

"One regular coffee. Milk and sugar?"

"Just milk."

"Just milk for the lady."

I laugh.

"What's so funny?"

"The thought of me as a lady," I say.

"Well," he replies, "you're very ladylike to me."

I just shake my head and sip the rich and delicious coffee, which is just as good as it would be in a coffee shop. "I might have to get one of those things."

"I must make a note of a new conversion," he says.

"Have there been many?"

"Oh, yes. You're at least my… first. Okay, I don't entertain much."

He leans on the counter with such an adorable lopsided grin that once again, that creeping feeling of guilt catches up with me. Something about my expression ruins the moment, because Mark senses my discomfort and moves away.

"Okay, so you have a cup of coffee, and we're alone. Sorry, that sounded weird. We're in a private place. The floor is all yours. What did you want to talk about?"

He's certainly easy to talk to, with that open face and those kind blue eyes, but still, I find myself drumming the edge of my coffee mug, trying to find the words. "Before I moved to Clifton, I was in a very bad relationship. It ended violently, suddenly, and ruined a few lives along the way. That person is still out there, and they are trying to find me. At least, I think they are. I've had to change my name. Lizzie isn't my real name. I'm sorry that I had to lie to you, and to everyone else I've met since moving here, but I have to protect Scott. I have to protect myself."

"I understand," Mark replies. "I'm sorry you went through that. There's no need to apologise for anything."

"Scott moved out, as you know. I'm living alone now, which is scary after everything that happened. And when I got home today, there was a dead bird on the doorstep."

"Oh." Mark seems confused, and I can't blame him.

"The person who is trying to find me is obsessed with birds. They used to draw me different birds and tell me the meaning. They had a pet magpie." I'm saying too much. My fingers wrap around the warm mug of coffee, and I stop. "I think it was… If it's them… I'm in danger."

"Hey, it's okay. You're safe here." Mark places a hand on my arm, and I let him keep it there for a moment before gently pulling away.

"This person is very dangerous indeed." I get to my feet and check the window. "You didn't see any cars following us or anything, did you?"

He shakes his head. "No, but I don't think I would have noticed if we were followed. I'm not the kind of person who checks that stuff."

"Maybe I shouldn't have come here if she knows where I live now."

"She?" Mark raises his eyebrows.

"It's not what you think," I say hastily, not that it matters. "I can't go into it all, but just know that even though this person is female, she's just as dangerous as any man, probably more so. And if she does know where I am, she'll be watching me, and she'll see you, and you will become a target. I think I should go. I should make some calls. This was a mistake."

Mark grasps me by the shoulders as I'm in the process of getting down from the stool at the breakfast bar. "Slow down. Breathe. I'm taking you home, and we're going to check your house together. If this person is as dangerous as you say she is, I don't want you to be alone. Can you call Scott and ask him to come and stay with you tonight?"

"I've already called him," I admit. "He thinks I imagined it. I have a history of imagining things, you see. And, honestly, I'm not sure if I did. There was this woman on the bus who mistook me for someone else, and it made me have a bit of a panic attack. And then the bird on the step… I don't know. I've been stressed out. It could just be the stress."

"Come on. I'm driving you back. We'll check out the house, order takeaway and make sure you're safe."

I don't argue.

CHAPTER 30

ISABEL

Your world is about to be turned upside down, dear Leah. You see, it didn't take very long for a photograph to emerge on the internet. *Leah Smith, I know her. We went to school together. I met her at university. We got off with each other in a nightclub. I can't believe it was her all along. I feel sick. She always seemed weird. Never liked her at all. I saw her in Hutton. Everything makes sense. It doesn't make sense. Are you sure it's her? I recognise her now. She was a bitch. But she was always so nice. #justiceforalison #leahsmith #thenurse #isabelfielding* The tweets have come rolling in thick and fast. Retweets, likes, replies, DMs. On and on it goes, rolling out farther and farther until people halfway across the world now know your face like the back of their hand.

Has anyone approached you yet, Leah? I wish I could be there when they realise it's you. What is your name now? I'd love to know. I want to send you these letters.

I've been drawing you birds. Here's Pepsi in the garden at Crowmont. Did I tell you that I still dream of the garden at Crowmont?

It wasn't much of a garden, some pot plants and a yellowing lawn. Not much of anything at all, really.

I'm blowing through the money I collected on train fare, but it's necessary. If I stay in one place too long, someone will recognise me, and that can't happen just yet, because I'm extremely close to finding you. The internet will do it for me. Got to love that hive mind.

Do you want to know something funny? I was bored in the library one day, and I logged into my mother's Facebook account using her email address and password, which she hasn't changed in a decade, only to find that your lovely little brother/son has been messaging my loony-bin pill-popping mother. Fascinating. You know what else I discovered? That Tom saw you with blood on your hands one night. Are you sleepwalking again, Leah?

That's interesting. Very interesting.

Where did the blood come from, Leah? You're not a cutter or a quitter. I don't think it was your blood. I think it was someone else's. Which makes me wonder if this relationship of ours was a little more equal than you were letting on. Has a bit of me rubbed off on you? Tell me, how are your dreams? Are they more violent now? Do you crave a bit of blood and guts?

I think you do. When we meet, I'm going to ask you all about it.

Aha! As I've been sitting here in the library writing to you, someone has tweeted something very interesting.

I know her! She works with me! But her name is Lizzie.

I think I might send that person a private message and see what I can find out.

I'm close to you now. Can't you feel that connection strengthening between us? I've felt bereft of you for too long. It's time for us to be together again. And, Leah, this time I think we should make sure that we're together forever. I've never told you this before, but I love you, and I think you love me too.

CHAPTER 31

This has happened before. This exact situation. As I stare down at the empty step, I remember, very clearly, the moment when Seb checked the kitchen windowsill for me. I remember how the birds were there one moment and gone the next. After that happened, I never found out if it was a hallucination or if it was Isabel, or another member of her family, playing tricks on me. Now, I'm not sure which is worse. Either my brain has broken again, or Isabel knows where I am.

No. That's a lie. I do know which is worse. Isabel. Isabel is always worst. If she knows where I am, I'll never be safe again.

Then I remember. This time it's different. This time I will have proof, because I've already thought about this exact scenario. "The camera." I turn to Mark in excitement. "I forgot about the doorbell camera. It records movement on the doorstep."

"Do you mean that camera?" Mark points to broken glass littered all over the step, and the empty shell that once was my security net. "Maybe it caught the person before it was destroyed."

Or maybe Isabel threw a rock at it from a distance to make sure it *didn't* catch the person who put the bird on the step. At least the broken camera was proof that someone had to be here. Security cameras don't just explode.

"I should call Tom," I say. "Just to make sure he's safe."

"Let's quickly check the house first," Mark suggests, gently taking my keys from my hand to open the door. He saves me the embarrassment of trying to open the door with shaking fingers.

The door is still locked, which I take as a good sign. The house is quiet as we move slowly through the hall and into the living room. Nothing. No one. Then the kitchen. Still no one. I move past Mark and try the windows to check that they're still locked. They are, as is the back door. Then we go upstairs and check the bedrooms. Despite the fact that the weather isn't particularly warm, I still find that I'm sweating slightly, and wipe the back of my hand against my forehead. My eyes roam over the room, investigating the area for any inconsistencies. Everything is exactly where it should be.

"There's no one here," Mark says. "You all right? You're little pale."

I nod, steadying my breathing in an attempt to control the emotions that are bubbling up to the surface. "I'm fine. I'm really sorry for the way I acted today. I swear I saw the… the magpie. I'm sure of it."

Mark slips an arm over my shoulder, and I don't stop him. He walks me back through the house. "Would you like me to put the kettle on?"

"Okay." A cup of tea would be nice. "I'm going to check the computer just in case the camera did pick something up."

The laptop boots up agonisingly slowly, finally loading the video just as Mark is setting down the mug of tea on the table next to me.

There's no feed right now, only a black screen. I go back, waiting for my doorstep to appear, and then click on *Play*. Mark leans over my shoulder as the video plays back. When a stone is thrown towards the camera, I jolt, every part of me tensing.

"Are you okay?" he asks.

I let out a breath. "As okay as I can be."

It takes a few attempts for the camera to be smashed, and all the while, someone hides just out of sight. Watching the angle of the stones, I can only imagine that they came from our next-door neighbours' garden and climbed through the small gap in the bush, then angled themselves away from the house with several rocks to throw.

"Jesus," Mark says. "This person was desperate to destroy your camera. But how did they even know it was there?"

"I guess they've been watching me," I reply, the thought making my spine stiffen. I can't stop thinking about Isabel out there with my mother's wedding ring on her finger. Isabel, capable of anything, sick to the core, twisted and disgusting, barely human…

"Do you want to talk about it? What happened today? Or the stuff in your past?"

I shake my head. "I can't. Sorry."

Mark lets out a short, breathy laugh. "You keep apologising, Leah, but I don't see anything you need to apologise for. What you went through must have been extremely traumatising. Maybe you have PTSD from what happened to you."

"I do," I say, more matter-of-factly than I intended to. "I have a therapist. I'm working through… stuff."

"I'm glad you have help. I think that's very brave."

"I should call Scott," I say, then take my phone and find his details. Tom's face pops up on the screen while I wait for him to answer. Five rings. Ten. Voicemail. No answer. I text him, warning him that the camera has been smashed.

He texts back: *How do you know you didn't do it yourself?*

I close my eyes and count to ten, willing the terror away. When Mark's arms wrap around my shoulders, I lean into his embrace for a moment, then pull away. I wipe my eyes and let out a long sigh. The truth is, Tom might be right. How do I know I didn't do it? Was what happened on the bus real? What if I didn't walk the last few stops, and instead I was smashing my security camera and putting a dead magpie on the step?

"Do you want to leave?" Mark suggests. "We could get some food, take it back to mine. I know being here is making you feel even more tense, and, honestly, I wonder if it's a good idea for you to be here."

But I shake my head. "No. I don't know that it's her."

"You should call the police," he says.

"I will. I have a number to call." I chew on my bottom lip. What if they remove me and not Tom? "Not yet, though. I need to stay and see if I can get through to Scott." I send a quick reply to him: *I was at work.*

It's not strictly true. My hallucinations have been in-depth and complex before. The more I think about what happened on the bus, the hazier it becomes. According to the time-stamp, I could have made it home around the same time that the camera was smashed.

"Why don't we work on Abigail's disappearance now you're here," I suggest. "I have the laptop open. We can continue to search for the Pierce family, or the children's home near Simon Blackthorn's place of residence?"

Mark nods. I log on to my fake Facebook profile to see if we can find out more about the Pierce family. Checking to see if someone has replied to my comments in the local history groups, but there's nothing

By the time our mugs are drained, we've also sent emails to any offices in the area who might have historic records, hoping that one of them might have some information on young girls of Abigail's age being admitted to children's homes in the area. The distraction is a good one, and I feel better for it. When the threat of Isabel feels more real, it's like I become a bystander in my own life. But when I'm actively helping another person, I have agency again. Yet, at the same time, I can't help wondering why I never seem to be able to apply that agency to my own life, my own future. My mind refuses to help, blocking me at every corner, making me hallucinate or reducing me to a panicked mess.

One day, I will change all of that. I just need to learn how to do it.

"Are you hungry?" Mark raises an eyebrow. "I'm starving."

I glance at the time, only now aware that it's well into the evening and I haven't eaten since lunch. The medication I'm on not only makes me feel groggy, it plays hell with my appetite.

"I've kept you here too long." I stand up, about to shut down the laptop and apologise again. Mark should go, and I should track down Tom and make him listen. I glance at my phone—still no response to my last text message.

Marks also stands. "Actually, I was thinking maybe a takeaway?" The suggestion is tentative. He stands with his hands open, his eyes pleading, as though he's afraid of my reaction.

"That sounds nice." And it does. The truth is, there's another reason why I suggested that he leave. I'm also a little frightened of him staying here too, while I'm vulnerable and lonely, and I'm not sure I'm ready for that. But I'm also not ready for him to leave me in this house alone. "I think I have some menus somewhere."

"Do you mind if I check my email on your laptop?"

"No problem." Now that I've mentioned the menus, I can't remember where I shoved them. Tom and I aren't usually takeaway people, having learned to be frugal with our food purchases, but I know I've kept them for a potential treat night. I slam one drawer shut and open another. "Found them!"

When I turn around to face Mark with the menus, the atmosphere changes in an instant. His expression is fixed, his eyes are hard, and the air around us chills. The hairs stand up on the backs of my arms.

"It was you," he whispers.

"What was me?"

I recognise this change in atmosphere. I've experienced it many times before as I cowered before my father in one of his drunken rages. Some people make the room feel smaller with their presence, but I never took Mark for one of those people. That cold expression on his face makes me think of Tom as he reached for that knife.

"You're a murderer."

The sound of that word makes my breath catch.

"I thought you were helping us because you're a good person." He stands, and I back away from the table. "But you're her. The nurse."

"Mark, I—"

"You have no idea who I am, do you? You have no idea what you've done to me. How *could* you? How could you let that girl out of the hospital?"

"What are you talking about?"

When he moves, I flinch, and it isn't because he's threatened me with any indication of violence. It's merely the rage coming off him in waves.

"I hate you," he says, visibly seething. "You're the reason I'm alone. You're a terrible person, and I hope you rot in hell."

"Mark!" I call out, but I don't follow him as he walks away.

The door slams, and finally I find I can breathe again. My fingers are shaking, and part of me can't help but wonder if what just happened actually *did* just happen. Slowly, as my muscles finally begin to release after the shock of the confrontation, I make my way to the laptop to try to make sense of it all.

Mark's Twitter account is still up on the screen. There's a tweet open on the page, with a picture attached. That picture is of me. And the caption above it reads: *Leah Smith. The nurse who let Isabel Fielding out of prison.*

CHAPTER 32

ISABEL

No more Thelma and Louise road trip for me. I'm a bus and train traveller now, Leah. What do you think of me getting on a bus? Settling down in my seat, one row down from a collection of rowdy men known as a "stag do", quietly reading my book—*The Peregrine*, by J.A. Baker, if you'd like to know. I might even lend you a copy. There was, of course, a worry that the beer-swilling, football-chanting group behind me might recognise me, but they've paid me little attention. One of the group attempted to make conversation, perhaps in an effort to work out if I'm "up for it", but as soon as he realised I wasn't, he went back to the group and commenced a new chant about someone called Harry Kane.

But don't worry, Leah. The delights of the Peregrine kept me distracted from the buffoonery behind me. That is, until the sea caught my attention.

It was at that moment that I realised my little road trip with

Chloe hadn't made the most of the delights of this country. Yes, we drove into the countryside. We drove to isolated pastures. We ate as much junk food as we possibly could. We listened to the radio playing loudly, and Chloe laughed when I didn't know any of the chart music. But we never came to the sea. Do you know how long it's been since I saw the sea? A long time. And even longer if you count the British coast. My parents preferred to spend their money abroad, on a craggy Greek Island or the luxurious French Rivera. Most of our holidays were such a dull affair that I contemplated throwing myself from the steep cliffs of Corfu, or perhaps throwing someone else into the dark depths of the sea.

Luckily for you, I never did throw myself from a cliff.

The sight was enough to make me put my book away and gaze out to the distance. It made me want to write to you, to tell you what a stunning view the sea is. Leah, I wish you were here with me so we could experience it together. What a wonderful last sight it would be. Don't you think?

I left the bus before the members of the stag do. No doubt they're on their way to a livelier seaside resort. I don't need that kind of energy. I'm happy with the quiet little place I've arrived at. Clifton-on-Sea. It sounds like the kind of place where Poirot would comb his moustache and totter around with his cane. It sounds like an excellent place to hide. Well done, Leah.

You put on a commendable show of attempting to escape me. I truly had no idea where you were, and you have been surrounded by protection at every turn. Even now, as I twiddle the gold ring on my finger, I am in awe of just how much the police have thrown into keeping you safe. The police stayed in Hutton for far longer than they were welcome. They checked up on your mother's grave. They brought you here, changed your name, and gave you a new life.

But do you deserve that life? How complicit are you in the

grand scheme of things? How responsible are you for the acts I've committed? I'm insane, Leah, or so the doctors have told me for many years. Does all the blame sit at my feet?

You, though you have your issues, are not insane. Your issues are the scratch of a troubled past. Not much to write home about. Nothing of any particular interest. And yet *you're* the one given a new life? *You're* the protected one?

There are plenty of small B&Bs to choose from in Clifton, but I would like somewhere a little more private. By the time I'm done walking to the caravan park, my stomach is rumbling, and after a strange little man wearing far too little for his age shows me to my van, I decide to raid the vending machines on the site. There are plenty of free maps of the area to choose from, too, and it doesn't take me long to locate Ivy Lodge, the care home where you work. Did they let you become a nurse again? More fool them.

I don't linger in the caravan for too long. It's far too reminiscent of the room in Crowmont. I do, however, bleach my hair. I practise the accent down here, making my voice sound a bit posher, a lot less northern. And then I get the strange little man wearing shorts at the front desk to order me a taxi. I want to see you, Leah. I want to see your face. It's been too long, and now I can barely picture it.

I can't wait to see you again. Can you say the same for me?

CHAPTER 33

I stand in the kitchen feeling stunned. The laptop is still open, and my face is still visible on the screen. It's the terrible photo taken for my ID badge at Crowmont Hospital, where the flash drained all colour from my face and my pale skin clashed with the wall behind me. How could anyone do this to me? How could they?

I'm shaking as I sit back down in the chair and begin to scroll through every tweet related to #justiceforalison. It takes less than a minute to find the one that means the most. *Her name is Lizzie James, and she works at a care home in Clifton-on-Sea. A fucking care home! #justiceforalison.*

My mouth fills with bile as nausea rises from my belly. What have they done? They've killed me, that's what they've done.

I grab my mobile phone and dial the emergency number I was given by Adam to use whenever anything like this happens, but I don't tap the call button. Instead, I come out of the screen and call

Tom instead. He needs to know first. He needs to get out before even Adam can set anything up. At least him being away from me makes him slightly safer.

But he's still dodging my calls. I have to leave a voicemail.

"Tom, it's Leah. I know you don't want to hear from me, but this is important. My name and photograph have been leaked on social media. They know the name Lizzie, and they know where I work. It isn't safe for you here. I'm going to call Adam so he can place us somewhere else. I think you should get out now. Keep in touch, Tom. This is serious. You know it is. Okay? I love you."

Then I call Adam. Three rings, no answer, and my stomach roils with concern. I can't stop thinking about the magpie on my front step and the rock flying through the air towards the camera.

Five rings. Still no answer. What's the point in an emergency number if there's no response?

Voicemail again.

"My name is out. People know who I am and where I work. I need to get out. I'm going to find a hotel to stay. Can you call me back? Please? Soon as you get this."

ISABEL

Ivy Lodge is disappointingly sweet for a care home, the name clearly inspired by the ivy that creeps up the front of the house and clusters around the door. I only stand in the carpark for a moment to see if I can see you, with no intention of going in. I could try sneaking past the security, of which I'm sure there isn't much. Perhaps I can steal a nurse's uniform, or find out the name of a patient and claim to be their granddaughter. But I don't plan on doing any of that, because nothing can risk the future I have planned for us both.

But something fortuitous happens. A visitor's pass slips from the jacket pocket of a guest as they're leaving. No one sees it. No one bends down to pick it up. I walk towards the building as though I'm about to enter, bend down, retrieve it, and hang it around my neck as though nothing has happened. Then I walk into the home, smile at the woman on reception, and ask for your name.

"Oh, I'm covering reception for her," says the short woman with spiky hair. "If you need her, she'll be in room six with George Hawker."

"George Hawker?"

"He's a patient here. Lizzie has been helping him find out what happened to his sister in the forties. She disappeared during a house fire all those years ago. It was very sad. Poor old George wants to know what happened to her before he passes on. It's very kind of her."

My lips form a smile. "She's such a lovely person, isn't she?"

"We all love her around here. Are you a friend of hers?" she asks.

"An old friend," I reply. "We go way back. We went to university together."

"Really? I didn't know Lizzie went to uni."

"She did," I say. "We're both nurses."

"A nurse?" the woman frowns. "She never mentioned she was a nurse."

"Well, I'd better be getting on. Thank you for the help." I walk away from the desk, smiling to myself. They didn't let you come back as a nurse after all. Instead, you had to get a job as a receptionist. Was that demeaning for you, Leah? Did you cry yourself to sleep?

Room six is deep within one of the corridors, with the door slightly open. I know I can't linger too long, but I'm curious about this new you. I see you're still poking your nose into other people's business. Remember when you thought I was innocent? Wasn't that a hoot? When will you stop letting people manipulate you into helping them?

I press myself close to the door and listen. The room is quiet, apart from the beeping from a machine. I wonder if I have the right room at all, but then I angle myself better in order to see through the slight gap.

And there you are.

It's only the back of your head, but it's wonderful to see you. A moment later, your hand stretches up and adjusts the blanket laid over the old man on the bed. As attentive as always, I note. I'm not sure how the idiots here haven't figured out you're a nurse. The signs are all there.

I long to reach out and touch you; my fingers stretch closer, but I know it's too soon. I only wanted to see you from a distance, and I have perhaps been too bold with my desires. This is too risky and could ruin my future plans if I don't act with caution.

As much as it kills me, I turn away and walk out of the home, dropping my visitor's pass at the reception desk on the way out.

But I've seen you, Leah. I've seen you. How wonderful it was to see you. Now, I need to figure out a way for us to meet. We need a proper catch-up, you and I, don't you agree?

LEAH

I stop by the fish and chip shop, but there's no sign of Tom; however, a surly man with a moustache tells me he isn't at work today. I even slip up and ask for Tom, then appear extremely strange by correcting myself to Scott.

Nowhere is safe for me now. My instinct tells me to get as far away from Clifton as I can, but I can't leave without Tom, and he hasn't told me his new address yet. I don't know where he is.

What if she has him?

No, don't think that. Don't think that at all.

First, I need to find a safe place to stay. There are plenty of quaint little B&Bs in the area, but I also know of a caravan park a mile or so back from the coast. It's cheaper, more isolated, but would the vans be safe? It would certainly be easier to break into a caravan than a B&B, but would she even think to look there? I just don't know.

I walk up and down the promenade, my head whipping from side to side. She could be anywhere. Watching me. The tendrils of her creep up to me and tickle the back of my neck. Every time I close my eyes, I see her in the loft at Hutton, sharpening her knives, a slow smile spreading across her face.

Fuck.

What do I do?

ISABEL

Clifton is lovely, Leah. I can see why you decided to stay here. There's a charming little chip shop on the promenade, and the ice cream is just splendid. There's also one of those pawn shop type places where you can buy old laptops and PlayStations. I decide to purchase a cheap tablet and pay for the wifi at the caravan park. I need to keep an eye on the #justiceforalison hashtag. The tweet hasn't quite gone viral yet, and I would be surprised if you knew your name and photograph is out there for everyone to see. No, I believe the photograph is being sent via personal messages to the trusted few lobbying for your punishment.

You have no idea I'm here. There you were, tucking in an old man, sitting dutifully at his bedside. Do you remember when you would sit dutifully outside my room? My guardian angel. My ticket out into the world.

But then I found myself out in the world, and I missed you. I've realised that the world doesn't want me, Leah, and I'm not sure I want to be in this world, either. Oh, I can have a bit of fun every now and then. The fun I had with Chloe was amusing enough. But there's nothing here that will sustain me for the long term. I knew that as soon as I abandoned your silly little car and ran away onto the moors.

I don't belong to this world.

What was I supposed to do at that point? I had no idea. All I wanted to do was go back and talk to you, to figure out what I was supposed to do. But deep down, I knew you didn't want me either.

And, well, Daddy and Owen… Yes, they understand. We're all the same, after all. But they were users. They wanted to exploit my talents. Daddy and I had quite the row, which was why I insisted that Owen spend some time in prison. Daddy frightened me at one time. I knew who he was. I see the newspapers now as they find his bodies all over the place. Skinny young girls like Chloe. No doubt their rotting skin is covered in needle marks. I suppose I'm turning into him a little bit, abusing the people who are never missed.

No, that's not true. Daddy never created art. All he cared about was the power, and that was easy for him, because he was the only one who needed to appreciate how powerful he was. But not me. I need someone to appreciate my art, and I'm not finding an appreciative audience.

At least I wasn't until recently.

There's another reason why the ridiculous #justiceforalison hashtag intrigues me. You see, the world is very presumptuous. They find a woman with her back all cut up, and they just *assume* that it was me. But, Leah, it wasn't. The only person I've killed since James Gorden was Chloe, and that was half out of necessity. I don't like my art to be rushed. I like to take my time, and afterwards I savour it for as long as I can. Little Maisie lasted until I became restless, for instance. I'm not an animal. I don't long to kill every mouse I find. I take my time, because I want to feel it from the inside out. It took a little while for me to want to kill Chloe, and I wouldn't do it unless I wanted to.

I never even met this Alison Finlay. I have no idea who she was at all. Which means someone else killed her. Someone who knows the way in which I kill.

I can think of very few people, Leah.

Do *you* know who it was?

CHAPTER
34

"Leah."

It's been a long time since I've heard my name spoken outside the bungalow or on the telephone. The shock of it causes me to go rigid all over. I grip the cold metal of the railing on the promenade and turn around.

"You wanted to speak to me."

Relief floods through me. I rush forward and grab him by the shoulders, pulling him to me. "I was worried. Did you get my message? My name and photograph are all over Twitter. Mark saw it and freaked out. Isabel knows. The bird on the doorstep—"

"We'll sort it out," Tom replies. His expression is impassive, but he runs a hand through his hair. The sun makes his birthmark even brighter against his skin. He's wearing jeans and a hoodie, with one hand pushed down into the pocket.

"We should leave. I can't get hold of Adam at all, so we'll have to go on our own and hope they can send us some money or something. I have a month's—"

"No." He shakes his head.

"Are you insane? We have to get out of here. You know how dangerous Isabel is." Right on cue, my scars begin to itch. I reach back under my t-shirt and try to scratch them, but I can't reach.

"I'm not leaving. Let her come." He shrugs.

I don't understand his reaction. He was adamant that I hadn't done enough to keep us safe, that I had been too passive, too accepting of our position, that I should have killed her when I had the chance.

"What?"

"I'm sick of running from her. I'm sick of being afraid. She's a short, skinny woman, and I've been going to the gym. I'm taller, heavier, fitter. I can take her."

"You're not seriously suggesting you fight a serial killer?" I lean in to him, my voice lowering in case any of the random walkers might overhear.

"Why not? She doesn't have members of her family helping her move bodies and capture people. When she kidnapped me, it wasn't her who knocked me out. It was her father, and I killed him."

The nonchalance of his words frightens me. "But not out of choice. You did it because you had to. Why would you want any of that to happen again?"

"I don't," Tom says. "But I also like it here, and I'm not running away. Look, I promise you I'm not being stupid. We can hide away somewhere. Get a hotel. Call Murphy and get the police down here. But I'm not running away, Leah."

There's a determination in his eyes that I haven't seen for a while, and for once, that unemotional haze seems to have lifted. Perhaps he's right. Perhaps it's time to stop running.

"All right. I'll make a call. We'll stay here. We don't go back to the bungalow, but we stay in Clifton."

The next step is to find somewhere to hide, but once we've examined the contents of both my and Tom's bank accounts, it's clear that our options are limited. My direct debits have already cleared, leaving me with the small amount of spending money I have per month, and most of Tom's money goes straight to the pub and the gym, something that I'm only just learning.

Most of the B&Bs around Clifton are boutique and expensive, tailored for young professionals or retired couples. The one budget hotel nearby is fully booked. Given all of that, we decide to head to the caravan park after all, despite the fact that it might not be quite as safe and secure as a hotel. It's better than the bungalow.

What I'm most worried about is her following me. We probably lingered too long on the promenade, where we were out in the open for anyone to see. One of the problems is that I don't know how Isabel is travelling around the town. Does she have a car? She certainly doesn't have a licence, but that hasn't stopped her before. Is she using buses? Or taxies? When we get on the bus to make our way to the caravan park, I make sure that we sit right at the back in order to examine every single person who gets on and off.

I'm a quivering mess of anxiety as I examine faces and body types. Could she be the skinny person in the hoodie? No, they get off at the next stop and are clearly a teenage boy. What about the girl reading her Kindle? Her head is bent low. Her hair is a different colour, but she could have changed it. Does Isabel have narrow or wide shoulders? How tall is she? I can't remember any of these things. Why can't I remember? I should have taken a photograph of her and kept it to remind myself. The mugshot used by the news is no good, because it's just her face, and I remember her face just fine.

When we get to the caravan site, a man with a moustache takes our money and walks us to the van we'll be staying in. It's a small static with a working toilet and shower; pokey, but nicely decorated. I pay cash and give him a fake name and address.

"We're from Watford," I lie. "Came for a few days away."

"Well, the sun's out for you," he says sarcastically, glancing at the drizzle that is just starting outside.

When we're alone in the van, I bite a thumbnail and listen to the phone rings add up while I try to contact DCI Murphy. Where is he? What is he doing? Where is Adam? Why is no one answering their phone?

Finally. "Hello?"

"It's Leah Smith. Isabel knows where we are."

"Hold on, Leah. What's happened?"

"Someone leaked my name and photograph on Twitter. That ridiculous 'justice for Alison' crowd. I think… There was a magpie on my doorstep. Someone must have recognised me and put up my witness protection name. She knows where we are."

"Are you sure?"

"I'm sure." I glance at Tom, who is watching me from the floral corner sofa. "She knows. I can feel her watching me."

"I'll get in touch with the local police now. And I'm on my way as quickly as I can," he says. "Are you still in the house? Where are you?"

"No, we've rented a caravan a mile or so out of Clifton-on-Sea. That's where we were housed by the programme."

"Okay. Stay in that van and don't leave, okay? If you do leave, stay in a public place. You'll have to take time off from work. Leah, this might be a good thing. We've had leads that have gone nowhere. She moves on between towns and cities as fast as she arrives. We haven't been able to pinpoint her location because she's always one step ahead. But she won't leave without finding you. That's always been her end game, and we know that. We can *use* that."

"I'm not bait," I snap. "I'm not risking my life so you can catch her."

"That's not what I'm saying. I just mean that at least now we know where she is, and we can track her down once and for all. This is going to end now."

I eyeball Tom and realise that he's right. This is going to end now, once and for all.

ISABEL

I'm not made for the trailer park life, Leah. Perhaps I need an American accent and a pair of denim shorts, I just don't know, but after a few days I'm already stir crazy. The internet is my only refuge from the drudgery of staying in such a small town. Of course I wander around quite a lot, hoping that I might see you somewhere and be able to follow you home. But I don't want to do that too much. I may be rather clever at disguising myself, but I can't escape the fact that the media love to print my face in every newspaper in the country. Which means I'm stuck in a tin can amongst the other tin cans, Twittering as much as I can to try to find out where you live. I know where you work, but I don't know where you live, and when I went back to your place of work, the pleasant woman on the reception desk said it was your day off. I had hoped to have followed you home then.

I don't know what car you drive or whether you even own one. I don't know where you shop or what you eat. No one on Twitter seems to know where you live. Where are you, Leah?

Vending machine food and fish and chips from the promenade have become my source of nutrition, if you can call it that, and after only a couple of days, my skin is greasy again. Ah, this is no way to live, is it? It puts me in a hurry to find you just so I can end this complete and utter monotony.

Give me a hint, Leah.

Stop pretending that you don't want to see me.

LEAH

The rain drums down on the metal roof as we hide away in the caravan. Adam finally calls back and tells us that the programme will liaise with the local police and he will make arrangements to get us out of here. But Tom is staring at me with piercing eyes, and I decide to trust in what we decided on the promenade.

"We're not going to leave. We've decided. DCI Murphy is finally going to catch her, and then we're going to stay here."

There's a pause, and I imagine the quiet man thinking, contemplating, most likely trying to figure out a way to change our minds. "Put a time limit on it. If Isabel isn't behind bars within the next three days, get out. She might want to play the long game. She might wait."

"No, I don't think she will. She wants to end this."

"Are you sure?"

I almost laugh. "No, I suppose not. I've not always been the best at reading her, but at the same time, I know her as well as anyone. She didn't wait before, did she? She could have been free for years before she came after me, but that didn't happen."

"That's true. Be careful, Lizzie."

"Thanks. I will."

"What did he say?" Tom demands, barely waiting until the phone is away from my ear.

"He said to give it three days, and if Isabel isn't behind bars in that time, to get out of Clifton."

To my surprise, Tom actually agrees. "Maybe he's right."

There's not much to do to pass the time in the caravan, and God knows we don't want to talk anymore. All our talks devolve into rows, and I don't have the energy to cope with them. Tom paces up and down, seeming taller than I've ever known him. Now that we're in a close environment, I notice that there's something different about him.

"You've had your hair cut. It's nice," I say.

He just shrugs. "Yeah, I guess."

"How are you settling into your new place? After all this has blown over, I want the address and phone number, okay?"

"Yeah, yeah."

"I wonder when the police are going to—"

"Maybe I should go and get some food," he interrupts.

I hesitate, a little hurt that his interruption was obviously designed to shut me up. It takes me aback. "I don't think that's a good idea. We should stay in the caravan."

"I won't leave the site," he insists. "There's a vending machine back near that visitor's centre with Mustachio on the desk. Come on. I need sugar. I'm starving."

I reach for my bag, fish out my purse, and retrieve a few pound coins. "Maltesers, then. And a coke."

"Coming right up."

As soon as Tom has ducked out into the rain, I take up his role of pacing up and down the small space. How long does it take for the police to come out here? Is this an emergency call, or the kind of deal where they come when they can? DCI Murphy will have a long drive from York. Will they get a helicopter out searching for Isabel? Where can she be hiding? Is she still out there roaming the countryside? The campsite is farther away from the sea, more into the country, though the sea is visible. She managed to lose the manhunt on the moors.

She might be able to do it again in the surrounding fields.

I pace and pace. How long is it since I ate anything? I never did have dinner.

The windows are dark, turning darker as the early evening evolves into night. Soon, the floodlights around the caravan park will come on. Will I see her if she comes for me?

I glance at my phone for the time. Tom has been gone too long, and my palms are beginning to sweat. Taking a deep breath, I scroll quickly through my contacts and pull up his number. The phone rings, cuts out, and I realise he's rejected my call.

Why would he do that? Our fight is over, and we're both in danger. Surely, he'd be sensible enough to pick up the phone.

A cold sensation washes over me, and I have to fight the nausea that rises from my stomach. But that cold, complete and utter terror focuses into a point. A resolve. I open the caravan door, and I walk out.

A quiet voice says, "Hello, Leah, sweetie. I knew you'd come to me."

And then the knife pokes against my side.

CHAPTER 35

"Where is Tom?"

"Be a good girl, and I'll take you to him."

"Fine. Lead the way."

I'm surprised by the strange sense of calm that spread through my body the moment I felt the knife in my side. This has been inevitable, filling me with such dread, that I almost feel relieved that it has finally happened. But at the same time, I'm terrified for Tom. I make a mental note of the time that passed between Tom leaving the caravan and Isabel finding me. She didn't have time to hurt him. Did she?

How did she find us? I was positive we hadn't been followed, but Isabel has outsmarted everyone else over and over again. Of course she knew where to find us.

"Good girl, Leah. Just keep walking. Keep doing exactly what I say."

"I could scream," I point out. "And all of these people behind those thin walls of metal will come running out to see what's going on."

"You could," she admits. "But then you wouldn't find out where Tom is, and let's just say that you might need to find him sooner rather than later."

Now the terror truly kicks in. "What's that supposed to mean? What have you done to him?"

The knife pokes harder, drawing a small amount of blood and making me wince from the pain. The heat of the blood spreads down my skin, hits my clothing and begins to cool. I think Isabel feels the knife cut into my flesh, because she lets out a tiny moan of pleasure.

"Just be a good girl, Leah, that's all I'm asking."

There are little roads built into the campsite, making it feel as though we're walking through a housing estate somewhere. The place is not silent, but it feels half-asleep. TVs and radios, conversations, dogs barking, the beat of music coming from the visitor's centre—all of it is strangely lacklustre as I walk alongside my serial-killer stalker. Where are the police? They should be here by now, shouldn't they?

A couple approach us arm in arm, walking their little Yorkshire terrier on a lead. The knife blade retracts slightly, and when I turn my head, I notice Isabel slip it back into the sleeve of her top. She stares at me, and I realise it's the first time we've locked eyes since she caught me outside the caravan. Despite having lost some weight, she appears to be healthy and well, with neat, blonde hair cut just below her chin, and even a little blusher on her cheeks.

"Tom," she whispers, not needing to utter anything else in order to make me behave myself.

"Evening," says the man, nodding his grey head. His waterproof jacket rustles as he walks. "Ced now the rain's stopped."

"Until it starts again," Isabel replies, rolling her eyes in a comical fashion.

"Have a good night," says the man's wife or female friend.

"You too," Isabel shoots back sunnily.

As soon as we've passed the couple, the knife is back, finding the tiny tear in my flesh from her previous cut. I hiss and pull away from her slightly.

She makes a tutting sound. "You were a little quiet there. What will they think of us? Really, Leah, I do hate to come across as the chatty one in this relationship."

"Shut your fucking mo—oh!" The knife digs in again.

"While that little show of spirit does amuse me, I think you're forgetting who has the knife. Like I said, *behave* yourself, Leah, or I'll gut you right here, right now, and Tom will die alone. Is that what you want?"

"No." The strange sense of calm that seeped through me at the beginning is now gone. My legs feel jelly-like and unnatural as I keep walking, and my heart pounds and pounds, so fast it's frightening.

I got us away from her once. I can do it again. But when we escaped last time, I knew my surroundings. It might have been pitch-black on the moors, but I had a vague idea of where to go and who could help me. *Seb.* My mind goes to him, as it often does when I'm in need of comfort. *Think*, Leah. My phone is in my jeans pocket. Isabel didn't think of that, did she? She forgot to take my phone. That in itself is strange. She's usually one step ahead. It almost seems as though she hasn't planned this.

I watch her carefully as we move through the caravan park. Her eyes roam left and right, and she hesitates at turnings, occasionally chewing on her bottom lip. Is Isabel nervous? I've seen her act nervous before. I've seen her pretend to be afraid, upset, and joyously happy. I've seen every range of emotion from her, but all of them were fake.

What if this was an unplanned attack? For all I know, Isabel was staying here in the caravan park, or at least very close to it. Her clothes are different this time around. Last time, she was dishevelled, and it was clear that she had been sleeping rough. She was wearing anti-scent jackets and tough, hardwearing boots. Today, she's in jeans and a blouse with a cardigan. No coat. Why wouldn't she wear a coat if she was planning on stalking me in the rain?

The most important part of all this: if Isabel's attack was one of fortitude and not planning, what has she done with Tom? He was gone no more than around twenty minutes. Isabel had time to frighten him and lead him away, but did she have time to set up something that puts his life in danger? There is no pulley system to tie him up. As far as I'm aware, there aren't any outbuildings in the area, and surely a caravan would be too risky. What has she done with him?

"How did you find me?" I ask, hoping that if I get her talking, she might begin to drop her guard and reveal further information. We're approaching the back of the park, which means we're about to leave the area. Surely, Tom can't be much farther away. We've been walking for at least five minutes.

"I got the internet to do it for me."

"So it was you who leaked my real name and photograph. And then you waited for someone to recognise me in Clifton. Clever."

Isabel's eyes flash to mine. "If I didn't know you better, I'd think you were trying to flatter me. You know it won't save your life."

"I know that."

She lets out a low chuckle. "See, this is what I love about you, Leah. There's always that little glimmer of hope that you latch on to and won't let go. What else are you hopeful about? I can't wait for you to tell me what you've been up to here. I went to where you work, and I saw you there." She swings open a small gate, letting us out of the caravan park and onto a footpath. She shuts it behind us and gives me a little push to keep going. "I saw you in a room with an old man, tucking him in like he was your baby. And the funny thing is, from what I heard, you aren't even a nurse anymore. But it seems to me that you have yourself a new project. I know you love a project. It used to be me. Who was it before me? Tom? Poor kid. When did you get bored of him? No, not Tom. I'm guessing a boyfriend. Or was it one of the gangsters you worked with in the *other* asylum for the criminally insane."

"That's not what they're called."

"Oh, forgive me for not being politically correct. I'm too busy trying to commit a murder."

I've only seen Isabel this gleeful once before, and it was when she was taunting me at the abandoned farm. And then I realise: "This is the only way you find happiness." I stop and stand, prompting Isabel to push the knife back into the wound she cut on our way out of the park. "The only way you can be happy is by being cruel to another human being. And not just any human being; the one you want. It's all about the hunt and kill with you. Is that what it was like for you when you hunted Alison Finlay down and killed her? Or that homeless girl you threw in a river?"

Isabel smiles, and the moonlight catches her pink lips. She shakes her head slightly as though she's laughing at a private joke. "First of all, I did not hunt Chloe, the homeless girl. Her death was a necessity, because she realised who I was. I couldn't have that, clearly, not if I was going to finally find you. And second of all…" She trails off, stopping suddenly and clutching my shoulder with one hand.

A surge of adrenaline runs through me. Is it the police? Have they finally shown up? Then I realise that Isabel is staring at a cluster of bushes to the right of the path.

"Here we are. Finally. I wasn't sure I'd actually find it again. Leah, be a doll and root around in those bushes. You might find something you want to keep."

I drop to my knees and push the foliage aside, groping the ground in the dark. First a shoe, then a pair of jeans and a muffled cry.

"Tom!" My hands grasp his legs, pulling as hard as I can. He kicks out with bound feet. "Tom, it's all right. It's me." He wiggles himself down as I yank his ankles free of the thickset bush. When his torso emerges from the bush, I grab hold of his bound hands and pull the rest of him out.

Tom sits up, wide-eyed and afraid, his mouth gagged with duct tape. I reach forward to remove it, but Isabel places a hand on my shoulder.

"Ah-ah. You can untie his feet, and that's it."

"If anyone sees us—" I begin.

"We're not going far," Isabel says. "I'm going to risk it."

I turn and face her. "You lied to me. You said he was in immediate danger."

"He was. He created an immediate danger for me. If someone had seen him…" She shrugs, smiling again.

"You haven't planned any of this, have you? You saw Tom in the caravan park, forced him to tell you which van we were staying in, then brought him here and tied him up. Then you came back to me. You don't have a plan at all. What's the matter? Struggling to be a first-class serial killer without Daddy here to help you?"

The knife finds a sensitive spot just beneath my rib cage, and when I cry out in pain, she slaps me round the mouth.

"Time to shut up now. Get him on his feet and follow me."

CHAPTER 36

As I help Tom to his feet, I hear the strains of a siren. Isabel stops dead, her eyes roaming the path. She remains unnervingly still and silent. It's like watching a hunter get the first whiff of its prey. Her eyes widen in surprise.

"You knew I was coming," she says. "That's why you're here at the caravan park, to get away from me. You've already called the police, haven't you?" She laughs. "I should've known."

"If you go now," I say, "you can get away without them finding you. You're a clever girl; you'll find a way to get out of the town without alerting suspicion. You could get abroad, even. You could live out the rest of your days in the sunshine, away from the rain and the short summers." As I continue talking, my voice turns pleading. Then I remember how she taunted me about my belief in hope. She's smiling now, as though I've proven her right again.

"You just don't get it." She retrieves a bag from the ground and starts walking as I help Tom move on his stiff legs. "You've never understood. What's out there for me?" The knife pokes me a little harder, searching for a place to stab.

But it isn't the knife that fills me with cold dread. It's those words. *What's out there for me?* It never occurred to me that I wanted Isabel to *want* to live. I want her to *want* to escape, because if she has the desire to escape and live away from me and Tom, we have a chance to survive the night. But Isabel doesn't want to live or escape; she wants to go down in a blaze of glory.

This is a suicide mission.

I've always been the suicide mission. When Isabel escaped from Crowmont Hospital, I assumed it was all in for her to go away and live a normal life somewhere. But what kind of normal life can a person with her desires have?

"You're giving up," I say.

The knife pokes in again, not hard enough to make me cry out this time.

"I wouldn't call it that."

"You never struck me as a quitter."

Another cold glare. Another poke of the knife. "Don't pretend to understand me. Half a dozen psychologists, therapists, and psychiatrists couldn't." She pushes me on in the dark, and my feet touch sand.

"I'm sure you're not the only killer they've worked with. You're not that special."

"Shut up, Leah."

"Why? Am I upsetting you?"

But she isn't listening, she's checking the beach. There could be dog walkers, couples on a romantic stroll, or joggers, but the unpredictable rainy weather seems to have cleared the beach for the night.

"This way," she says.

I wrap an arm around Tom, guiding him through the dark, trying to smile at him to tell him everything is going to be all right. But he'll know I don't mean it. His eyes are those same little magpie eyes I saw back in the bungalow, cold and unemotional. What could he possibly be thinking right now?

But now isn't the time for that. I turn my attention back to Isabel, not knowing whether talking to her is helping or not. Still, I have to try. Isabel may have teased me about the glimmer of hope I always cling to, but it's better than despair.

"Why do you think you have nothing to live for? Surely, you don't care enough about this world to want to die. You weren't built to care, were you?"

"You've already answered your own question," she replies. "And I don't like repeating myself. In there."

I feel as though my body is crumpling up from the inside, folding inward. Isabel has led us to a craggy cove surrounded by cliffs. I know this spot. There's a cave built into the cliff that's only accessible during the low tide. Come high tide, the sea floods into the cave, making it easy to drown. The place is extremely dangerous and covered in warning signs, which Isabel is about to ignore. It's also isolated, far enough away from civilisation that our screams won't be heard.

As we make our way into the cave, there's a *shuck-shuck* sound coming from above. I crane my neck back to see the police helicopter beginning a sweep along the beach. Isabel spots the chopper at the same time and pushes Tom into the cave first, following up with me. As she pushes me, I fumble in my pocket for my phone, hoping I might be able to navigate through the settings to get to DCI Murphy's number. My phone is on silent, as it usually is, and no doubt I have a number of missed calls by now. The police must have found our caravan empty and discovered that Isabel is staying here, probably under a fake name.

The pitch-black of the cave is interrupted when Isabel lights a match and lifts it to reveal her pale face in the darkness. She takes a candle from her bag, ignites it with the match and half-buries it in the sand.

"It appears that you're quite popular." She raises the knife and gestures for me to take Tom to the back of the cave.

"So, you did plan this after all."

"I did," she admits. "It just happened a little quicker than I anticipated. I should have known you'd suspect I was here as soon as the internet went nutty over your identity."

"And there were the birds, too," I remind her.

The corner of her lip twitches up as though she's amused. "Oh, yes. The magpie."

"You're nothing if not predictable," I say, helping Tom down to the ground.

"Unlike other people here. Oh, you can remove his gag now if you want."

I carefully peel the gag away from Tom's mouth, and he gulps in a big breath of sea air. "Fuck you, Isabel," he spits.

Isabel ignores him and continues staring at me. "Poor kid. Knowing you is a hazard, isn't it, Leah? First, your mother. Then the greasy blogger from that terrible website. Tom, of course, and…" She lifts her knife and smiles at it knowingly.

"And?"

She shrugs. "I suppose you'll have to wait and see on that one."

"What have you done?" I demand.

"Like I said, you'll have to wait and see."

"Is it Seb?"

"If I told you, I'd be spoiling the surprise, wouldn't I?" she says.

"I hate you." The realisation hits me like a punch to the stomach. This woman, this *young* woman, has made my life a living hell. "You should've died."

"What, you mean when you pushed me off a cliff? I did scratch my arm on a rock on the way down," she says. "I had quite a large scab. And a migraine that lasted days. But you know what? I'm the kind of bird you can't kill."

"You're no bird," I reply. "You're a cockroach. A plain, uninteresting, run-of-the-mill cockroach that refuses to be squashed. The fact that you keep coming back isn't because you're special, it's because you're relentless." That isn't strictly true, but I'm hoping to get some sort of rise out of her. If I can distract her long enough to be able to dive at her, knock her off-guard, take the knife somehow…

Inside my pocket, I've tried going through the steps I believe will take me to calling DCI Murphy. Now I can only hope he's on the other end of the line, listening to this conversation.

"I know this place," I say in a clear voice. "The locals call this cave 'Dead man's Den'. And what's the cove called?"

Isabel shrugs.

"Reverend's Cove." If they heard that by some miracle through my pocket, then maybe the police will find us. "You have to be careful, Isabel. The tide will make its way in here at some point. Have you checked the tidal table?"

She shrugs again. "You know, I don't care." Though her knife remains aloft, she manoeuvres her body in order to see out of the cave. "It's not a bird's death, drowning. But it has a noble quality about it. Perhaps my body will be lost to the sea."

"You've gone through all of this just to give up? Breaking out of Crowmont? Chasing me? Why?" I ask.

"Because she knows she can't keep getting away with it," Tom replies. "She can't even control herself enough to get out of the country for a while and wait until people have forgotten about her."

"This isn't a film, little boy. I couldn't leave the country even if I wanted to," Isabel says, her voice cold and cutting. She's pissed off now, which might work in our favour. "I can't buy a house or even rent a flat. I can't get a job. Everyone knows my face. I change as much as I can, move differently, dress differently, but still I see the side glances of people when they suddenly think, *Where do I know her from?* And then I have to move, quick as a swallow in flight, to another town, another city, in a stolen car or on a bus, forever wondering when they'll catch up with me. Tell me, is that any kind of life?"

"Do you expect us to feel sorry for you?" Tom's voice is almost a growl. Sometimes I forget how much he has grown up since the last time we were with Isabel like this. "A washed-up, failed serial killer. Poor you, not being able to get a job or a house. Poor, poor you."

"I don't care about you." When Isabel says this, I believe her. "I don't care what you think. I won't go back to that prison, and it's clear I can't live outside of it. That leaves me with one other option." She sits down on a rock and rests the knife on her knee. "Perhaps I made a mistake by coming after you so soon after escaping from Crowmont. That was Daddy, getting me wound up, reminding me of everything I could be. His little killer. He was keen to go after you because of the way you turned up at our house. I think he felt the way I feel right now, the selfish bastard. He could have warned me he wanted to end it all. So I decided to go along with his plan because it was you, and you were always going to be my reward for escaping." She stands up and takes a few steps towards me. I instinctively position myself between her and Tom. "You are *such* a blank canvas. I can't wait to finish what I started."

"Let Tom go," I insist. "You don't want him. He won't go to the police, I promise."

Isabel cocks her head. "Always the mother."

Every muscle in my body tenses. I forgot what I told her that night on the moors.

"He doesn't know, does he? Tell me, Leah, who was the father?"

Bile rises in my throat. I cough, almost vomiting onto the cave floor.

"What is she talking about?" Tom's voice is as cold and hard as Isabel's. I can't look at him.

"Leah, tell your son who his father is."

Finally, I lift my head to meet Isabel's gaze. "I'm going to kill you."

"Leah, just fucking tell me what's going on." Tom hits his bound hands against his knees.

Tears spring into my eyes as I take his hands in mine and hold them tight. "This isn't how I wanted you to find out. We were both going to sit down when the time was right and talk it all through."

"Just tell me."

I can barely look at his face, which is stone-like and impassive. "I gave birth to you, Tom. I was very, very young, and I was afraid. Mum agreed to raise you as her own, and I promised to always be your big sister."

"What the *fuck*." He pulls his hands away from mine, and tears begin to roll down my cheeks. "Who is my father? Who is it?"

"Whatever happens, I'm still… I'm still Leah, okay? And you're still the kind, sweet boy you were when we were growing up."

"No, I'm not." His voice is low, menacing. It sends ripples of panic through my body, like electric shocks. "Just tell me."

"I don't want to," I whisper.

"Did someone… God, you could only have been…" I watch desperately as Tom begins to piece everything together. "Someone raped you."

"Yes."

"A boy at your school?"

I shake my head.

"A man? Someone I knew. Someone in our family?"

A nod is all I can muster.

His face is pale when he says, "It was Dad? He raped you, didn't he? I'm a child of incest, aren't I?"

Another nod. "I'm sorry I didn't tell you, Tom." An uncontrollable, racking sob shudders through me. When I reach for his hand, he shuffles away from me, his gaze fixed on the floor of the cave. "It doesn't change anything." But even I know that's a lie.

"What a twist in the tale," Isabel says with a mocking laugh.

"At least I won't be dying a virgin, like you." Beyond the agony I'm feeling, I still have enough rage to turn to her and see a little flicker of emotion travel across her face. What was that? Anger? Sadness? I smile at her, hoping it's just as much of a twisted smile as the one she just gave me. *Yes,* I think, *I can be a monster, too. Let's see which monster wins, shall we?*

Isabel grabs hold of my hair, pushes the knife under my chin, and drags me away from Tom.

It has begun.

CHAPTER 37

"I want to show you something," Isabel says. She pushes me onto the rock and cuts a tiny slice of skin beneath my chin. Then she takes a step back and shoves her left hand under my nose. "See it?"

On her wedding finger is a slim gold band.

"I see it."

"Do you know where I found it?" She taps the ring with the blade of her knife.

"Of course I do."

"She pulled it off the corpse of my *grandmother*," Tom says in a voice that almost sounds bored.

"Ten points to Tom!" Isabel crows. "Well done."

"I didn't tell you because I didn't want you to be upset," I say quietly. He just shakes his head.

"It seems as though you've failed at being a mother," Isabel points out with glee. "Just like you failed at being a nurse. And a daughter. Anything else you've failed at? Driving test? GCSEs?" She pulls back my hair, forcing my head back roughly, and draws the knife along my jawline. As the knife cuts into my skin, I scream at the top of my lungs, but she warns me, "That won't help you now."

It's been months since my ordeal in the abandoned farmhouse, and yet the face I see before me is the same face that has haunted my dreams. The same smile, the same wide, open eyes, the same expression of pure joy. Isabel amidst blood and knives is like a child opening her Christmas presents.

"I... pity... you." The blood dribbles down my neck to my collarbone.

"I know," she says simply. "That's always been a huge problem for you, hasn't it? If you hadn't pitied me to begin with, none of this would've happened."

The knife travels down and begins to cut through my top. My heart is beating hard against my ribs, my head is in agony, but still I find enough strength to try to push her away. That knife moves as fast as a greyhound on a track, slashing at my palm.

"Bad Leah," she chides, tutting like a schoolteacher. Backing away slowly, Isabel bends down and pulls a length of rope from her bag.

This does have me panicking, because as soon as I'm tied up, there'll be nothing I can do. While Isabel is low to the ground, I take a chance. I dive straight for her, knocking her onto her backside.

"Tom, run!" I yell.

The force may have toppled her over, but she still hasn't released the knife from her grasp, and as I lie on top of her, Isabel drives the knife beneath my ribs, pushing it deep into my flesh. This isn't a minor wound; it's a real stab, a blow meant to kill.

But I don't care. I wrap my bloodied hands around her neck, squeezing hard, watching her eyes widen in surprise. She opens her mouth to speak, but only a spit bubble makes it out. Then the knife is out of my side, and her hands are pushing me back. She manages to raise the knife for another stab, this time in my upper arm, slicing down to the bone. The pain from the wound causes me to lose my grip on her throat, and she kicks me away from her with both feet.

"There's my killer," she says. "I knew you had it in you."

"Tom?" I whip my head from left to right, trying to find him. In the chaos of the fight, I didn't even notice Tom escaping the cave. Good. At least now he can get help.

Isabel sits panting on the ground in front of me, bloody marks on her neck from where I tried to strangle her. A throbbing pain is radiating from my ribs, and when I look down, I see blood gushing from a deep wound. I immediately press my fingers against the wound to stem the bleeding.

"I know you're a killer, Leah. Have I been in your dreams since we last spoke? Do you still wake up and not know where you've been or what you've done? Have you ever dreamt of blood and guts?"

I want her to stop talking. Her voice is making me remember, and God, I do not want to remember.

"I didn't kill her, Leah. Cross my heart and hope to die. I didn't kill her. Not Alison. It wasn't me. I carved up Chloe and dumped her in the stream, but the first one wasn't me."

"You're lying."

"I'm not," she says. "What do I have to gain by lying?"

"You're trying to make me think I did it, because…"

"Because what? Why would you think you did it?" For once, she appears genuinely interested.

"Because I do dream about it. The violence. I dream about it, and I sometimes think I want…"

The blood on my hands. It was the night Alison was murdered.

"You want what?" she prompts.

"To hurt someone."

"Me?"

"Yes."

She smiles. "You already have hurt me. You've hit me, pushed me off a cliff, strangled me. You're a little killer, Leah. Just like me."

"Shut. Up."

"Yes, you're quite right. We don't have time for this anymore, do we? Now, be a good girl and turn around."

"I can't move."

For the first time, Isabel stares down at the wound under my ribs with utter dismay. "Now, why did you go and make me do that?" She moves across to me and places a hand over mine, the blood coating her fingers, thick, dark blood. "It ruins everything." She sighs, almost tenderly. "Now I can't torture you."

Despite everything, I start to laugh deliriously. My head is light, and the pain is beginning to ebb away. It's strange—the blood seems to have spread below me, too, onto the ground. But when I manage to move my head far enough to see the ground, I realise that it's water.

"The tide's beginning to come in," I say.

Isabel nods. "So it is." She manoeuvres herself to sit beside me. Then she rests her head against my shoulder. "You know that I care very little about you, or Tom, or the world in general, don't you?"

"Yes."

"Good. I want you to know that I do care about the fact that you were one of the few people on this earth to show me genuine kindness."

I don't know what to say in return. The hate is still there, simmering beneath the surface, and yet at the same time, there is love, and I can't explain the love. I hate myself for it. I *hate* it. I thought the love was for a girl who didn't exist, but now I see that parts of that girl are in Isabel, and I can't escape the fact that I still have love for her.

"Shall we watch the tide come in together?" she asks.

There's nothing more for me to say. At least I made sure that Tom got out before the water began making its way into the cave. At least he can get to safety. Part of me wonders whether this was inevitable and whether perhaps I deserve to die, but just as Isabel said, I still maintain that glimmer of hope that Tom found the police, or that I actually did manage to call DCI Murphy using the phone in my pocket.

The rock is hard against my back, and Isabel is heavy against my shoulder, both things a pleasant distraction from the low throbbing in my side. Then I realise that numbness is spreading all through me, alongside the freezing cold. I begin to shiver uncontrollably, but Isabel doesn't seem to notice.

Water seeps into the cave, first about an inch, and then, a few moments later, at least two inches, then some more. It's coming in quickly. I wonder how long it will take for the water to fill the entire cave. An hour? More? Less? Part of me wants it to sweep me away, out to sea.

As Isabel relaxes, she lets go of the knife. She lets out a contented sigh, relaxing into what I assume is the fate she has resigned herself to.

Her guard is down, and I recognise that I have one moment in which to act. I don't pause to wonder whether I have the strength to do it before I lean over her and snatch the knife from the water. The pain is excruciating, but I push myself through it. Moving quickly, before she has time to react, I plunge the knife into her throat.

Isabel's eyes open wide in shock. Then, oddly, she smiles. I yank the knife from her throat, trying not to see the jet of blood being expelled from the wound. I push her head down with my other hand, into the water.

"I'm sorry. I have to."

I hold her head down as she writhes against me. Her fingernails dig into the flesh of my thighs. My head is light, woozy; I'm barely keeping hold of consciousness. Isabel begins to stop struggling as the water floods in, almost covering my legs now, and then a bright light comes with it.

I close my eyes, let go of her head, and the world slips away.

I'm ready to float away to sea, but instead I begin to cough, and once I've started, I can't stop. The world comes to me in flashes. In one flash, a man's face looms over me. In another flash, fluorescent lights are flickering above me. Then there's another flash in which several people are tugging at parts of my body. I try to swat them away with my hands, but they won't stop. Finally, the flashes stop, and I slip into a dream where I'm walking along the beach with Isabel. Pepsi the magpie lands on her shoulder and begins pecking at her flesh. Isabel just laughs and laughs and laughs…

"Leah?"

The world comes back again, and this time I can tell that it's back for good. The man sitting next to me is DCI Murphy, and I'm immediately disappointed.

"Where's Tom?" I ask.

"He went home to fetch you some things. How are you feeling?"

I gesture to my sore throat, and he passes me a glass of water. "You need to stop visiting me in hospitals," I say after taking a sip. "People will talk. Oh, I'm okay, I guess. I've been better." I glance down at the place where Isabel stabbed me.

"All stitched up. You lost a lot of blood and had to have a transfusion. The doctor will need to have a long talk with you, no doubt. Best asking her rather than me." He leans forward and rests his elbows on his knees.

"Did the phone thing work? Is that how you found us?"

The detective shakes his head. "The phone thing?"

"I thought I'd pressed the right buttons in my pocket." I let out a little laugh. "I guess not, then. Was it Tom?"

He nods. "It was Tom. He called from a phone box and told us where you were."

I lick my lips as I build up to the next question. We both know what it is, and we know how it worked out last time. My pulse quickens in preparation for the answer. But I have to know.

"Isabel?"

"She's in intensive care. Unconscious."

"This hospital?"

He shakes his head very slowly. "No."

"Good."

"She's monitored 24/7. Leah, I won't let her out. We have her now. It's over."

But I'm not sure I believe him. "I can't believe she's alive. I thought… I honestly thought I'd killed her."

"You fought back," he replies. "You hurt her badly." Then he says pointedly, "In self-defence." As his eyes penetrate mine, it's almost as though he's pleading silently.

I just smile and nod. "Of course it was."

CHAPTER 38

How far away are any of us from becoming murderers? One psychotic break could eliminate your ideas of morality and control.

We choose not to kill people every day. We converse with other people, kiss them, touch them, shake their hands, brush their hair, and we choose not to hurt them. But we're all strong enough. Even little children can inflict pain on each other. We choose not to kill because to do so would remove us from the tribe. Only occasionally do we possess a motivation strong enough for us to kill another human being and not care about the tribe.

Sometimes a sickness causes that lack of remorse. Sometimes, in gangs and wars, killing is fundamental to being part of the tribe. Other times, a desire to live or a passionate rage overrides any remorse we might feel. Isabel, I now realise, knew that what she desired more than anything would isolate her for the rest of her life and condemn her to a miserable existence, either prison or poverty. She can't be part of society and do the things she wants to do.

I understand that now.

What I can't understand is what happened to Alison Finlay. I keep thinking back to the morning I turned on the television and the reporter announced the discovery of the body. Where was I that night? All I remember is the blood on my hands, washing them in the bathroom, and wondering what had happened.

A doctor comes to see me to inform me of the damage to my intestines and the difficulties I'll be experiencing for the foreseeable future. The words "colostomy bag" are particularly jarring.

I've been awake for two or three hours at this point and still haven't seen Tom, who is apparently at home gathering my things. I can't stop thinking about the cave, especially Tom's anger when he found out the truth. His anger in general has become a terrifying thing. Maybe he's never coming back. Can I blame him? Maybe he's better off out there on his own, without me around.

When the room door swings open, I hold my breath in anticipation, but it's DCI Murphy back again to see how I'm doing.

"I wanted to let you know," he says, "that Isabel regained consciousness this afternoon. Her throat is pretty torn up, but she was able to speak a little. She requested the presence of a police officer, and she confessed to the murders of Maisie Earnshaw, James Gorden, Alison Finlay, and Chloe Anderson. She also confessed to the kidnapping and assault of you and Tom. That was all she could say, but she hinted that she will be giving us more details and telling us how Owen and David Fielding came into play with the murders."

Stunned, all I can do is nod. "She confessed to them all?"

He nods. "She confessed to them all. It's all over, Leah. And this time, I'm going to do everything in my power to ensure that Isabel goes into a maximum-security prison, not a psychiatric hospital. She won't be getting out ever again. You have my word on that."

"Don't make a promise," I say. "Just... don't."

"All right, then, I won't. But you have to promise—okay, try, at least, to live a normal life without even thinking about Isabel Fielding, because you can do that now."

I force a smile. "All right, then."

"There's something else I wanted to talk to you about. That missing girl from the forties, Abigail Hawker. I did some research, and I found the family who disappeared, the Pierces. They're both dead, obviously, but I found a relative, and here are their details. Now, I have to warn you, if it was them, Abigail did not move away with them alive. They lived without children until they died. The relative is a descendant of the wife's niece. Great-grand-niece, or something like that." He hands me a piece of paper.

"Thank you." I take the paper and pop it into my bedside table for later. "I mean it. You've been... Well, you know."

As he nods, tears begin to well up, even though I don't want them to. I never used to cry like this. Perhaps it doesn't matter how often you cry when you've been to hell and back.

"I'll have an officer come in to take a statement about what happened with Isabel in the cave. A nice officer. Remember, though, it was all self-defence. Isabel had stabbed you, after all."

"She had."

As he walks out of the room, I wonder what he saw entering the cave. A helpless Isabel drowning and me pushing her head down into the water? Or did they arrive in time to see me stab her, too? I'm not sure how far away they were when it happened, and it's all such a blur.

When I wake, there's a pile of freshly laundered clothes on the chair next to my bed, including pyjamas and slippers. My bag is on top, and I search through it to find my keys and wallet. Up till now, I haven't thought to check my phone, which I discover is in the little table. It's dry now, though it obviously would have been wet during the event with Isabel. I have plenty of missed calls, nearly all of them from DCI Murphy. But there are also two missed calls from Mark, and one from work. I grit my teeth and begin working my way through the voicemails, dreading the messages that will no doubt transport me back to that night.

Murphy's voicemail begins by assuring me that the police are on their way. Not long after that, he left another message about the caravan number. After that, the messages are all asking where I am. Later, he stops leaving messages and just hangs up.

The message from Mark is an apology, along with a promise to explain his reaction the next time he sees me.

The one from work is disturbing. They tell me that George suffered a minor stroke and that he might not have much time left. I knew he'd been failing recently, but according to the message, his sudden deterioration was a surprise. Of course, the elderly suffer strokes like this very commonly, but I can't help but feel suspicious, because now I remember what Isabel said to me.

She said she'd seen me at work. And later, she said I would be in for a surprise. Did Isabel hurt George?

I long to get out of this bed, but I can barely move. Instead, I decide to call Mark and ask him how George is doing.

After a brief conversation with a tired-sounding Mark, he promises to visit today before the end of visiting hours, and I'm left waiting alone, wondering. *Where is Tom?*

A nurse comes in to check my dressings. Her rough fingers poke and prod me, but I know it's nothing personal. Sometimes a little pain is an unpleasant side-effect of being cared for.

"Have you seen my little brother? Well, he isn't little anymore. Tom?"

"With the dark hair? Quite tall? Late teens?"

"That's him."

"He dropped off some clothes for you about an hour ago," she says, turning me slightly so that she can clean me up. "And there was a note, I think."

I didn't notice the note. As soon as the nurse has left, I pull the chair closer so I can rifle through the belongings Tom left for me. Sure enough, tucked between clean underwear and a pair of jeans is an envelope. With a sense of dread, I tear it open and devour the contents.

Leah,

It's nothing you said or did. I just need to go.

I brought you some things. The police have my statement. I need time, okay? Don't try to find me.

Tom

Isabel might as well have driven that knife into my intestines again. No love. No well wishes. Nothing. The note is cold and emotionless, just like he has become. I put the note back in the envelope and press my fingers against my eyes to block out the light. *Don't try to find me.* How long is he planning on being away from me? After everything that's happened, he's left me. Gone. And now I have no family left.

"Is this a bad time?"

Mark is standing halfway into the room, holding the door open. His face is etched with worry, and his smiling eyes have turned tired, but I'm surprised by how pleased I am to see him.

"Come in," I say. "Sorry. I just found out that Tom... I mean Scott; that's the name you know... He's decided to leave."

"While you're in hospital?" Mark steps closer and hovers near the bed. "Jesus."

"I know." I shake my head. "Maybe he needs time alone."

"He should be taking care of you." He reaches down and gently pats my hand. "I'm sorry about everything. About that day in your house. If I hadn't left you alone, Isabel might not have—"

"Or there would be another person in the hospital," I point out. "I'm glad you didn't end up involved with this. Especially now. I'm sorry to hear about George. How is he doing?"

Mark shakes his head. "He's stable, but he's confused. He keeps claiming that a blonde woman tried to kill him."

Blood drains from my face, but I remain silent.

"I think he's just confused. He was unconscious for a little while, and I think he had some bad dreams. He says someone held a pillow over his face and he couldn't breathe, but we think that might be his brain reacting to the stroke."

As Mark regards me with eyes that remind me of his grandfather, I find that I simply cannot tell him what Isabel hinted at outside the cave. I'm sure she did try to kill George. Perhaps she thought she had, if he lost consciousness. Of course she would go after George. She said she saw me at the care home. She must have been jealous, seeing me tend to another person.

"Are you feeling okay? You've gone a bit pale," Mark asks.

"I'm fine. The wound makes me tired, that's all."

Mark finally decides to sit. "You've been through a lot. Do you want me to go, if you're tired?"

"No, stay, please. I'm going out of my mind with boredom."

"Actually, there was something I wanted to get off my chest." He smiles. "That day when I flipped out about your real identity. You see, it's very strange, but I have a connection to the woman Isabel killed. Alison Finlay. She was my ex-girlfriend's therapist. We used to live in a pretty little cottage in Dinlabyre a few years back, then moved back to Clifton six months ago. When my ex-girlfriend heard the news, she was very upset. There were cracks in our relationship going back a long time, but my ex had a hard time dealing with change, and Alison's death was the kind of change she finds difficult to handle. She cheated on me not long after, and the relationship died. I kept following that ridiculous hashtag on Twitter, and I think I convinced myself that you and Isabel were to blame for the death of our relationship. I'm sorry about that. It was all completely random. Small world, I guess."

"Ripples," I say.

"What?"

"Nothing. Just a thought. About how events ripple out, affecting everyone in their path."

"I suppose I'm one of those ripples. Or just an arsehole."

"Hmm. Yes, maybe." I can't help but laugh. "It's all understandable. I just hadn't realised that Alison was a therapist. We never learn about the victims, do we?"

"No, I suppose not."

I take Mark's hand and give it a squeeze. "I found out more information about Abigail. Do you want to hear it?"

"Yes, absolutely."

CHAPTER 39

It's one week later, and I'm bundled into a wheelchair. Mark drives the thing as we make our way into Ivy Lodge to rapturous applause. I nod warily, waving at the nurses as they crowd around me.

"It's nice to meet you, Leah," my boss says, tongue in cheek.

They've bought cake. Sandra from physiotherapy made scones. They pat me on the back and ask me how I'm doing, throwing out a few medical terms here and there, and nodding gravely as I tell them about the damage to my intestines. But the big news is that Isabel has been caught. She's going to be put away for a long time, and the people of Britain can sleep soundly again. I'm the reason why they caught her. I'm the one who stabbed her, played the hero.

But I couldn't feel anything further from a hero. All I feel like is a killer.

Mark wheels me in to see George, who can't sit up any longer, but who reaches for my hand and squeezes it tight.

"No need for tears," he says softly, his voice slightly slurred. "I won't be crying any time soon. It's my time now, you see. But that's all right."

And of course I cry harder. I'm not just crying for George, but for Tom, too, and everything that has happened. Even Mark is taken aback by the force of my tears, but after a while they finally subside, and we bring a slice of cake to George, who enjoys it immensely.

A few hours and it's over, and I'm left feeling tired again, as I often am these days. Mark takes me back to the bungalow, and I waddle my way into the bedroom to sleep.

I dream of Alison Finlay and blood. Lots of blood.

Another week later, I'm back on my feet somewhat unsteadily. It's better than getting wheeled around by Mark, anyway. We're going on a special trip together today. We're going to Dover to meet Francesca Adams, an apparent descendant of the Pierce family. It's my first time travelling since the stabbing, and I'm nervous. But the colostomy bag is no more, and I feel physically stronger than I have for a while. More importantly, George is still deteriorating. Mark could have gone on the trip without me, but he waited until I was well enough, insisting that this is as much my story as it is his family's at this point.

We travel along the A2 amidst a patchwork of green fields, and for the first time in a long time, I miss Hutton village, with the long stretching moors and the narrow roads. Now that Isabel is gone, I can go back there. I can see Seb again, and the thought makes me feel conflicted. Will he want to see me after everything I've done?

Killer.

I put those thoughts out of my mind because this is a time to do good, to clear some of that guilty conscience of mine. Mark turns the radio up and rolls the window down, showing me the beautiful bright sunshine outside. I just wish my mind wasn't clouded with darkness.

The café where we meet has a portrait of the white cliffs on the wall. Francesca is sitting below the picture, a pot of tea resting on the table in front of her. She's tall, slim, somewhat severe in appearance, with a pointed mouth and rosebud lips, but she smiles politely and gestures for us to take our seats. Mark helps me into mine. I keep an arm pressed over my wound, as though I'm protecting it.

"It's nice to meet you," I say. "Thank you for agreeing to help us."

"Not at all," she replies. "Aren't you the nurse—?"

"I am," I interrupt. "But that doesn't have anything to do with today. This is all about Mark and his grandfather, who lost a sister in 1944. There was a fire, and Abigail's body was never recovered." I glance at Mark, unsure how to proceed. It's never easy asking people if they believe their relatives may have kidnapped a child many years ago.

But Francesca is more forthcoming than I expected. "Yes, I know about that. My mother died a few years ago, and I was sorting through some old photographs. My Uncle Steven—my mother's brother—explained to me about my Great-Aunt Marie and Uncle Clive and the small town they used to live in. Clifton-on-Sea. I did some research into Clifton and discovered the fire and all of the rumours that surrounded it. I also saw that some people thought my ancestors took Abigail Hawker because they couldn't have children of their own." She takes a sip of her tea and leans back in her chair. "I… I have to be frank with you. I thought these rumours might be correct. My Great-Uncle Clive was not a good man. According to Uncle Steven, they had to leave Clifton because Clive had had an affair with a sixteen-year-old student."

"Do you think he might have been a paedophile?" I ask as gently as it's possible to ask such a question.

"It's possible. The girl was very young indeed, and I believe it to be true, so I suppose he was. I don't know if he did anything with anyone younger, or if it was just that girl." She shakes her head. "I'm sorry."

Mark shows her photographs of Abigail and the mysterious Mary. "What about these? Do you recognise the people in these photographs?"

Francesca shakes her head again. "I'm sorry, no. I don't. I checked through all of our photo albums and all of the letters kept from that time, and there's no sign of a young girl matching your missing girl. If my great-uncle did take this Abigail, he… Well, he didn't take her to Dover, anyway."

The unspoken implication is clear. He could have killed her and dumped the body somewhere else before the family ran away from the town. But is it possible that after all these years, Abigail's body was never found?

Mark and I leave the café feeling somewhat dejected, but before we leave the town, we drive to the cliffs and eat fish and chips while gazing over the Strait of Dover. The vinegary grease tastes good after being on a restricted diet for weeks.

"We might have to face the fact that we'll never know." Mark chucks a chip towards a group of seagulls, and we watch them fight over it.

"There's still the children's home. I have some replies to my emails from a few weeks ago. Why don't we stop off in Canterbury and see if we can find anything else out?"

Mark's shoulders sag, and I place a hand on his shoulder to comfort him. "I want Grandad to find peace," he says in a very small voice.

"Let's go to Canterbury," I urge.

On the way to Canterbury, I pull up the emails sent to me by the various records offices and libraries. Most have come back to tell me they found nothing, but there is one from a lady claiming to have found a young girl the same age Abigail was at the time. As Mark drives back the way we came, I call the lady, Geraldine Abbott, and ask if we can call in this afternoon. Time is rushing ahead and it's after four already, but she agrees to stay late for a chat with us.

I can tell from Mark's silence and the tense line of his shoulders that he's feeling dejected after meeting Francesca, but I have a better feeling about this. Geraldine doesn't strike me as the kind of woman who would stay late at the office just to tell us she hasn't found anything after all.

There you are, Isabel. I'm hopeful again. No matter what you say about me, I'll always be hopeful. You're not the only cockroach around, you know.

I'm a little disappointed that the office is out of the town centre, as I had hoped to see the cathedral and the Tudor buildings. But that does make it easier to park, and doesn't take us too far out of our way home.

When we reach the records office, I'm sweating from the long day. Even walking across the carpark takes it out of me, but I still feel energised as I press the buzzer and wait for Geraldine to answer.

Ever since working at Crowmont Hospital, I've had a hatred for buzzers. They always remind me of that first day. Mark jangles his keys in his pocket, and I place a hand on his elbow to calm him. When the door opens, we discover that Geraldine is a tiny woman wearing bright pink lipstick and thick-rimmed glasses. Her voice suits her frame: it's high-pitched, but not shrill.

"You must be Lizzie," she says, holding out a hand for me to shake. "And this is Mark. He's George Hawker's grandson."

"Oh." Her eyes widen. "It's a pleasure to meet you, then. Come in."

The offices are small, crammed with furniture and bookcases overflowing with books. There are a few desks stacked high with files, mugs left on desks and ancient computers that desperately need an update. Despite the dustiness and the tea rings, the place feels cosy, and light gushes in from the large window.

"Take a seat. I won't be a moment."

I find an armchair with wooden armrests, and Mark pulls up a desk chair to sit in. Geraldine rustles through some papers on her desk, muttering to herself as she goes.

"I'm sorry to bother you late in the day," Mark says as she works, filling the silence. "We've just been to Dover to speak to someone else we thought might know more about Abigail."

"Oh, really," Geraldine says, sounding slightly distracted. "Did you find anything out?"

Mark sounds older when he says, "No."

"But we're still hopeful," I add. "If there's anything you can help us with, it would be fantastic."

"Actually, there is." Geraldine produces a piece of paper that I can see is a scan of some handwriting. The handwriting is in columns, with names on one side and dates on the other. "This is a copy of the register for Canterbury Catholic Children's home, where a lot of displaced children were sent during and immediately after the war. Now, I didn't find anyone called Abigail on the list, but I did find an Annemarie, aged twelve, who was sent to the children's home around the same time as the fire." Geraldine passes me the scanned image, and I immediately see the pencil marks where Geraldine has highlighted the name.

"Mary," I whisper, handing the sheet to Mark. There's a lump in my throat as I say, "Um, Mary is a name we believe might be connected to Abigail as she grew older. Someone sent a photograph to George of a woman who might be Abigail, and on the back it just said 'Mary.'"

"Oh, I see." Geraldine nods. "That's interesting. I actually have some more information for you. It's noted here that Annemarie was injured when she came to the children's home. Head trauma. It was her uncle who brought her to the home and claimed that she'd been hurt during the Blitz in London. According to these records"—Geraldine gestures to more handwritten notes—"Annemarie didn't remember her own name."

"What was the name of her uncle?" Mark asks, finally lifting his eyes from the paper before him.

"That wasn't recorded, I'm afraid," Geraldine says. "But it is recorded that she was sent money and clothes by the same uncle and was occasionally visited by him. Does any of this sound plausible to you?"

I find myself nodding. "It has to be Simon Blackthorn. He had the connection to the family. He was most probably Abigail's father. Maybe she saw him start the fire and he snatched her, hurting her in the process. When he realised her memory was gone, he also realised he wouldn't be able to care for her and sent her to the children's home. What do you think, Mark?"

"I think it makes sense. What happened to Annemarie after she left the children's home?" he asks.

"She left in 1952." Geraldine lifts up another sheet of paper. "Here, it's written that the home arranged for her to work as a maid for a household called the Colemans. Her surname is listed as Prior."

"Annemarie Prior. I wonder how she got that name," I say.

"If this Simon Blackthorn did kidnap Abigail like you think, perhaps he had papers forged," Geraldine suggests. "With the chaos of the war, it might have been much easier to do it then."

I glance down at all the information again, but instead of thinking about Abigail, I find myself thinking of Tom. Will I have to track him down one day? Two weeks, and not so much as a phone call.

"Thank you for your time." Mark stands and shakes Geraldine's hand, new energy giving him a spirit that's wonderful to see.

"Yes, thank you so much," I add. "You may have helped figure out what happened to Abigail, and it will make an old man very happy." I almost pull Geraldine in for a hug, but shake her hand instead.

CHAPTER 40

Mark slips his hand in mine as we walk back to the car. He gives me a little squeeze, and I squeeze back. That bit of pressure tells me everything I need to know. It's gratefulness, not love, or lust, or attraction. It's relief. We've been through this together, and now we're about to come to the end. The mystery of what happened to Abigail Hawker is about to be solved. We've tracked down the Colemans.

They live on a farm estate just outside Canterbury. Rather than waste any more time, we've decided to drive there now.

The drive from Geraldine's office to the Colemans' farm is a relatively short one, without incident thanks to the sat nav. Here, the countryside is fecund green, and the farmland spreads out among the dry stone walls. I open the window and let the smells in, good and bad. If I close my eyes, I'm back at the Braithwaites' farm, with Seb waiting for me at the cottage.

"We should manage our expectations just in case nothing comes of this," Mark says as he pulls onto the drive. "They might not be in. They might not talk to us. Annemarie might not be—"

I place my hand on his arm. "Now is the time to be optimistic. Now is the time to hope." We lock eyes. "We're going to find out what happened. Okay?"

He nods. "Okay."

On the way down to the farm, my shoe catches on a loose stone, tripping me forwards. The quick movement pulls on my stitches, resulting in a sharp pain that's a lot like the knife Isabel stuck in me. At least while I'm here, away from the caves of Clifton, I can try to forget, even for a moment or two, about everything that happened. I need to practice what I preach—as always—and allow myself a moment of optimism.

Somewhere on the farm, a dog barks, and the sound echoes back to us. A horse nods its head in the paddock to our left, occasionally twitching its ears away from the flies. A curtain moves on the ground floor of the farmhouse. I imagine that the Colemans are not expecting visitors, especially not ones who walk slowly while holding their insides together.

Mark knocks firmly on the door, and a jolt of electricity travels through my body. It's perhaps thirty seconds before the door is answered, and during that time there's an instant when I feel like running away. But then I realise that the jolt of electricity isn't fear, it's excitement. This is the kind of nervousness that should be savoured, because it leads to something positive. For the last few years of my life, that sense of nervousness always led to bad experiences. Not anymore. Today, that changes.

"Hello?" The woman who answers is wearing an apron and has her hair tied back in a bun. She frowns, clearly wondering if we're here to sell something or try to convince her to switch religions.

"I'm sorry to bother you," Mark says, and it just now strikes me as the most often-spoken phrase in Britain. "My name is Mark Hawker, and I was hoping you might have some information about a young woman who worked here in the fifties and possibly the sixties. Annemarie Prior."

"I'm just a housekeeper," she replies. "You probably want to speak to Maeve. Just wait here a moment, and I'll see if she wouldn't mind talking to you. She's in her eighties now, you see."

"Thank you."

There's the sound of a chain moving across the lock as she closes the door. I don't blame her at all. As I think about locks and safety, my mind wanders back to Isabel again, always close to me, always there.

The chain shifts, and the door re-opens with a creak.

"She remembers Annemarie." The housekeeper appears surprised as she informs us of this. "And she will see you, but only for a few moments. She hasn't been very well recently."

"Thank you," Mark says, and for a moment I think he might actually hug her.

The housekeeper swings the door open and leads us through into a real farmhouse kitchen with an old Aga and horseshoes nailed to the beams. We continue on, and it's clear that the farmhouse is kept tidy but hasn't been redecorated for a few decades. Old books are stacked up in the windowsills with jam jars of wildflowers resting on top, the carpet is worn but still retains its deep red colour, and each of the chairs in the living room is in a different floral pattern. In the background, a grandfather clock ticks away ominously.

There's a creak from an old armchair, and a small woman with a grey head leans forward. She's tucked in up to the chest with a blanket, this one patterned with purple embroidery.

"Who did you say you were?" Maeve's fingers point vaguely in our direction, and I can see from the milky surface of her eyes that she can't see very well.

"My name is Mark Hawker. My grandfather is George Hawker, and we're from Clifton-on-Sea. When my grandad was young, his mother died in a fire and his sister disappeared. We've been trying to find out what happened to his sister, Abigail. We think she might have been taken to a children's home in Canterbury, and that she might have been called Annemarie Prior."

The woman's eyebrows lift. "Annemarie. Yes, I remember her. Mary."

"Mary?" I blurt out. "Is that the name she went by?"

"Oh, yes," Maeve says. "She didn't like Anne. She wanted to be a Mary. She was young, you know. But I was too. She cleaned for my mother and father and made bread in the mornings. Very pretty, she was. I remember wishing I had those long legs." Maeve begins to chuckle. "Of course, I still got the boys. Didn't I, Sophie?"

The housekeeper nods. "Yes, Maeve, you were quite the catch in your day."

"Show them the photograph," Maeve demands.

Sophie subtly rolls her eyes but still reaches for the photograph on the mantelpiece above the log fire. Maeve was indeed a catch. Hands on her slim waist, eyes open bright and wide like a movie star, a little mischief in her smile. Slim, beautiful, and cheeky.

"Gorgeous," I say.

Maeve nods. "Oh, I've still got it."

Mark glances at me with an expression of horror, but I just pat Maeve on the shoulder. "Of course you have. Is there anything else you remember about Mary? Did she work here for long? Do you remember if she moved?"

"Oh, no," Maeve said. "Mary didn't move. She married my brother. They lived in the cottage near the south field for years."

"Did she ever move to Leeds?" I ask, wondering how the photograph of Mary ended up coming from Leeds if she'd stayed here in Dover.

"Oh, do you know, I think she visited a relative there once," Maeve replies. "In the sixties. I think it was her uncle." She pauses. "Or was is some sort of weekend away *with* the uncle? I can't remember now, it was a long time ago."

"Is... is Mary still alive?" Mark sits slowly down in the chair opposite Maeve, his mouth set in a tense line.

"No. She died five years ago, and my brother went the year after."

Mark presses his hands against his knees before he glances across at me. "Well, it was a long shot."

"But my niece still lives there," Maeve says. "And her husband."

"They do?"

"Oh, yes. Valerie and Gavin. They have two children, Rosie and Sam. Rosie has just had a baby, Oliver, and Sam is away at university in London. Maybe you can meet them some time. Here, let me write down Valerie's phone number for you. She'd love to know more about her mother."

"That's very kind of you." There's a shine of dumbstruck emotion passing over Mark's face as he takes a scrap of paper with a number scrawled on it. Sophie, who was assisting Maeve with the pen and paper, sits back down.

"Did you know Mary well?" I ask. Surely, if Abigail—who then became Annemarie, or Mary—was Maeve's sister-in-law, the two of them must have known each other very well. I want to know everything I can about this woman we've been chasing for the last few weeks.

"As well as anyone, I suppose," Maeve replies. "Mary and Bobby got married in 1960, I think it was. Or maybe it was 1961. I was a bridesmaid. I had ringlets in my hair." She smiles and mimes the curl of her hair with her fingers. "There was only one man on Mary's side. An uncle, she said. And a few friends from the town. Some of them she said she knew at the children's home. The uncle was a strange one. He walked her down the aisle and then left before the reception, without talking to anyone."

"Did Mary mention anything about her background?" I prompt.

"Well, she had grown up in the children's home. She always said that she was in some sort of fire before that. There was a burn up her right arm, and she often wore long sleeves to cover it up. She said her parents died in the war, but she couldn't remember much before she got to the children's home. The uncle would visit every now and then." Maeve pauses. "She was very pretty and sweet, and… loyal, but—" She shakes her head a little and sighs. "Didn't have much up-top. They told her in the home that she'd been hit on the head with something. Falling debris or whatnot in the war, you know? Whatever tragic accident she was in hurt her head, and her mind never recovered. She forgot her own name, so she said. Had to learn everything all over again. She'd wake up in the morning and be confused for a while. Even after she married my brother, she'd forget things. She was terrible for numbers and dates. I don't think she even knew how old she was."

So that was why Abigail never went back to George and his dad. She couldn't remember them.

"Do you know the name of her uncle?" Mark asks.

Maeve shakes her head. "I'm sorry, I can't remember. Most of the time, Mary just called him 'my uncle'. I'm sure I was introduced at the wedding, but he left early."

"Do you have any photographs of Mary?" Mark, with his hands on his knees, still clutching the small piece of paper with the phone number, is flushed pink, with watery eyes.

"I have. Sophie, the second drawer in the bedroom cabinet."

"On it." Sophie unties her apron and makes her way out of the room.

A few minutes later, she arrives back with two large leather-bound photo albums. "Which one, Maeve?"

"The one with the maroon binding is the oldest. Maybe that has a few from when Mary was young."

I find a spot to perch on the chair next to Mark, awkwardly bumping knees and elbows. From my pocket I produce the photograph George kept for all those years of the woman he assumed to be his great-aunt, the young girl who disappeared in such mysterious circumstances.

"I think the wedding is in that one," Maeve says. "Go to about halfway through. That should be Mary and Bobby's wedding from there."

Mark skips through the album until we reach Mary's wedding just like Maeve told us to, and there, smiling in her white dress, clutching a bouquet of roses, is the girl in the photograph.

"Abigail," Mark says softly.

I have to take a deep breath to quell a sob as we finally know what happened to her all those years ago. Then I reach across and place my hand on Mark's arm.

"George will be elated to know that his sister went on to live a full life." I nod at Mark, but he's staring at the photograph in the album on his knee. "What is it? Is something wrong?"

"Yes," he replies. "That man, standing behind Mary, is that her uncle?"

"Yes, I believe it is," Maeve says. "My eyes aren't what they used to be, but I remember the photograph well."

"That's my great-grandfather," Mark says. "The man who raised grandad. That's him."

CHAPTER 41

"Do you want to talk about it?"

The silence hangs between us, thick and suffocating. Mark hasn't spoken since we got back in the car and began our journey home. The sight of his great-grandfather has confused and upset him, and I know why. How are we going to tell George that his own father knew Abigail's location the entire time? How can we break that kind of news to him?

"No," Mark says at last. "Let's talk about something else. Tom. What are you going to do about Tom?"

"I'm going to try to find him." What else can I do? I can't leave him out in the world, alone and upset. He might play at being an adult, but deep down I know he isn't. "Even though he says he doesn't, I think he needs me, and I suppose I have to hope that I'm right."

"Well," Mark says, "if you need a friend to help you, I will. God knows I owe you a favour."

"Thanks." I pause. "It was Tom's eighteenth birthday yesterday."

Mark turns to me. "Really? And you heard nothing from him?"

I shake my head, trying hard not to cry.

"Why did he do it?"

"Tom? He left because of what he found out," I reply. "The truth about our father and… me." My face flushes red. I told Mark everything while I was in the hospital, but even now it's difficult to bring up.

"Oh," Mark says. "Sorry, I didn't… I was talking about my great-grandfather."

I shake my head, embarrassed. "Yes, sorry. Of course."

"I just don't get it. From what Grandad has said, his father loved his mother very much. Why would he kill her in a fire? And why would he make Abigail disappear? I just don't get it. We're missing something."

He's right. But I can't figure out what we're missing.

It's a week later, and I wake up to the sound of the sea near my little bungalow. I wake in my bed, in the deep blue room that I love. There hasn't been an instance of me sleepwalking since Isabel was captured, and even my usual anti-psychotics are making me feel much better. The grogginess is finally fading away, and I feel sharper than ever. There's an ache in my belly and the scars on my back itch, but apart from that, Isabel is far from me today.

She's never gone, you understand, but she's far away. Right now, at least.

And today is a good day, because I'm going to Ivy Lodge for what might be my last time. And, no, I refuse to feel sad about that, because this visit is a happy occasion. It's a celebration.

I'm halfway through a slice of toast when the doorbell rings. I hurry towards the door, chomping the last half before I get there. Mark greets me, appearing slightly dishevelled but excited.

"All set?"

"Let me just lock up." I grab my coat from the rack behind the door, shove my keys into my bag, and slip into a pair of pumps, chewing on the last bit of crust as I get myself out of the house and lock the door.

Mark walks with me down to his car, sounding slightly out of breath. "Mum is already there. I took her before I fetched you. But she's under strict instructions not to let anyone in until you're there."

"You didn't have to—"

"No, I did," he insists. "We can't start without you. That's the rule."

I have to admit I'm relieved. After all our hard work, I want to see how it all ends. And for the second time in a few weeks, I have the good kind of nerves that tickle at your stomach and tell you something wonderful is about to happen. I'm beginning to enjoy those nerves.

When we arrive at Ivy Lodge, Susie is waiting patiently in the reception area with a group of people milling all around her.

"Leah!" She calls me over, and I lean down to hug her. "It feels strange calling you by your real name. But it suits you much better than Lizzie." She pinches my cheek affectionately before gesturing to a woman standing to her right. What strikes me immediately is the fact that this woman has the same Hawker eyes I've become accustomed to. "This is Valerie."

"It's really nice to meet you." I take her hand and shake it limply.

"You must be the good Samaritan who managed to track me down. Who would have thought that I'd find new members of the family in my forties? It's amazing. You must meet my family." Valerie takes me around the family, introducing me to her children, her daughter's husband, and her son's girlfriend, as well as the baby sleeping soundly in his pram. And then, though I promised myself I wouldn't, I feel sad about the family George has never had an opportunity to know.

At least he'll know them now. He'll know Abigail was happy, and that's what counts.

There's more that I know, but I won't tell George any of that. I haven't even told Mark yet, though I will when I think the time is right. That isn't today.

"Is everyone ready?" Mark asks, reacting to the chorus of "Yes!" followed by tentative laughter. He leads the way, pushing his mother's wheelchair along the corridors.

I quickly say hello to the nurses, wave at the patients, and enjoy the tickle of butterflies in my stomach. This is what it feels like to know something good is going to happen. I want to hold on to this feeling, because I don't know how long it will last.

Mark opens the door to George's room, and everyone piles in. "I have some people to meet you, Grandad."

That's when I begin to cry.

Throughout the course of the afternoon, there are photographs taken, photographs shared, jokes, smiles, and tears. In the midst of it all, George watches happily. He holds the baby, ruffles the hair of the children, holds hands and tells tales, while I sit sniffling in the corner, overwhelmed and unable to take much of it in.

Then, partway through the meeting, when everyone has grown quiet for a moment, George finds me across the room with his roaming gaze. "This is all you, Lizzie."

I haven't explained who I am to him yet, but somehow it doesn't matter.

"That's right." Mark puts a hand on my shoulder. "This is all because of you. You've brought family to us and helped solve a mystery that has upset my grandad for too long."

"What a guardian angel you are," George says.

But not for my own family, I think. Not for them.

You're a killer, Leah.

I'll never forget what I am.

These are the things I know:

After we arrived back in Clifton-on-Sea after our road trip to Dover, I received a new email from Francesca about her family. She'd taken our conversation to heart and had gone through a number of old boxes containing all sorts of belongings from the Pierces. It was in one of those boxes that Francesca found a diary belonging to Clive Pierce. In that diary, all the details of Abigail's abduction were laid out, except that the kidnapping was actually an arrangement. George's father, Anthony Hawker, had reached the end of his tether when it came to threats from his wife's ex-husband. Not only that, but he was well aware that Simon was Abigail's real father. According to the diary, *both* of George's parents agreed it would be best to get Abigail away from Simon, and they thought that faking her death in a fire would be the best thing to do. Clive Pierce would look after her for a few weeks while her parents sorted out the mess from the fire, got George, and met them in a safe location.

But none of that happened. In the chaos, Claire Hawker couldn't find George. It was George who had left his room in the night to go to the bathroom, and it was George whom Claire ran back to find. When he told me the story of that night, he must have been mixed up, inserting his anxieties about Abigail from the night she disappeared.

Not only did George's mother die in the fire, but Clive Pierce found Abigail much more difficult to take from the house than he'd thought. When she continued to scream, he hit her over the head to knock her out, stupidly giving her brain damage in the process.

Anthony, reeling from the backfiring of the plan, told Clive Pierce to take Abigail to a children's home, claiming that he couldn't take care of her if she had special needs. Abigail couldn't even remember her own name at this point.

Francesca sent me the excerpts of the diary in the Pierces' own handwriting, so I had no reason to doubt the events they recalled, strange though they were. But I couldn't help but be stunned by what I was reading.

The photograph from Leeds was the result of Mary going on a short holiday with Anthony, still posing as her uncle. He sent the photograph to Clive Pierce before he died, who then sent it on to George. Perhaps Anthony wanted Clive to know she was safe, but I don't know. It seems cruel to send that picture, after letting George search for his sister for so long. Perhaps Clive thought that if George thought Abigail was happy and well somewhere he'd drop the whole thing and move on. The action smacked of desperation. Given the terrible organisation of the crime itself, I'm not at all surprised that Anthony and Clive handled the aftermath with the same disorganisation. Poor George.

Coming from a violent home, I always assumed that bad blood flowed from one generation to the next. I know I have it, and I think Tom does too, as much as I hate to admit it. But I always assumed that George's father had been a good dad to him. Now I knew he wasn't. The plan might not have been meant to cause anyone harm, but it was still a reckless and outright stupid thing to do, resulting in the pointless death of Claire Hawker.

Yet no one has a bad word to say against a man like George.

Maybe it *is* possible to be a decent person despite coming from dirt.

These are the other things I know:

Isabel is psychotic, relentless, smart, and a murderer. She's still in hospital recovering from the injuries I inflicted upon her. DCI Murphy informs me of her progress daily. She is never out of the sight of the police, yet I still worry, and I will until she is locked away.

Isabel has also admitted to the murder of Alison Finlay, even though she told me the opposite. Why would Isabel do that?

She called me a killer.

On the night Alison Finlay died, I left my bed, and I cannot remember where I went.

I could have killed Alison. It could have been me.

I could be a killer.

I could do it again.

I should turn myself in.

But I can't. Because of Tom.

He's out there, and I don't know where he is. I've been to visit his friends from the chip shop, his manager, his old school friends—if you could call them that—and his foster family. No one has heard from Tom, least of all me. I don't know where he is, but I know he needs me.

Maybe I'm afraid, and that's the real reason I haven't told anyone about my fugue state on the night Alison Finlay was killed. Maybe my motivations are purely selfish and I've tried to convince myself otherwise. Some days, I just don't know.

If it was me, will I ever do it again?

I don't know.

Pye the cat jumps out at me as I walk down the path to the front door. I step across the top step in one big stride, avoiding bad memories, and knock loudly. The door creaks as it opens, still sticking a little despite the many times it has been fixed, but it opens quickly, and there he stands.

"You're back."

I nod. "Yes."

"Tea?"

"Yes."

And I walk in.

There he is, filling the kitchen with his size, moving with those calm, languid motions. The room hasn't changed except for the large tub of butter left out on the table and the dirty mugs in the sink.

"You live here now, then?" I ask. "They told me at the house."

"It was sitting empty, so…" He shrugs.

When he turns away from me, I realise that my abdomen is throbbing, but it isn't from the healing laceration below my ribs. I hadn't realised I missed him this much. I place my hand on his forearm, and he freezes.

"Forget the tea," I tell him. And my arms swing up around his neck.

Clifton-on-Sea almost felt like home, but it was missing one vital ingredient: Seb.

EPILOGUE

TOM

You should be here, Leah. You'd love it. The sun rose an hour ago, and now the fields are bathed in an orange glow. Is this why Yorkshire is God's own country? Maybe it is, if God exists, which I'm not sold on, I have to admit.

There's a lot I need to tell you, but I won't be telling you any of it for a very long time. One day, I will sit you down and explain to you how it's all your fault. I didn't used to think that. I thought you were a victim, but that version of me was weak. You see, the moment I stuck a knife into flesh, I realised that I was changed forever, and at first I wanted to fight it, but then I changed my mind and decided to embrace it, because I discovered that my blood is tainted.

How can I be anything but bad, given how I came into this world? I overheard you, Leah. Do you remember that time in Newcastleton when I was supposed to pick you up from the therapist? I actually turned up a few minutes early. The receptionist at the office was on the phone and not paying attention, giving me an opportunity to listen at the door. I heard everything.

Tom is my son. He's my son and my brother. Sometimes I look at him and all I see is our father raping me, and there are times I wish he'd never been born, because then he wouldn't have been through everything we've been through. Our parents. Isabel. So much violence. I can't stand it. I pity him.

The truth was finally laid out before me. For the first time, I knew who I was, and I hated myself. But what you don't know, Leah, is that I knew I was bad anyway. I'd been fighting it harder and harder every day, but at last I knew I could embrace it because of who I was. You see, ever since I killed David Fielding, I'd imagined doing it again. Killing David Fielding was the one time in my life that I felt any power at all. It was the one time in my life that I managed to change this world somehow. Before then, all I could do was watch as our father killed my mother—my grandmother, I suppose now—and as the bullies picked on me at school, and as you tried to claw our way out of poverty. And as Isabel tortured you.

I finally did it. And I wanted to do it again.

But I realised that I couldn't just go up to a person and stab them. If I was going to do it, I had to do it right. I had to do it in such a way that I wouldn't get caught. That's when I came up with the idea.

There was a murderer on the loose. Owen Fielding was in prison for killing Maisie Earnshaw, but after the kidnapping and torture of me and you, it was pretty well-established that Isabel had had some sort of hand in Maisie's killing. Of course we knew the truth, because she'd confessed to us. The public suspected she'd done it, too. Which means if a young woman turned up dead with bird wings carved on her back, they would assume that Isabel was the murderer.

But in order to get away with it, I had to do something to you that I felt quite bad about. I switched your medication. Instead of your anti-psychotics, I gave you sleeping pills every now and then. The pills were a very similar shape, and when I brought them to you with a cup of tea, you didn't even notice. I had to be sneaky about it to make sure that you didn't sleep all day. I couldn't do it all the time, just when I wanted to go out at night and find the right girl.

Alison was a therapist who took evening patients until quite late at night. Do you remember those martial arts classes we attended? She had an advert in the village hall for her group therapy sessions in the evenings. She was also an environmentalist without a car who used to walk home near to a stretch of fields. The road was quiet and rural, with no CCTV around. I didn't take any chances. I wore dark clothing. I hit her over the head with a stone, and I dragged her into the field. I killed her quickly, and then I left her. But I'd forgotten to wear gloves. There was blood all over my hands, and it took a long time to wash away.

You almost ruined my plans. As I came back to that tiny little house, I saw you sitting up in the lounge in the darkness. I swear my heart stopped beating for a second. I even opened my mouth to confess everything to you, to lie at your feet and beg for forgiveness. But I didn't. I walked up to you, and I smeared the blood all over your hands.

Then I stood back and said, "What did you do?" before walking away from you.

The next morning, I thought you were going to say something to me, or at least suspect me when the body was found. But you said nothing. I wasn't sure if you remembered the blood or not, you were so out of it. But even without the memory of the blood, you took the blame for something you considered Isabel's doing. You blamed yourself.

And I let you.

It felt like my little secret. My only fear was that someone would find out, and I would go to prison. I was frightened you might find out, or that you'd notice a change in me, that you'd see how powerful I'd become.

I did everything I could to throw you off. I argued with you about Isabel, and I kept making small changes to your medication, switching the occasional pill for a painkiller or a sleeping pill. You found yourself sleepwalking every now and then, and I could tell there were times when you couldn't decide what was real and what wasn't. Eventually, I decided to leave because I couldn't keep doing it to you. If I stayed, you were going to figure it out. I know you were. I couldn't control my temper anymore, no matter how much I went to the gym.

But even after I moved out of the bungalow, I was paranoid that you'd figure everything out. The only thing I could do was make you think you were crazy again. I didn't want to, Leah, I hope you understand that. It was me who planted the magpie on the step. It was me who broke the camera outside the front door. You see, I didn't want to kill anyone else. I'd done it and tried it out, and I decided that the power of the killing wasn't worth the fear of being caught. The adrenaline rush wasn't worth it. But there were times when I felt like someone was telling me to do it. They pointed out how awful people are. We're all sinners, aren't we?

I have another confession to make. I didn't believe Isabel had come to Clifton until I went out to the vending machine to buy food for us both. She slipped that knife softly against my flesh and I knew I could disarm her, but I didn't. It was me who allowed her to take us both. Me who let her tie me up. I pretended I was afraid, but I wasn't. Part of me was curious about what Isabel would do. Part of me wanted to watch you die. And part of me also wanted to die.

I've been looked down on my entire life. I've been called a fairy, a cow, a monster, a fatty, a faggot, and a poof. I've been punched, beaten, kicked, and often by my own father. You don't know how bad it got after you left me with him. But when I sliced through skin, I was powerful. And don't try to tell me that poor little Alison didn't deserve it, because everyone deserves it. We're all rotten deep down. It was only a matter of time before she did something despicable.

I'm a murderer, Leah. That's just who I am. Who you *created*.

Now for the big question: what am I going to do now? For a long time, I decided that I would never murder again. The risks were too high. I'm aware of the life I've taken, though I do believe that no one is innocent in this world. Taking a life is merely sparing the rest of the world from the monster they will no doubt become. If not today, then tomorrow, or the next day, or the next day. We're all nasty, spiteful creatures; I'm just more honest about my spite.

Then Isabel threw me a lifeline. I don't know why, but she confessed to the murder, putting me in the clear. I had been terrified of leaving DNA behind, or you, Leah, remembering something about that night. But now, with Isabel's confession, the police won't even bother to keep searching for clues. The case is closed. Isabel will soon be behind bars, and everyone can move on.

And what will I do now?

I'm not sure.

But I know I'll be watching for a while. Watching you. Watching everyone. I think I may have started something I can't finish. Not yet.

Sleep tight, big sister.

Or should I say Mum?